ACCl

MW01148130

A Picture of Love

"Beth Wiseman's *A Picture of Love* will delight readers of Amish fiction. Naomi and Amos's romance is a heartfelt story of love, forgiveness, and second chances. This book has everything readers love about a Beth Wiseman story—an authentic portrait of the Amish community, humor, the power of grace and hope and, above all, faith in God's Word and His promises."

—AMY CLIPSTON, BESTSELLING AUTHOR OF *THE FARM STAND*

A Beautiful Arrangement

"Wiseman's delightful third installment of the Amish Journey series (*Listening to Love*) centers on the struggles and unexpected joys of a marriage of convenience . . . Series devotees and newcomers alike will find this engrossing romance hard to put down."

—*PUBLISHERS WEEKLY*

"*A Beautiful Arrangement* has so much heart you won't want to put it down until you've read the last page. I love second-chance love stories, and Lydia and Samuel's story is heartbreaking and sweet with unexpected twists and turns that make their journey to love all the more satisfying. Beth's fans will cherish this book."

—JENNIFER BECKSTRAND, AUTHOR OF *THE PETERSHEIM BROTHERS SERIES*

Listening to Love

"Wiseman is at her best in this surprising tale of love and faith."

—*PUBLISHERS WEEKLY*

"I always find Beth Wiseman's books to be both tenderly romantic and thought provoking. She has a way of setting a scene that makes me feel like I'm part of an Amish community and visiting for supper. I loved the title of this book, the message about faith and God, and the heartfelt romance between Lucas and Natalie. *Listening to Love* has everything I love in a Beth Wiseman novel—a strong faith message, a touching romance, and a beautiful sense of place. Beth is such an incredibly gifted storyteller."

—SHELLEY SHEPARD GRAY, BESTSELLING AUTHOR
OF THE SEASONS OF SUGARCREEK SERIES

"*Listening to Love* is vintage Beth Wiseman . . . Clear your calendar because you're going to want to read this one in a single sitting."

—VANNETTA CHAPMAN, AUTHOR OF THE
SHIPSHEWANA AMISH MYSTERY SERIES

Hearts in Harmony

"This is a sweet story, not only of romance, but of older generations and younger generations coming together in friendship. It's a tearjerker as well as an uplifting story."

—*PARKERSBURG NEWS & SENTINEL*

"Beth Wiseman has penned a poignant story of friendship, faith, and love that is sure to touch readers' hearts."

—KATHLEEN FULLER, AUTHOR OF THE MIDDLEFIELD FAMILY NOVELS

"Beth Wiseman's *Hearts in Harmony* is a lyrical hymn. Mary and Levi are heartwarming, lovable characters who instantly feel like dear friends. Once readers open this book, they won't put it down until they've reached the last page."

—AMY CLIPSTON, BESTSELLING AUTHOR OF *THE BAKE SHOP*

Amish Celebrations

"Wiseman's (*Amish Secrets*) collection of timeless stories of love and loss among the Plain People will delight fans of the author's heartfelt story lines and flowing prose."

—LIBRARY JOURNAL

Home All Along

"Beth Wiseman's novel will find a permanent home in every reader's heart as she spins comfort and prose into a stellar read of grace."

—KELLY LONG, AUTHOR OF THE PATCH OF HEAVEN SERIES

Love Bears All Things

"Suggest to those seeking a more truthful, less saccharine portrayal of the trials of human life and the transformative growth and redemption that may occur as a result."

—LIBRARY JOURNAL

Her Brother's Keeper

"Wiseman has created a series in which the readers have a chance to peel back all the layers of the Amish secrets."

—RT BOOK REVIEWS, $4^{1}/2$ STARS AND JULY 2015 TOP PICK!

"Wiseman's new launch is edgier, taking on the tough issues of mental illness and suicide. Amish fiction fans seeking something a bit more thought-provoking and challenging than the usual fare will find this series debut a solid choice."

—LIBRARY JOURNAL

The Land of Canaan Novels

"Wiseman's voice is consistently compassionate, and her words flow smoothly."

—*Publishers Weekly* on *Seek Me with All Your Heart*

"Wiseman's third Land of Canaan novel overflows with romance, broken promises, a modern knight in shining armor, and hope at the end of the rainbow."

—*RT Book Reviews*

"In *Seek Me with All Your Heart*, Beth Wiseman offers readers a heartwarming story filled with complex characters and deep emotion. I instantly loved Emily, and eagerly turned each page, anxious to learn more about her past—and what future the Lord had in store for her."

—Shelley Shepard Gray, bestselling author of the Seasons of Sugarcreek series

"Wiseman has done it again! Beautifully compelling, *Seek Me with All Your Heart* is a heartwarming story of faith, family, and renewal. Her characters and descriptions are captivating, bringing the story to life with the turn of every page."

—Amy Clipston, bestselling author of *The Bake Shop*

A
PICTURE *of*
LOVE

OTHER BOOKS BY BETH WISEMAN

A
PICTURE *of*
LOVE

THE AMISH INN NOVELS

BETH WISEMAN

ZONDERVAN

A Picture of Love

Copyright © 2020 by Elizabeth Wiseman Mackey

Requests for information should be addressed to:
Zondervan, *3900 Sparks Dr. SE, Grand Rapids, Michigan 49546*

Library of Congress Cataloging-in-Publication Data

Names: Wiseman, Beth, 1962- author.
Title: A picture of love / Beth Wiseman.
Description: Nashville : Zondervan, [2020] | Series: An Amish Inn novel ; 1
   | Summary: "In the first novel of Beth Wiseman's new Amish Inn series,
   matchmaking widows ensure that two young artists have a second chance at
   love"-- Provided by publisher.
Identifiers: LCCN 2020015639 (print) | LCCN 2020015640 (ebook) | ISBN
   9780310357223 (paperback) | ISBN 9780310363170 (library binding) |
   ISBN 9780310357230 (epub) | ISBN 9780310357247 (downloadable audio)
Subjects: LCSH: Amish--Fiction. | GSAFD: Christian fiction. | Love stories.
Classification: LCC PS3623.I83 P53 2020 (print) | LCC PS3623.I83 (ebook) |
   DDC 813/.6--dc23
LC record available at https://lccn.loc.gov/2020015639
LC ebook record available at https://lccn.loc.gov/2020015640

Zondervan titles may be purchased in bulk for educational, business,
fundraising, or sales promotional use. For information, please email
SpecialMarkets@Zondervan.com.

Printed in the United States of America

HB 04.22.2021

To Sharon and Linda, you two wild and crazy sisters! Love you both.

GLOSSARY

ab im kopp: crazy, off in the head

ach: oh

boppli: baby

bruder: brother

daadi haus: a small house built onto or near the main house for grandparents to live in

daed: dad

danki: thank you

dochder: daughter

Englisch: those who are not Amish; the English language

fraa: wife

Gott: God

grossdochder: granddaughter

grossmammi: grandmother

gut: good

Gut nacht: Good night

haus: house

kaffi: coffee

kinner: children

lieb: love

maedel: girl

mei: my

mudder: mother

nee: no

sohn: son

schweschder: sister

Wie bischt?: Hello, how are you?

ya: yes

ONE

OCTOBER

MONTGOMERY, INDIANA

"I THINK HE'S DEAD." LIZZIE CRINKLED HER NOSE AS SHE
easedcloser to Gus Owens. She bent at the waist and leaned
down to within a few inches of his face. Loose strands of
gray hair fell from beneath her prayer covering as she shook
her head.

Esther rolled her eyes at her sister and swiped at her own
silvery tresses escaping in the cool breeze. "He isn't dead."

"Wishful thinking on *mei* part." Lizzie sighed.

Their grumpy English renter was slumped in a rocking
chair on the front porch of his cottage. His gray hair was pulled
back in a ponytail, the way he always wore it, and his beard
needed grooming. Gus reminded Esther of the Santa Clauses
she'd seen in malls, but when the English took their children

1

to sit on Santa's lap, the man in the red suit was always jolly and smiling. There was nothing jolly about Gus Owens, and he never smiled.

Gus had rented the cottage for the past ten years, but the only reason he was still there was because of a promise Esther and Lizzie made to their dying mother—that Gus would be allowed to live in the cottage for the rest of his life.

Lizzie straightened and slapped her hands to her hips. Esther's younger sister scowled, deepening the lines of time that feathered in every direction on her face. Those same wrinkles stared back at Esther each morning when she looked in the mirror. And that was where their similarities ended. Esther was several inches taller and a bit stouter than Lizzie, whose frame was much more petite. Esther still had all of her own teeth, crooked as they were. Lizzie boasted a set of straight pearly white dentures—when she actually wore them. They were new and she often shifted them back and forth in her mouth, saying they didn't fit well, despite three trips back to the dentist. He'd said it would just take some time for Lizzie to get used to her new teeth.

"He's breathing." Esther had trekked across the field and past the pond to reach the cottage. Barely visible from the main house, the small home had been on their family's property for as long as Esther could remember. When she and Lizzie were children and it wasn't rented out, the cottage had served as their playhouse.

"You don't think he got into our cough medicine again, do you?" Lizzie's nostrils flared as she glared at Gus.

"*Nee*, I don't think so." Esther pulled her black sweater snug, then cleared her throat. "Maybe if you didn't put so much rum in the honey mixture, he wouldn't be drawn to it." She scratched her face, the soft skin covering cheekbones that used to be much higher than they were now.

"I use the same amount *Mamm* used." Lizzie pulled back one of her small legs and, before Esther could stop her, she kicked Gus in the shin.

"Lizzie!" Esther loved her sister, but sometimes she acted like a child. "We do not kick people!" *Not even Gus.*

When the elderly man still didn't move, Esther's chest tightened. She couldn't rule out the fact that Gus might be drunk. He didn't make a habit of it, but it had happened before. Not in a long time, though.

"Maybe we need to get him to a doctor."

"Nah. Ain't nothing wrong with Gus that a good swift kick in the—" Lizzie pulled her leg back again.

"Stop it!" Esther yelled this time, and Gus opened his eyes just as Lizzie's foot made contact with his shin again.

"Woman, are you out of your mind?" Gus slowly lifted himself from the chair. He had recently celebrated his seventy-fourth birthday, making him only two years older than Esther. He looked bigger each year—taller, broader, and rounder. He towered over Esther, but since Lizzie was so tiny she looked like a child standing next to him.

"We thought you were drunk or something." Lizzie straightened her prayer covering and backed away from Gus—Grumpy Gus, as they called him.

"I haven't drank in years, and you know it." Gus's jowls jiggled like small water balloons on either side of his face. "Can't a fellow just take a nap on his front porch?" He waved a dismissive hand at Lizzie. "Get on back to your house and leave me alone."

Esther had been playing referee between Lizzie and Gus since before their mother died four years ago. The man was unpleasant to most everyone, but he and Lizzie butted heads the most. Gus had always treated their mother with respect when she was alive. Maybe because he needed a place to live and their mother didn't charge him much to rent the cottage. Esther wished Gus didn't know about the promise they'd made her. He seemed to think he could treat her and Lizzie any way he wanted. Some days he was downright nasty. Other times Esther swore she saw a tiny glimpse of what Gus might have been like at another time—almost kind.

"We just came to tell you that we have overnight guests coming." Lizzie's mouth thinned with displeasure. "So don't come calling for anything."

Gus groaned as he stretched and yawned. "I ain't got no business at your place." He grinned before he winked at Lizzie. "I think you just make up excuses to come see me."

Esther covered her mouth with her hand, attempting to stifle a giggle. Lizzie was sure to go off on him now.

Lizzie clenched her fists at her sides, her nostrils flaring. She opened her mouth to say something, but slammed it shut. After staring at her bare feet for a few seconds, she slowly lifted her chin and stretched to appear taller.

"The Good Lord is punishing me for something." She shook her head again. "Because not a day goes by that you don't irritate the daylights out of me." Spinning on her heels, she marched down the porch steps.

"You gonna head over to John and Mary's place now?" Gus had a deep voice, and whether he was angry or not—and he was usually angry—his voice had an air of authority that didn't fit the man he was. "You gonna go kick them too?"

John and Mary Lapp had moved to Montgomery for a job opportunity recently and were renting the third house on the property. They were a sweet young couple who had been married for five years. They stayed to themselves a lot, but they waved and were friendly to guests who came to stay at the main house. The same couldn't be said about Gus. Folks would wave or call out a pleasant greeting if Gus was on the porch and awake. He would wave them off, grumbling as he stood up, then he'd slam the door when he went in the house. It wasn't the impression Esther and Lizzie wanted for their guests.

Lizzie didn't answer as she continued walking back to the main house.

"Have a *gut* evening, Gus." Esther had learned that it was better not to engage Gus in conversation, but she refused to let her manners slip just because he didn't have any.

Growling, Gus went inside the house and slammed the door.

Esther followed the worn path back to the house she and Lizzie had grown up in. A few months ago they'd turned the hundred-year-old home into a bed and breakfast. Business was slow so far, but word was spreading. Some of their patrons were Amish folks visiting friends or relatives. Others were English tourists who said they wanted to "live like the Amish." Esther hoped the cooler temperatures October brought would also bring more guests. July and August had been unusually hot, and while the English might think they want to live like the Amish, they don't want to live without air conditioning.

Esther didn't see what all the fuss was about with outsiders showing such an interest in the way they lived. But Lizzie insisted Montgomery was slowly bringing in more and more tourists.

As Esther walked up the porch steps, she wondered if they'd ever have much business. Turning the house into a bed and breakfast hadn't been about the money. After their mother died, the home sat vacant for almost four years. They paid a caretaker who tended to the house and yard since they hadn't been able to face selling it. They both thought Gus should do the work, but he insisted he had a bad back that prevented him from strenuous activity. In truth, the man was just lazy. Esther had seen him carry huge armfuls of chopped wood into his house for the fireplace. His back seemed just fine when it suited his own needs.

But when Esther's and Lizzie's husbands died within a few months of each other last year, they sold their houses and moved back into their family home. It was Lizzie's idea to have the house remodeled to accommodate guests.

Esther shared her sister's passion for the project. It provided a reprieve from their grief—and opportunities to play matchmaker. Single Amish visitors from other communities could be introduced to the unattached young people in Montgomery, which was too small to offer many options for courting. Esther and Lizzie had been known to dabble in people's love lives, but now it was like having a full-time job, a sense of purpose again. If there was a downside, it was Grumpy Gus. He hadn't been happy when the renovations started, or when the sisters moved back into the house. Esther and Lizzie could have done without Gus on the property too.

When the caretaker was no longer physically able to tend the yard or house, Esther and Lizzie began looking for help. Naomi Byler applied for the position of housekeeper and cook, and Esther and Lizzie were excited for her to live in the spare room they'd set up for such a person.

More importantly, Naomi was a young woman nursing a broken heart and had sworn off men. Esther and her sister couldn't let that continue. Lizzie was as crazy as a rabid coyote and often took things to the extreme, but Esther tolerated her sister's over-the-top antics. Sometimes young people just needed a little coaxing to find true love.

The sisters had each lived their own love stories. Esther was married to her beloved Joe Zook for fifty-two years before he passed. Lizzie had shared her life with Rueben Glick for fifty-one years.

No one should miss out on the blessing of true love. Especially Naomi Byler.

After the dining room table was set for four, Naomi stood back and eyed each place setting. An Amish woman and her son from Ohio were coming to town for a wedding and staying through Sunday, and two Englisch ladies had left a message saying they would like a room for this evening only. The bishop allowed phones for business purposes, but he preferred the devices be installed away from the house. Esther and Lizzie kept their telephone and answering machine in the barn, but it was the only electricity in use on the entire eighty acres.

Naomi went back to the kitchen just as Esther and Lizzie came into the house. After dropping their shoes by the front door, the women crossed through the living area and met Naomi in the kitchen.

"Everything is ready," Naomi said. "The pot roast and vegetables are keeping warm in the oven, along with a loaf of bread. And there is a fresh pitcher of tea on the counter, next to the shoofly pie I made earlier in the day."

"Everything looks *gut*, Naomi. *Danki*." Esther folded her hands in front of her. "I suspect our guests will be hungry after their travels, but we'll give them the option to get unpacked and settled before they eat, or vice versa."

Lizzie's lips were puckered with annoyance, an expression that surfaced any time she'd been around Gus. She walked over to a cabinet, lifted up on her toes, and began to inspect the medications they kept on hand. She pulled out the homemade cough syrup and held it up to the window.

"Unless one of you developed a cough and chugged a third of this bottle before I got up this morning, Gus has been up to no good." Her glare ping-ponged between Esther and Naomi, who each shook their heads.

Esther sighed. "Lizzie, I think we would have heard Gus come into the *haus*, and he surely doesn't get moving in the morning until well after sunrise. Someone is usually up here by five o'clock. He's not nipping on the cough syrup."

"If you say so." Lizzie put the bottle back in the cabinet and turned to lean against the counter. She wiggled her teeth back and forth in her mouth a few times, eventually spitting them out in her hand. "Stupid teeth."

Naomi stifled a grin. Esther was always calm, predictable, and polite. Lizzie was the complete opposite. Naomi had known the women all her life, and she loved them both. They'd been like family since her parents died five years ago. Esther and Lizzie had been married to wonderful men who had also embraced Naomi like a daughter or granddaughter until their deaths. Maybe they had endeared themselves to Naomi because neither couple had been able to have children of their own. The offer to work at the inn and live with Esther and Lizzie couldn't have come at a better time. Naomi's fiancé had suddenly broken off their engagement and left town four months ago.

"Lizzie, please keep your teeth in your mouth when our guests arrive." Esther frowned as she reached for jars of chow-chow and jam from the refrigerator, which reminded Naomi that she needed to check how much propane was left in the tank. "And keep your tongue in check."

"I know, I know." Lizzie tapped her bare foot as she spoke with a lisp. "No telling inappropriate stories. No making fun of what the two *Englisch* women might be wearing. No sarcasm when they ask about our way of life. No telling them to mind their own business. And no asking the Amish woman and her *sohn* if they like their bishop, then sharing all the reasons why I don't like our bishop." She folded her arms across her chest. "Did I miss anything?"

Esther smiled at her sister as she headed to the dining room with the jams. "*Nee*, I believe you've got it."

Naomi turned away from Lizzie and smiled to herself as she recalled how all the things Lizzie listed had happened at some point over the past few months. Each time Esther reprimanded Lizzie for her behavior, she promised to do better next time. Naomi knew Lizzie didn't mean to lie, but those promises were usually forgotten.

Naomi could tell Lizzie made Esther nervous, but Naomi found the younger of the sisters to be a welcome distraction from the sadness that had wrapped around her. And to Lizzie's credit, she'd been kind and caring to a lot of their guests, especially those who had recently lost a loved one. It was as if God placed the words in Lizzie's mind, told her exactly what to say to help someone who was grieving. Esther had once mentioned that it was worth the trade-off. If Lizzie helped one person for every person she'd angered, how could Esther forbid her to interact with their guests? Naomi wished God would give Lizzie His wisdom regarding her own situation—that He'd tell Lizzie, or someone, how Naomi would ever recover from her breakup with Thomas.

They heard a car pull into the driveway, and Esther made

her way to the window. "It's Anna Mae Lantz and her son, Amos. They're here for Suzanne and Isaiah's wedding on Thursday."

Lizzie shuffled to the window and pressed her nose to the glass. "We don't know them, do we?"

"*Nee*. Distant cousins of Isaiah's, I think. Anna Mae told me on the phone that they'd be hiring a driver to pick them up from the bus station. They're planning to stay through the weekend."

Lizzie gasped before hurriedly placing her teeth back in her mouth. "Her *sohn* is a grown man. Look how handsome he is." She nudged Esther, then looked over her shoulder and smiled at Naomi.

Oh no. Naomi had no interest in a romantic relationship. She'd never love anyone the way she loved Thomas, but that didn't stop Esther and Lizzie from constantly trying to play matchmaker for her. Lizzie had even told Naomi she was practically an old maid at twenty-five. Their people married young, sometimes as young as seventeen or eighteen, but Naomi didn't think she should be labeled an old maid just yet. Maybe in a few years she would have to accept the title since she had no plans to marry anyone else. Unless it was Thomas, returning home to tell her he'd just had cold feet and wanted to spend the rest of his life with her. Naomi was losing hope that was going to happen. But what haunted her most was that she didn't understand why he'd left her.

Lizzie and Esther were both widows, and it was unfortunate that neither woman had been able to have a child. They'd already told Naomi they were bequeathing their property to her and that they considered her their granddaughter.

Naomi was honored, humbled, and incredibly grateful. Otherwise, as a single orphan, she wasn't sure how she would continue to support herself. The little bit of money her parents had left after the accident was long gone. That small chunk of cash and funds from the sale of their family home had been spent paying creditors Naomi hadn't even known about. Financially and emotionally, Esther and Lizzie's timing with a job couldn't have been more perfect. She'd only had to stay with her cousin for a week before Esther extended the offer. Her cousin had eight children in three bedrooms, so it was already a tight squeeze without Naomi, and she didn't know the family well. They lived in Orleans, a town too far to travel to by buggy.

Someday Naomi would be an old spinster running The Peony Inn. She would never change the name in honor of Lizzie and Esther. The sisters had chosen the name because the peony is the state flower of Indiana, and it was also their mother's favorite.

At least they had their memories of long, happy marriages to reflect on. And they'd been blessed to have their mother until she passed a few years ago at ninety-four. Naomi wondered what she would have to reflect on when she was their age.

∞

Amos helped his mother out of the car, then paid the driver, who'd already gotten their two suitcases out of the trunk.

"This is a lovely property, *ya?*" Anna Mae turned to Amos and smiled. "I'm excited to see *mei* cousins I haven't seen in years. You've never even met some of them."

Amos forced a smile and nodded. He could have done without this trip, but his mother insisted a change of scenery would do him good. His two brothers worked several different jobs and hadn't been at them long enough to earn vacation time. Amos owned a small construction company that gave him the flexibility to take off when he needed to. His father's back problems would have made a trip like this difficult. Amos just wished the event were anything other than a wedding.

When they reached the porch, his mother knocked on the door, and an older woman pushed open the screen door. She was almost as tall as Amos, probably pushing six feet.

"Welcome to The Peony Inn. I'm Esther." She stepped aside, then motioned for them to follow her toward the stairs. "You have the two rooms at the end of the hall on the right. Supper will be served in about thirty minutes, or we are happy to keep it warm in the oven until you're ready."

"I think we are ready to eat. *Danki,*" his mother said. "It smells delicious."

Amos was glad to hear his mother's response. His stomach had been rumbling for hours.

He followed his mother as they crossed through a spacious living room. It was simply furnished with two tan couches, a couple of rocking chairs, and an oak coffee table. There was a large hutch against one wall, but it was the fireplace that stole his breath. It was enormous and enclosed in white rock with a mantel that spanned its entirety. He wondered if they would have a fire later as the temperature cooled down. His boots clicked against the wood floor as he followed his mother up the stairs. At home they dropped their shoes by the door, but Esther hadn't said anything or given them time to do so.

He set his mother's red suitcase just inside the first room, a no-frills space with one exception. The quilt on the bed was bursting with enough color that it practically reflected the sunrays streaming into the room. There was a small writing desk and chair, the traditional hooks on the wall for hanging clothes, and a gas heater in the corner. A bookshelf graced one wall, filled with a variety of reading options. Even in its simplicity, the room was charming. Lace doilies sat atop the desk and nightstand, and the lanterns gleamed as if freshly polished.

"This is perfect," his mother said as she took in her surroundings. Amos knew she'd been looking forward to this trip for months.

He carted his own suitcase to the next room. The setup was similar, except there was a trunk propped open in the corner next to a rocking chair, instead of a bookshelf like in the other room. The weathered trunk held blankets, throw pillows, and a few books tucked to the side. For a few long moments, he eyed the beautifully crafted wedding quilt. The pastel colors would have a calming effect on most people. For Amos, it was just another reminder of all he'd lost.

His mother peeked into the room. "Are you ready to head downstairs?"

Amos nodded. "*Ya*, I am." The alluring aroma would be a welcomed reprieve for his hunger pains.

The same woman—Esther—met them at the bottom of the stairs and directed them through the living room and into a large dining room. Two middle-aged English women were already seated at the dining table set for four, although the large oak table could have easily accommodated twelve guests. A small woman, in comparison to Esther, introduced herself as Lizzie, Esther's sister. She began filling glasses of tea just as a much younger woman entered the room.

Amos locked eyes with her and couldn't seem to look away. She was beautiful with dark brown hair and big doe eyes that reeled him in like a fish on a hook. He couldn't remember a woman looking at him like that in a long time, nor had he relished the thought of anyone doing so.

His reasons for staring at her went beyond her outward beauty. It was her eyes—the gateway to the soul, he'd heard—and this woman seemed to be looking right through him. What did she see? The truth?

Amos recognized her expression of an internal pain that was hard to hide. Whatever her story was, she suffered from the same ailment as Amos.

A broken heart.

Two

Naomi forced herself to look away from their male guest. Her heart had briefly flipped when she laid eyes on him, a reaction she hadn't experienced since her breakup with Thomas. She wouldn't be human if she didn't notice the Nordic blue of his eyes, the way his dark hair framed a square jawline, and his broad shoulders, proof of a man who did physical work. His fading summer tan shone on his face, but that wasn't all she could see. There was pain in the lines that ran across his forehead, and somehow she sensed a raw hurt that hadn't healed. Or maybe she was completely off the mark because of her own situation.

Most of the available men in their small district, and even some from surrounding communities, had tried to court Naomi since Thomas had left. Each time she politely declined. She had no interest in pursuing a relationship with anyone.

16

Thomas had stolen her heart like a thief who took a part of her—maybe all of her—when he'd broken off their engagement and left town.

Amos Lantz possibly found her attractive, but this man wasn't in the market for love either. And unless she was wrong, that meant she wouldn't have to put up with his pursuit of her affections. He felt safe, even if it was due to a loss in his life. Such suffering tended to recognize company.

Naomi stood in the corner of the dining room in case anyone needed a tea glass refilled. Esther fielded questions from the two English women, which included the usual inquiries from outsiders. Since Lizzie had been instructed to behave, she stood quietly beside her sister. Naomi was glad to see she had her teeth in this evening.

"But if a person hasn't been baptized, then they can't be shunned, right?" One of the English women, a plump woman wearing too much makeup, posed the question to Amos's mother, Anna Mae, who nodded.

"*Ya*, that's correct," Esther injected so Anna Mae could finish chewing her food.

From there Esther suggested several places for the women to visit since they wanted to do some sightseeing.

"Stop 'N Sea is run by Amish folks." Esther folded her hands in front of her. "They have a variety of things on the menu, but they are most popular for their hot fish sandwiches."

Esther told them about other eateries and shops in the area. Thankfully Lizzie remained quiet. Naomi loved both the women equally, but Lizzie's unpredictable behavior had made for some interesting dining experiences in the past. Particularly when an English family had shown up with their fifteen-year-old daughter wearing very short pants and a low-cut sleeveless blouse. Lizzie brought the girl's attire to her attention right away, telling her that she looked like a walking advertisement for— Luckily Lizzie had stopped mid-sentence, but the damage was done. The mother defended her daughter, saying it was a hundred degrees in the house. Lizzie had responded by saying, "It's July and you're staying in an Amish *haus*. What did you expect?" That couple and their daughter left first thing the following morning.

Naomi drifted in and out of the conversation, hearing bits and pieces as she sneaked glances at Amos. The more she tried to feel something other than physical attraction for this handsome fellow, the more defeated she felt. She didn't have even the tiniest interest in getting to know him, but how nice it would be to entertain the possibility of love again. He was handsome, and though he barely smiled, when he did, the ground probably shook beneath most women's feet. Not Naomi's. Without a beard, he was obviously unmarried. Why?

It doesn't matter. Thomas had been her one true love. She'd waited for years until she was old enough to date. Her father had a strict rule against dating before she turned eighteen. Naomi was an only child and thought the rule was unfair. Most girls were allowed to date when they turned sixteen. Thomas was three years older than Naomi. He'd found someone to court before she turned eighteen. She dated a few other young men, but no one she could imagine sharing her life with. When

Thomas broke things off with his girlfriend, Naomi's heart had sizzled with the prospect that maybe he would ask her out. And he did. After six months he proposed. Then he left her broken, like scattered pieces of a life she'd never have an opportunity to live.

Later, after the kitchen was cleaned, Naomi walked onto the porch to feel the crisp fall air as she eyed the orange-and-yellow hues settling in around the house. October was her favorite month. The heat of summer was past, and the busyness of the holidays hadn't arrived yet. It was a peaceful time of year since most crops had been harvested, and it was also beautiful. There were a few cornfields—like the one behind their pond—where the stalks still stretched high.

Someone cleared his throat behind her, and she jumped as she swiveled to face him. "*Ach*, I'm sorry. I didn't see you."

Amos sat alone in one of six white rocking chairs on the front porch.

"Can I get you anything?" Again she hoped for a tinge of excitement, a swirl in her stomach, or the nervousness of being in the presence of someone she found incredibly attractive. *Still nothing.*

"*Nee*, I'm just enjoying the view." He grinned, and for a moment Naomi wondered if he was talking about her, but he pointed to the hill on the other side of the pond. "That's quite a display of color."

"*Ya, ya.* It's a lovely time of year." Naomi wanted to know if her speculations about this man were right. She was sure Esther and Lizzie were already scheming ways to set her up with him. If Naomi knew Amos's sad story, she could halt the sisters' efforts.

"May I join you?" She pointed to one of the rocking chairs, two spots down from where he was sitting.

He nodded. "*Ya*, sure."

Naomi wasn't good at small talk, and now that she had an opportunity to ask him why he looked so sad, she realized how nosy and inappropriate that would be.

"Are Esther and Lizzie your aunts, or is one of them your *grossmammi*?" He twisted slightly in the rocking chair to face her.

"*Nee*, we aren't blood related, but I still think of them as family. *Mei* parents died five years ago." Naomi paused, pushing away the images of the crushed buggy next to a blue car that she'd seen when she'd arrived at the scene. "It was an accident. They were hit and killed instantly by an oncoming car. The driver is actually in jail." Although that hadn't done anything to quell the pain she'd suffered at the time, it saddened her that a young woman, who was only nineteen at the time, would spend a long time in prison because she'd been drinking and driving. That woman's life had been taken from her as well, but at her own doing.

Amos didn't take his eyes off her. "I'm so sorry."

She could tell by that single expression, the way he reacted with such sincerity, that the loss he'd suffered was the passing of a loved one.

"*Danki*," she said as she kept her eyes fused with his. "It was five years ago, and I miss them every day, but time does lessen the pain. The hurt doesn't feel as raw and unmanageable now. I'm able to reflect on the *gut* memories more often." She didn't understand how, though time had lessened the blow of her parents' death, she couldn't shed her sorrow about Thomas leaving. If anything, it just got worse as the days went by. She had to hope that time would eventually make a difference and open her heart to love again. But hope had very little room to breathe, not much room to grow, and was constantly snuffed out by doubt and self-pity.

"I understand that type of loss." He finally pulled his eyes from hers and stared somewhere into the distance, maybe eyeing the colorful foliage again. But still lost somewhere. "I was engaged to be married until *mei* fiancée was diagnosed with a rare form of cancer and died almost a year ago."

Naomi wasn't sure what to say. She was feeling sorry for herself daily because Thomas had left her. The woman this man loved had died. "I'm sorry for your loss," she said, barely above a whisper.

"*Danki*." His eyes found their way back to the distant place he must retreat to when memories so unbearably tragic threatened to overtake him. Then he turned back to her. "Somehow I knew you were in mourning as well." He shrugged. "I'm not sure how, but I suspected you had gone through a difficult time."

She tried to smile. "You picked up on that even though we just met?" It was an ironic thing to say since she'd read the sorrow in his expression too.

"I was hoping I was wrong." He smiled a little, sympathetically, and Naomi thought she needed to fess up.

"In a way, you were wrong." She swallowed hard as she stared at her bare feet for a few seconds before looking back at him. "Please understand how much I loved *mei* parents. But it was five years ago, and over time, I've learned to function again." She took a deep breath. "I will always miss them, but the source of *mei* current pain is more recent. I feel badly even saying anything because it's not nearly as tragic as what you've been through." The weight of his pain pressed down on her shoulders. At least Thomas hadn't died.

Amos struggled to read her expression, but it had shifted and changed so much in a matter of minutes that he was confused. He waited for her to go on.

"*Mei* sadness stems from a bad breakup." She lowered her head again. "I know that's not like a death, but . . ." She blinked, and Amos hoped she didn't cry. If she did he'd have no choice but to pull her into his arms, or comfort her in some way, and she might mistake his kindness as something other than sympathy. "We were engaged." She finally looked up at him, and there were tears in the corners of her eyes.

"I suspect it felt like a death in much the same way," he said, unsure if that was true or not. He'd had breakups before, but nothing could have prepared him for Sarah's death.

Naomi looked at him as her jaw dropped briefly. "You are the first person who has ever said that to me. Again, your situation must be so much worse, but I appreciate that you do understand how I feel." She paused, biting her lip. "In so many ways, I do feel like he died."

But he didn't die, so maybe there was hope for her. "Is there any chance of a reconciliation?"

She shook her head vigorously, her face drawn into another confusing expression that portrayed a mixture of hurt and anger. "*Nee.* I don't think so. He broke off our engagement and left town." She pressed her lips together, and her eyes seemed to fill more. *Please don't cry.* "I feel like he took a part of me with him, a slice of *mei* heart that I'll never get back, and I don't ever want to feel that way again. I don't want to ever fall in *lieb* again."

Now she was speaking his language. "Nor do I."

They sat quietly for a while. This woman was convicted in her desire to never fall in love again. It was sad since she was incredibly beautiful and seemed like a nice person. But he was relieved that she wouldn't be flirting with him. Even as he had the thought, he realized how arrogant it sounded. But he was so tired of people trying to fix him up with their eligible friends, and women bringing pies and casseroles in hopes Amos would want to court them. No one wanted to talk about how horrible he still felt. As a man he felt he should keep those emotions inside. But sometimes he wanted to talk to someone other than God. He'd relied heavily on the Lord to get him through that difficult time, but not long after Sarah's funeral, friends stopped mentioning her name. He wanted to shout to the world sometimes that she had existed, that she'd been real, the only person he'd ever loved, a life not to be forgotten but remembered.

"Do you want to take a walk?" He quickly jerked his head

in her direction. "This is not me coming on to you. This is me feeling very grateful that I find you so easy to talk to about a subject we both seem to understand."

She smiled a little. He probably shouldn't have said that, but how could they be friendly with each other over the next few days unless Amos laid his cards on the table? No pretenses. No prospect of romance.

"No one ever wants to talk about it." She lifted her shoulders and lowered them slowly. "Sometimes I want to talk. But I must warn you . . . I can be fairly unpleasant when I do. Lots of self-pity." She chuckled a little. "No wonder no one wants to listen."

Amos smiled. There was something very real about this woman. "Did I see a pond on the back of the property when we were driving in? I bet the view of the sunset is wonderful. And I can deal with your self-pity as long as you don't get mad and punch me or something."

She laughed. "I promise not to hit you."

"Okay, then." He stood, and so did she.

"Just let me put on *mei* shoes." She scuttled to the other end of the porch and slipped on a pair of black loafers.

Then they set out across the front yard and toward the setting sun.

Esther stood at the window with Lizzie, watching Naomi and Amos walk across the yard toward the pond.

"Going on a walk doesn't necessarily mean anything, Lizzie." Esther tried to tame her sister's overly optimistic opinion. From the time she saw Naomi and Amos looking at each other in the dining room, Lizzie had them married off.

"Don't be so negative." Lizzie spit her teeth in her hand and pressed her nose to the glass. "Didn't you notice how handsome that fellow is? If anyone can mend Naomi's broken heart, it's him."

"Looks aren't everything, and you know that." Esther prayed for Naomi every day, that the girl would find love again. "You know I love a *gut* love story as much as you do, but we don't know a thing about that man."

"Well, here comes someone who does," Lizzie said in a whisper as she nodded toward the stairs. The two English women had gone out after supper, so it could only be Anna Mae.

"*Wie bischt,*" Lizzie said before she dropped her teeth, picked them up quickly, and forced them back into place.

Esther cringed, glad Naomi had swept the wood floors before their guests arrived.

"Would you like to join us for *kaffi* and shoofly pie?" Lizzie attempted to smile, but she obviously didn't have her teeth in correctly again, which gave her a lopsided smile that was comical. Thankfully Anna Mae was gracious and didn't stare.

"I don't think I can eat one more bite of food. Supper was wonderful, and I overdid it." Still smiling, she said, "But *kaffi* would be nice."

Lizzie motioned for her to follow them into the kitchen

where they had a small table and four chairs. It was where she, Esther, and Naomi ate most of their meals. The dining room was for guests and decorated fancier than anywhere else in the house. Naomi had a knack for arranging lovely place settings. Their kitchen was cozy and functional, and Esther felt sure Anna Mae would feel comfortable.

After they were seated and each had a cup of coffee, Lizzie sliced herself a large piece of pie. Like Anna Mae, Esther couldn't eat another bite. She didn't understand how Lizzie stayed so tiny. The woman ate all the time.

"Your *sohn* is a fine-looking fellow." Esther opened the conversation since Lizzie was shoveling pie into her mouth as if she hadn't just eaten a huge meal.

"*Danki*." Anna Mae took a sip of coffee, then circled the rim of the cup with her finger. "He's had a hard time." She glanced at Esther, then back down at her cup as she frowned. "His fiancée died of cancer about a year ago, and the boy can't seem to get over it." She paused before she looked at Esther again. "Sarah was a wonderful young woman, and he loved her so much. But unfortunately, he's cut himself off from available women and says he will never love anyone but Sarah." She shook her head. "His *daed* and I are hoping time will heal his heart. But for now, he just isn't interested in a romantic relationship."

Lizzie stopped chewing and shook her head. Esther shared her sister's disappointment. "I will pray for his heart to mend," she said. "Our Naomi is going through a similar situation. She was also engaged until her fiancé broke up with her and left our community. Naomi isn't blood-related to us, but we think of her like a *dochder*, more like *grossdochder*, I suppose. And we hate to see her so sad all the time."

Anna Mae glanced out the kitchen window and the hint of a smile played on her lips. "Naomi is lovely. Perhaps there is a friendship brewing at the very least. It's not like Amos to take off on a walk like that with a woman. I'm afraid that back home he's practically stalked by women who consider him quite a catch."

Esther caught the pride in Anna Mae's statement, but she had to admit, if the man was half as nice as he was attractive, she could understand him having a lot of female admirers.

"Naomi is as beautiful on the inside as she is on the outside." Lizzie had finished her pie, wiped her mouth, and managed to get her teeth straight. "It's a shame you and your *sohn* won't be here longer than a few days. Maybe those two would get to know each other and . . ." Lizzie raised both eyebrows and smiled.

Anna Mae blinked her eyes dreamily. "*Ach*, how I would love for Amos to find love again." She shook her head. "But I just don't see it happening. At least not any time soon." Smiling at Lizzie, she said, "But I wish we could stay longer, too, just to give them a chance and see what happens."

"Then stay." Lizzie straightened in her chair, grinning. "We won't charge you for any extra days," she said in a whisper, almost as if she was trying to keep Esther from hearing, even though she was right across the table.

"*Nee*, I couldn't do that. If we stay longer, I will pay."

Anna Mae spoke with enthusiasm, and hope found its way into Esther's heart as well.

"Please stay as long as you'd like." Esther glanced out the window. The young people were out of sight.

Lizzie pressed her palms together and lightly clapped her hands. "Watching the sunset is romantic."

Anna Mae nodded in agreement. "*Ya*, it is. Even if those two don't take to each other, I'd love to spend more time with *mei* family I haven't seen in a long time."

Esther was afraid to be too hopeful. But fear blocked the voice of God and was never a good emotion to cart around. She would try to pray her doubts away. It sounded like she and Lizzie had an ally, someone equally as interested in playing matchmaker. But then Anna Mae frowned.

"I'm afraid Amos won't want to stay longer than we agreed on. He owns his own construction company, and it's a slow time of year for him. I could only get him to commit to the trip if we returned Sunday." Anna Mae sipped her coffee. "It's a shame. Naomi seems like a lovely *maedel*. But, in truth, Amos just isn't ready yet."

Esther's hope fizzled, but Lizzie strummed her fingers on the table, lips pressed together and eyebrows drawn inward. Lizzie's hope hadn't floundered one bit. If anything, she was already plotting ways to get the young couple together. Esther admired her sister's determination, but Anna Mae knew her son. And she sounded certain he wasn't ready for love. Still, Lizzie's compassion for someone who had lost a loved one was always well received. Maybe she could help Amos with his healing process. That could be God's only plan for Amos right now. But Esther was going to try to keep her cup half full with hope that maybe a romance was on the horizon as well.

THREE

Naomi and Amos sat down on the bench near the pond. Lizzie and Esther called it the courting bench, and Naomi recalled all the time she'd spent on this bench watching the sunset with Thomas. She hadn't been back to this spot since he'd left. The only other person who used the bench was Gus. Naomi had seen him fishing here a couple times. There was an area between Gus's cottage and the *daadi haus* Mary and John lived in, where the bench was visible. It was otherwise hidden from view behind a cluster of trees.

"This is a great spot to watch the sun set." Amos stared straight ahead. "The colorful backdrops of those trees behind the corn are reflected in the water. This would be a perfect scene to paint, to capture the beauty of the sunset."

Naomi arched an eyebrow. "Do you paint?"

Amos turned to look at her and grimaced. "I used to. It

relaxed me and challenged me to reproduce the beauty of a great landscape." He paused, looking back over the water. "I haven't painted in a long time."

Naomi assumed he hadn't painted since his fiancée died. "I paint," she said before she bit her bottom lip. "At least, I used to."

"I haven't painted since Sarah died."

Naomi took a deep breath. "I haven't since Thomas left."

They were both quiet.

"Did you ever paint this?" Amos waved his hand across the pond just as a duck fluttered its wings and landed amid the colorful hues, followed by three more who gracefully landed atop the sun-kissed water.

"*Ya*, I did. Several times." She turned to him and smiled. "But it's so hard to capture the beauty of what God created. I'm actually not a very *gut* painter, but like you, it relaxed me and challenged me."

"I'd like to see one of your paintings." His gaze met hers. "You can tell a lot about a person through their art, whether it's putting a brush to canvas, writing a book, or some other form of creative outlet." She felt her cheeks begin to flush, as she was strangely flattered.

"I-I've never shown anyone the painting I consider to be my best one. The canvas is underneath *mei* bed." She frowned. "Probably covered in dust."

"I understand. I never thought *mei* paintings were worthy replicas of the landscapes I attempted to recreate. Do you paint with oils or acrylics?"

She was glad he didn't push the issue about seeing her painting. "Acrylics. What about you?"

"Same." He rubbed his chin as his eyes stayed on her. "Oils take too long to dry, in *mei* opinion."

They were quiet, both turning their attention to the sun making its final descent. It would be dark in about thirty minutes.

"I'm dreading this wedding on Thursday." Amos shook his head, still peering out over the pond. "I know that's a terrible thing to say, and I should be rejoicing for Suzanne and Isaiah." He chuckled. "Although I've never even met these cousins of mine, and I'm still not sure how we're related."

Naomi squeezed her eyes closed before she turned to him and sighed. "I'm dreading it, too, and it feels so freeing to say that out loud. I'm not related to Suzanne and Isaiah, but I've known them all of *mei* life. They are a lovely couple, very much in love, and so deserving of all the happiness in the world." She paused as she attempted to explain her feelings. "But if it were up to me, I'd sit this one out."

"Um . . . I hope I'm not being too forward by asking this, but will your, uh . . . The man you were supposed to marry, will he be at the wedding?" Amos scratched his chin again. "I would think that would make it unbearable."

Naomi had mixed feelings. A part of her longed to see Thomas. Had he missed her? He hadn't written to her since he moved. Would seeing her rekindle their romance? She reminded herself the reason he gave for breaking up with her and decided that seeing him would only twist the knife that was still in her heart.

"I don't know if he will be there." She squinted as the sun lowered even more, casting powerful rays directly into their eyes.

Amos took off his hat and laid it gently atop her prayer covering, tilting it slightly downward to block the glare. "I'm a carpenter and work outside all day. I'm used to the bright sunlight."

Naomi didn't think his eyes were any more accustomed to the intense glare than hers, but it was a nice gesture.

He laughed. "It's a *gut* look for you." He gently tapped the rim of the hat, and Naomi giggled.

"You're lying, but *danki.*"

I laughed. And it felt good. But just as quickly as joy tried to force its way into her heart, the door slammed. Her thoughts returned to the wedding in two days. Would Thomas be there?

∞

"I don't know why you bother being nice to that cantankerous old coot." Lizzie thrust her chin forward, pushing her lip into a pout.

"Language, Lizzie." Esther finished covering a plate of leftovers from supper. She briefly put a hand across her stomach and took a deep breath. Something wasn't right. She'd had a burning, nauseating feeling on and off since supper. "Besides, there was a lot left, and the man has to eat."

"Ha!" Lizzie said much too loudly. "Look at him. He ain't missing any meals."

"I'm sure he misses an occasional home-cooked meal."

"Well, you're a better person than I am. Every time we do anything nice for him, he returns our kindness with bitterness and no thanks at all."

"That doesn't mean we should stop being kind."

"Well, there is the old saying . . . Kill 'em with kindness." Lizzie grinned. She'd already shed her teeth for the evening and was in her nightclothes. "So, go kill him." She snickered as Esther left the kitchen.

Esther couldn't help but smile. This house would be a dull place without Lizzie in it. She was often inappropriate and sometimes rude, but not a day went by when there wasn't laughter—either *at* her or along with her.

Naomi had wandered in just before dark, Amos by her side. And the girl was smiling, which was rare. Esther tried not to swim in the pool of hope too long, but it was hard not to keep the emotion afloat, at least a little.

She put on her black cape since the night air would be chilly, hoping the pangs in her tummy would settle soon. Then she began the walk to Gus's cottage, her steps lit by the propane lamp in the yard, and then only by her flashlight. She stepped onto the worn path that connected the three properties. In the distance, she saw a glow from a lantern. It was early, and Gus was probably still awake. Even though he wasn't Amish, the cottage had never had electricity, so Gus had to suffer through the hot summers like the rest of them. Tonight he likely had his windows open to enjoy the crisp breeze.

Esther slowed her stride and took a few moments to appreciate a cloudless sky filled with stars, then she breathed in the scent of burning wood. Mary and John already had a fire going so early into fall. She glanced at the *daadi haus*, and all was dark. Esther smiled. The couple was likely tucked in early and trying to make a baby. They'd been married five years, but the Lord had yet to bless them with a child. Esther had overheard Mary weeping about it more than once, and a few times she'd even cried on Esther's shoulder. They were all on God's timeframe, but Esther prayed Mary would become pregnant soon.

She lumbered up the steps to the cottage and knocked on the door. Esther preferred to leave nonperishables in a tin on the porch—muffins, cookies, or other snacks—to avoid a conversation, more like a confrontation, with Gus. But when she brought him an occasional hot meal, she thought it best to hand it to him directly.

She took a breath and braced herself. Their renter would likely accuse her of disturbing him from whatever mundane task he'd been doing, something he would insist was very important. And as Lizzie had said, the old grump had never once said thank you. Esther did her best to tolerate him, and Gus seemed more tolerant of her than Lizzie. Maybe because Esther didn't kick him or provoke him the way her sister did, but Gus was still insufferable.

Esther would always be bewildered why her mother took pity on this man. She and Lizzie had asked about it not long after Gus became a tenant in the cottage, citing the disrespectful way Gus treated people. Their mother's response was vague but firm, saying only that he needed a home. Regina Yoder was a good woman, but Esther's gut told her there was more to the story.

The door flung open, and Esther's jaw dropped as she took a step backward. She blinked a few times, not sure it was Gus in front of her. He held up a lantern. There was plenty of light. It was him.

Then a string of curse words flew from the man's mouth, language so foul that Esther almost dropped the plate of food. She set the meal on a small table next to Gus's rocking chair, then covered her ears. When he appeared to be done with his obnoxious rant, she lowered her hands.

"What have you done?" Esther should have turned and high-tailed it back home, but she was too curious not to ask.

Gus pointed to his gray hair, no longer in a ponytail, but chopped raggedly to his jawline. He'd shaved his beard and had two nicks trailing blood from his chin. She wondered if maybe he had gone mad. To Esther's knowledge Gus had never cut that ponytail. Lizzie used to constantly tell him he needed a haircut, but he'd counter, saying he'd cut his hair if she did. Since Amish women don't cut their hair, that usually ended the conversation.

"I tried to cut my hair!" Gus shouted, but as he pointed to his horrendous haircut, it was hard to miss his fingernails. They were usually long and dirty, but tonight they were trimmed and clean.

"I see that." Esther awkwardly cleared her throat and pointed to the small table. "I-I brought you leftovers from supper, and—"

He abruptly turned around and pointed to the back of his head. He'd tortured those tresses even worse than in the front. Then he started throwing curse words all over the place again. Esther covered her ears again before rushing down the steps.

"Woman, where are you going?" he yelled.

Esther spun around, stomped back up the stairs, and pointed her finger at him. "Gus Owens, I will not tolerate that language." Her stomach cramped even more as anger built. "And 'Woman' is neither *mei* name nor Lizzie's. Do you hear me?"

It was unlike Esther to lose her cool this way. She prided herself on staying calm, no matter the situation, but she had listened to years of Gus's trashy talk. And the fact that she wasn't feeling well left her less tolerant of his behavior.

To her surprise, he didn't start hollering back at her, and she turned to leave, expecting him to lash out before she got very many steps away.

"Wait!"

Esther kept going.

"Wait!" he yelled again. Then Esther heard a faint "Please?"

She stopped but didn't turn around, instead glancing at the sky again to make sure it wasn't a full moon. Did she just hear Gus Owens say please?

Turning around slowly, she didn't move toward the cottage, but she shone the flashlight in his face. He quickly put a hand up to block the glare.

"What do you want, Gus?"

"What do you think I want, Woman? I need some help!"

Esther didn't think she'd ever cursed in her life, but this

moment was trying her patience as she spun around and starting walking again. Whatever was going on with her stomach was becoming a priority, and she wasn't in the mood for Gus.

"Wait, Esther. I'm sorry I called you 'Woman.' Thank you for the food. Now will you please get back here and help me?"

Sorry. Thank you. Please. All in one sentence. Tempted to keep walking, she turned and trudged back to the cottage, laying a hand across her stomach again. "Think before you speak, Gus. If I turn around to leave again, I won't be coming back." She flinched. Blood was drying in a trail down his chin.

He stepped aside so she could go into the cottage. Usually the smell kept her from ever stepping inside, but now she noticed a welcoming aroma, something lemony. And when Gus held up the lantern, Esther dropped the flashlight. She was too shocked to immediately reach for it.

"The cottage is clean." She looked at him, again wondering if he'd gone mad or was drunk. "It, uh . . . looks quite nice." Finally, she bent to get the flashlight.

"Oh, oh." He went back outside and returned with the plate of food. He stashed it in the refrigerator, then with pleading eyes, said, "Can you fix my hair?"

"Is it clean?" Esther reminded herself that sometimes she needed to think before she spoke, too, but previously she'd wondered what might be growing in that hair and beard.

"Yeah, it's clean!" He grabbed a stool and carried it from a small bar separating the kitchen from the living room. Slamming it on the floor, he went back to the kitchen and returned with a small pair of shears, the kind used for trimming bushes.

Esther laughed. "You're sure you want me to cut your hair with those?"

Gus's face was so red he looked like he might explode, but he got up again and returned with a pair of utility scissors. She'd cut Joe's hair throughout their entire married life, so the only haircut she knew how to give was cropped bangs with the back trimmed above the collar. But she'd used scissors that were made for cutting hair and smaller than what Gus held out now. She supposed he was sprucing up for Suzanne and Isaiah's wedding on Thursday, but that didn't explain the clean house.

"I've never given a haircut to an *Englisch* man before, but I'll do *mei* best." Esther held out her hand, and right before Gus handed over the scissors, he pulled back. "You're not going to stab me or anything, are you?"

She grinned. "Now, Gus, why in the world would you ask that? You've been nothing but pleasant and kind to us for all these years."

He grumbled.

"Give me the scissors. I don't have all night." Although she really did. The only thing waiting for her at home was a book about gardening. It wasn't very interesting. Maybe because it wasn't gardening season, but lately, she had trouble falling asleep, and reading helped sometimes—especially if the book wasn't holding her attention. Lizzie had a library of books, but they were all a bit too steamy for Esther's taste.

After Gus handed her the scissors and sat on the stool, Esther willed her stomach to settle and got busy straightening the jagged haircut.

"Don't move or I might *accidentally* nip off part of your ear." To her surprise, Gus didn't respond and sat so still that Esther wondered if he was breathing.

When she was done, she ran her fingers down the sides, smoothing it out, which seemed strange, to touch the man. Then she handed him back the scissors.

"That's the best I can do." She stepped back to have a better look, and even in the dim lighting, the improvement was nothing short of amazing. Beneath all that hair and beard, Gus was a fairly attractive man for his age, even with his jiggling jowls and protruding belly. "You might want to wash that blood off your face."

He grumbled some more as he carried the stool back to its spot. After he stashed the scissors in the drawer, he took a napkin, wet it, and dabbed at his chin.

Esther folded her hands in front of her, hoping for any type of acknowledgement, but he threw himself down on the couch and ran a hand through his short hair. It was silly of her to expect thanks. Saying it twice in one night might cause Esther to faint.

"Goodbye, Gus." Esther shook her head as she moved toward the door.

"Wait!" His voice had that frantic edge to it again.

Esther drew in a long, deep breath. *What now?* She turned around and held up a palm. "Gus, I've fixed your hair. I think it's lovely that you are cleaning yourself up for Suzanne and Isaiah's wedding, and—"

"Wedding! Woman, are you out of your mind? I hate

weddings. I hate churches even more." He waved a hand in the air. "Yeah, yeah, I know your people get married in barns and houses, but weddings aren't for me, no matter where they're held. What would make you think I'd do all this for a wedding?"

Esther held her arms stiffly on either side of her as patience abandoned her.

But he just groaned. "My daughter is coming for a visit."

Esther's mouth fell open. "Daughter? *What* daughter?"

"The only one I've got." He snickered. "That I know of. She'll be here tomorrow."

"I didn't know you had a daughter. How long has it been since you've seen her?"

His expression sobered as he rubbed his clean-shaven chin.

"Uh, not since she was fifteen and told me she never wanted to see me again." He growled. "I'm sure she only said that because her no-good mother told her to."

"*Ya*, I'm sure that was it." Esther pulled a Lizzie and rolled her eyes. She'd heard rumors that Gus had been married once, a long time ago, but even her mother hadn't been sure if it was true. "What is her name? How old is she?"

"Her name is Heather." He closed his eyes, tapping his fingers together, barely moving his lips as if he was counting. "Let's see . . . I'm seventy-four. She was fifteen . . ." He opened his eyes and started counting on his fingers, mouthing numbers. Esther was trying to process this new information. He opened his eyes and snapped his fingers. "She's fifty-four."

Esther glanced around the one-bedroom cottage. "Where is she going to sleep?"

"I guess on the couch. I'm too tall to sleep on it."

"What if she is tall too?" Esther tried to picture Gus's grown daughter, what she might be like, and more curiously, why did she want to see Gus now, after almost forty years? "Why don't you invite her to stay at the main *haus*?" At least Esther could make sure the woman had meals to eat and a bed to sleep in.

"I ain't paying for a room when—"

"Free, Gus. She can stay for *free*." It was a good thing she and Lizzie weren't in need of money, since they were offering a lot of free rooms this next week.

He slowly stood up and shuffled toward her, scratching his cheek. His expression left him more vulnerable than Esther had ever seen him.

"What if she doesn't like me?"

Under normal circumstances Ether would have burst out laughing, but something in Gus's eyes tugged at her heart. This was important to him. But what could she say—be yourself? The woman would run back to where she came from within the first five minutes.

"Just . . . be kind."

And this time Esther left, closing the door behind her, and half expecting Gus to rush out onto the porch to thank her. It was a hope she didn't cling to for long.

As she reached the steps to the main house, she tried again to picture what Gus's daughter might be like. How she'd love to be a fly on the wall to witness that meeting. But when she climbed into bed later, she felt called to pray for Gus and his daughter's reunion to go well.

Gus has a daughter. It still seemed surreal.

FOUR

NAOMI PULLED THE CANVAS OUT FROM UNDER HER BED and blew the dust into a plume that revealed just how long the painting had been there. She had other paintings stashed in the basement, the ones she didn't feel were very good, but she wasn't willing to throw them away. She brushed away more dust, each swipe bringing fall foliage on the other side of the pond into clearer view. This painting had the cornstalks in between the pond and the trees, when the landscape was at its best.

Naomi hadn't brought much with her when she moved in with Esther and Lizzie, but her paintings made the cut, along with her bedroom furniture, personal knickknacks, and her grandmother's cedar chest, which was against the far wall in her bedroom. She recalled the times she used to visit Lizzie and Esther, having attained permission to paint on their property whenever she wanted. Those were happier times.

She eyed the painting some more. It was her favorite. And it was something that wasn't tied to Thomas in any way. For a while everything she'd ever done with Thomas, or any place she'd ever been with him, caused her torment. But she'd painted this scene late one afternoon, months before she and Thomas started dating.

As she recalled being at the pond with Amos, she was surprised that Thomas hadn't consumed her thoughts since she and Amos had spent time there together.

After she propped up the canvas against the headboard, she walked around to the foot of her bed and tried to decide if it was worthy enough to show Amos. She'd never shown it to anyone, not even Thomas. It was also the largest painting she'd ever completed, rising two feet high and stretching almost three feet wide. As she wondered what Amos would think, her chest tightened. Was it too personal to show him something she'd never shown anyone? She gingerly picked it up and carefully slid it back underneath the bed, making a mental note to at least clear the dust from it every now and then.

Downstairs, dishes were clanking in the kitchen and as the aroma of bacon wafted up the stairs, she realized someone had started breakfast. She glanced at the clock on her wall. She wasn't late, but she scurried down the stairs, crossed through the living room, and hurried into the kitchen.

"Lizzie, I'll do that." Naomi sidled up to the small woman and gently eased the fork from her hand and began flipping the bacon. Lizzie tended to burn it. It was Naomi's job to get breakfast started, but they never served before eight o'clock when they had English guests. Traditionally Amish women and men started the day around four in the morning. Lizzie said traditions were meant to be altered, and Esther hadn't argued. Nor had Naomi. Sleeping until seven was a welcomed change after spending most of her life getting up much earlier. Even when they didn't have guests, they'd all taken to sleeping in until the sun had risen.

"Only the two *Englisch* ladies for breakfast." Lizzie took some eggs from the refrigerator and placed them on the counter. "Anna Mae and that handsome *sohn* of hers left early to have breakfast with Isaiah's parents." Naomi detected an odd twinge of disappointment as a heaviness centered in her chest. "I told Esther to stay in bed a while longer. I heard her up in the night with stomach problems again."

"Maybe she needs to see a doctor." Naomi began cracking eggs into a bowl.

Lizzie shook her head. "You know she won't go. Stubborn woman." She slammed her hands to her hips. "And we talked briefly in the hall after one of her trips to the bathroom. Guess who has a child?"

Naomi gasped. "Is Mary pregnant?" They'd all been hoping she and John would be able to conceive a child soon. Mary was a lovely person, and Naomi had hoped they would become friends. But after Naomi's split with Thomas, she preferred to be alone. Apparently Mary did too. Esther told Naomi that Mary's focus was on conceiving a child, so much so that she had detached herself from most everyone and slipped into depression. Maybe if Naomi and Mary had already been friends before Mary and John moved into the *daadi haus,* they would have been able to comfort each other during these trying times. Now, it felt like too much effort. Naomi didn't know how to make herself feel better, much less anyone else. But she prayed for Mary.

Lizzie glowered. "*Nee.*" She waved a frustrated hand in the air before it landed back on her hip. "Esther, being the *gut* woman she is, took Grumpy Gus a plate of food last night, and she ended up cutting his hair because his *dochder* is visiting him today."

Naomi spun around, her eyes wide. "He has a *dochder?*"

Lizzie wrapped her arms around herself and closed her eyes. "Just the thought makes me shudder. I mean, what kind of offspring could someone like Gus produce? And who'd have him anyway?"

Naomi turned back to the bacon. "Now, Lizzie, there is someone for everyone." Her heart sank a little. *Maybe not.* She used to believe that.

"And that sister of mine actually helped him get all spruced up for the visit and said his *haus* is even clean." Lizzie groaned. "She's too *gut* to that man."

"Maybe he hasn't always been the way he is now. Maybe seeing his *dochder* will brighten his disposition and make him a happier person."

"Well, since the *dochder* ditched him almost four decades ago—when she was fifteen—I can't imagine why she's seeking him out now. Esther told him the woman, who is fifty-four, can have a room upstairs." She chuckled. "For free." Rolling her eyes, she added, "Did I mention that Esther is too nice for her own good?"

"I can't wait to meet her." Naomi stirred the eggs, then added a little salt, pepper, and cheese. "Forty years is a long time. I'm sure she's nothing like Gus. But if he let Esther cut his hair, and the house is clean . . ." Naomi smiled. "He must be excited about her visit. Does Esther know when she'll be here?"

"Just sometime today. She filled me in best as she could before she went back to bed. And before I forget, it's just you, me, and Esther for meals today. The two *Englisch* ladies only made reservations for one night, so we won't see them again after they check out this morning. And Anna Mae and Amos won't be back until after supper time."

Naomi nodded. "*Ya*, okay." She felt a strange and unexpected hint of disappointment again, but it didn't last long. Today would be an easier day than normal. Naomi would prepare simple meals for herself, Lizzie, and Esther instead of the lavish ones she created for their guests. After breakfast she'd collect eggs and tend to the animals—two goats, two pigs, and three horses. She mentally ran through her list of daily chores. She'd dusted and swept the day before. Washday wasn't until Monday. After she stripped the beds, there were only a couple mending projects to work on. *Then what?* Did she really want an easy day? Staying busy was the best therapy, although she knew there was no cure-all for how she was feeling.

Lizzie cleared her throat. "Amos owns his own construction company. His *mudder* said his fiancée died of cancer." She paused, and even over her shoulder, Naomi could tell Lizzie was adjusting her teeth. Her words sounded garbled, and there was a sort of spitting noise when she talked.

"*Ya*, he told me about his fiancée." Naomi recalled the ease of their conversation the evening before.

"Seems like you have something in common. Not exactly the same, but you've both lost someone you love."

Here we go. Naomi spun around and pointed the spoon at Lizzie, drops of egg hitting the floor. "No matchmaking. Do you hear me, Lizzie?"

Lizzie grunted as she shook her head. "Now, dear. Would I do such a thing?"

This was one area where Esther was as guilty as her sister, but Lizzie always took things a step too far. "*Ya*, you would. Don't you remember locking me and that man from Lancaster County in the basement? We were down there together for hours before someone let us out."

"That was an accident," Lizzie said under her breath as she batted her eyes at Naomi.

"Ha. That's a lie." Naomi turned back to the eggs. "No tricks. And you best ask *Gott* to forgive you for not telling the truth."

Lizzie didn't say anything. Her intentions were good, but Naomi had made it clear to both sisters that she wasn't interested in a relationship.

"I'll be anxious to meet Gus's *dochder*," Naomi said to break the silence and change the subject. She wasn't sure if she'd made Lizzie feel bad or if Lizzie was busy brewing up an attempt to push Naomi and Amos together. It didn't matter too much. Amos and his mother would be leaving Sunday anyway.

The bigger concern was tomorrow. The wedding. And would Thomas be there?

∞

Amos enjoyed visiting and getting to know his relatives. He'd thought they were going to hire a driver to cart them around town, but instead, they borrowed one of Esther and Lizzie's buggies. It was a beautiful day and not much distance between the families they had visited.

Since they were leaving Sunday, his mother was trying to fit in as much visiting as she could during the trip. Amos could barely remember when his great uncle and some other family members decided to leave Ohio to move here. And no matter how many times his mother told him how they were all related, Amos couldn't keep it straight. He just knew they'd made the move in search of a quieter, less populated community.

"This is a fine animal," Amos said as he pulled the buggy to a stop in front of the main house. "It was nice of Esther and Lizzie to let us use one of their buggies." He glanced at his mother, but her eyes were fixed on the house. Amos wasn't sure she even heard him. When he got out of the buggy, he was surprised to see Esther, Lizzie, and Naomi all looking out the window. "Why are they staring at us?"

His mother stepped out of the buggy and started across the yard, picking up her pace. "I don't know. I hope everything is okay."

Amos gave an awkward wave, since it was obvious he and his mother could see the three women peering out the window. When he heard car wheels crunch atop the gravel road that led to the small cottage, he looked over his shoulder at a small white car.

As soon as they walked into the house, Naomi cleared her throat and turned to face Amos and his mother. Lizzie and Esther said hello but kept their eyes presumably on the car.

"We weren't staring at you." Naomi's face turned a delicate shade of pink as she spoke directly to Amos. "We were waiting to see Gus's *dochder* get out of the car."

Amos hung his hat on the rack by the front door, again wondering if he should take off his boots. But there were never any shoes near the entryway. Probably since they often had English guests staying at the inn. Lizzie, Esther, and Naomi were barefoot most of the time, even though the temperatures were dropping. Amos took off his shoes as a courtesy.

"Well, the wait is over." Lizzie stomped a foot. "And it isn't Gus's *dochder* who stepped out of the car."

Amos wasn't sure why the visitor's arrival was so important to the ladies, but Lizzie groaned. Esther turned to Naomi and sighed.

"It's a man, and there's an insurance name written on a sign on his car. I'd hate to be a solicitor and have to face off with Gus. Whether it's someone selling insurance or Gus's insurance agent, it definitely is not Gus's *dochder*," Esther said before she turned to Amos's mother. "*Mei* apologies that you caught us gawking at our neighbor this way, but we've known Gus a long time, and we never knew he had a child. A grown woman now, and she's due to arrive today." Esther smiled and waved an arm toward the kitchen. "I know you said you were eating with family, but there are plenty of leftovers in the refrigerator, and I left two pies on the table—apple and pecan. Please help yourselves to anything you'd like."

Amos and his mother thanked Esther at the same time. As the sun began its descent, Amos recalled his pleasant conversation with Naomi down by the pond the day before. He wanted to invite her to walk to the water again, to sit on the bench and talk more. But it sounded forward in his mind, and he worried she might think he was making an attempt at courting.

His mother covered her mouth as she yawned. "Pardon me," she said before she lowered her hand. "I'm going to excuse myself and retire for this evening. *Danki* again for letting us use your horse and buggy. We had such a lovely time and are looking forward to seeing many of our cousins again at the wedding tomorrow."

Amos wasn't looking forward to that part of the trip, and the only one who seemed to understand was Naomi.

As his mother started up the stairs, Amos wondered if he should excuse himself as well. He lingered, though, and walked to the window, then commented about what a nice view they had of the sun setting.

"You two should go take a walk," Lizzie said, grinning.

Amos turned around. It was difficult not to chuckle when Lizzie spoke sometimes. She seemed to have a hard time with her false teeth, which was comical, but he never allowed himself to crack a smile, which might hurt her feelings. But she was also clearly playing matchmaker by suggesting the walk. What Lizzie didn't know was that he and Naomi had already set the boundaries for their relationship. Friendship. But he wouldn't mind having someone to share his feelings with about the wedding tomorrow.

He turned to Naomi, but she avoided his eyes as she put a hand on the back of her neck. The rejection was coming. He reminded himself that it didn't matter, but his male ego kicked in and he forced a yawn.

"I think I'm going to have to pass." He kept his eyes on her to catch her expression, which didn't give away much. She just lowered her arm and nodded. But then her eyes softened, and she parted her lips slightly.

Amos told his feet to move toward the stairs, but there was almost a longing in her beautiful eyes, and he found himself drawn to her in a way that surprised him. He opened his mouth to tell her he'd changed his mind.

"*Gut nacht*," she said and moved toward the stairs.

He watched the graceful way she carried herself, even caught her looking back at him once, her eyes meeting his . . . and he realized he'd made a mistake. It wasn't longing in her eyes. It was sorrow. He recalled their conversation.

It would be impossible not to think of Sarah the entire

time. But Naomi might have to actually face the person who broke her heart. Sarah snuck into Amos's dreams, and seeing her was always wonderful. Until he woke up and stretched his arm across an empty bed.

He wasn't sure what to pray for Naomi. Maybe if her ex— Thomas was his name, he remembered—showed up, there would be a chance for them to work things out. But if the guy did show up and with no desire to get back together, that would be even worse for Naomi.

When he got to his room, he sat on the bed, then lit the lantern. He decided all he could do was pray that God's will be done tomorrow. *But, please, Lord, help Naomi and me both stay strong.*

Esther waited until she heard Lizzie snoring in the bedroom next door before she eased out of bed. She tiptoed to the living room and took her black cape from the rack. The October days had been warmer than usual, but the night air would be crisp and chilly, so she chose to put on her black bonnet as well.

She'd seen Gus's lantern in the cottage and knew he was still up. Unless he'd fallen asleep in his recliner inside. If he could fall asleep in a wooden rocker on the porch, she supposed he might be asleep. Esther had worried for years that Gus would knock over a lantern one day when he fell asleep without extinguishing it.

With a flashlight illuminating the ground in front of her,

Esther made the trek to the cottage. She tried to step softly as she held the handrail and ambled up the steps.

Gus flung the door open before she had a chance to knock. "What do you want?"

Esther drew in a calming breath. Lizzie would be furious she'd come to check on Gus. And by the tone of Gus's voice, Esther wished she hadn't bothered. "I didn't see your *dochder* arrive today. We had a room prepared for her. I-I just came to see if you were all right."

Gus clenched his fists at his sides, and even in the dim lighting, she could tell his face was as red as a freshly painted barn. "Why wouldn't I be all right?" He grunted, but relaxed his hands, then looped his thumbs beneath his suspenders. With his new haircut, he almost looked Amish, minus the beard. Esther shivered at the thought. She didn't even know if Gus believed in God, and she was sure a man like Gus would never be able to adhere to their ways. She'd been shocked when he first moved into the cottage and didn't fuss about not having any electricity.

"*Ach*, very well. I'm glad you're fine." Esther fought the urge to roll her eyes, but when her stomach began to churn, she put a hand across her stomach and bent slightly at the waist. She always carried a tissue in the pocket of her apron, but she didn't have her apron on, only her cape over her dress.

"Yeah, well I am." Gus dismissed her with the wave of his arm, but Esther couldn't move, and when she coughed, blood spilled into her hand.

"What the . . . ?" Gus narrowed his bushy gray eyebrows and leaned his head over.

"I need a tissue," Esther managed to say as she spit in her hand again, unintentionally.

Gus growled and mumbled something under his breath as he went into the house, leaving the door open. He came back with half a roll of toilet paper and pushed it toward her.

Esther pulled off several squares and held them to her mouth. "*Danki*," she said in a whisper before she tore off a longer wad this time, dabbing her chin and avoiding Gus's glare. When she finally looked up at him, his cold dark eyes pecked at her attempt to regain her dignity.

"What's wrong with you?" He scratched his cheek where a shadow was already laying the foundation for the beard he would probably grow back. There was a hint of concern in his expression, but the scowl on his face remained.

"I don't know." She'd been having stomach troubles for a while, but she'd only coughed up blood like this one other time, about a week ago.

Gus folded his arms across his chest, his stomach doubling as a perch. "Maybe you need a doctor." His tone was husky and stern, but not completely uncaring.

"*Ya, ya.* We'll see." Esther was terrified of anyone in the medical field and had been since she was a child. She'd managed to go seven years without visiting a doctor. Wagging a finger at him, she said, "Gus Owens, don't you speak a word about this to anyone, especially Lizzie." Esther's sister had gone to the doctor for a splinter once. Another way they were complete opposites.

Lizzie wasn't afraid of doctors—or much of anything—

and she disliked having anything wrong with her. She always bypassed any natural remedies and went straight to the English doctors, saying God would understand and that they'd had more training than the holistic people here. She'd have a fit if she knew Esther was having this much trouble with her health.

Esther shot Gus her fiercest attempt at rage, pressing her lips together and squinting her eyes at him. He needed to understand that this was her business, and she'd share it if and when she was ready. "I mean it. Not a word about this to anyone." She'd probably overshot her point, since Gus smirked.

"I'm glad you think this is funny." She spun on her heels, clutching the toilet tissue, and pointed the light in front of her as she stomped down the steps. Her emotions spiraled, caught somewhere between fear and anger.

"I won't tell her."

Esther turned around on the bottom step. "*Danki*, I appreciate that." She wanted to believe him, but she had her doubts. Her stomach still roiled, and she just wanted to get home.

"You make pies every day. One generous slice per day, and I'll keep my mouth shut." He puffed his chest out as he lowered his arms to his sides, grinning.

Esther bristled with indignation. From anyone else, this request would be a shock. It was a stretch even for Gus. Why couldn't he just do something out of the kindness of his heart? But Esther managed a coy smile. "Of course, Gus. I'll bring you a slice of pie every day." She paused, her eyes crinkling in the corners. "Aren't you worried I might poison you or something?"

He chuckled. "Nah, you ain't got it in you." Now he was the one pointing a finger at her. "But that wicked sister of yours, I wouldn't put it past her to lace my pie with arsenic."

"Nor would I." She shook her head and started home.

"You gotta be the one to bring it every day, not ol' Lizzie. At the very least, she'd spit on it."

Esther didn't turn around, but she smiled. Gus was right. Esther could never poison anyone, and in reality, neither could Lizzie. *But spit on his pie?* Now, that was tempting.

FIVE

IT WAS NEARLY ELEVEN WHEN NAOMI COVERED HER HEAD
with a scarf, slipped into her robe, and stepped into the hallway. Esther had installed battery-operated lights along the
floorboards every few feet. They attached to the wall and lit
the floor and stairs just enough to see. She also put a flashlight on every guest's night table. The English weren't used
to feeling their way around in the dark. Lizzie always said
Amish folks had cat eyes, from maneuvering in the dark all
their lives.

Naomi had only taken a few steps down the hall when she
wished she'd put on socks. The wood floors were cold against
her bare feet. After she crossed through the living room, she
thought about whether she'd have apple or pecan pie. *Maybe
both.*

"*Wie bischt.*"

Naomi gasped. "What are you doing up so late?"

Amos set a fork on a plate with a slice of pecan pie. "I guess the same thing you're doing. Couldn't sleep, and I kept thinking about these pies calling my name." A corner of his mouth lifted on one side. "I already had a slice of the apple, so now I'm working on pecan."

The kitchen held more battery-operated lights. Naomi had often wondered how much money the sisters spent on batteries, but she supposed the safety of their guests didn't come with a price tag.

Naomi had wanted to feed her anxiety with a giant slice of pie, then have a good cry afterward. Now she'd have to be more ladylike and select a smaller serving.

After she took a plate from the cabinet, then a fork from the drawer, she pulled out a chair across from Amos. She cut a dainty slice of apple pie, and once it was on her plate, she forked a bite and savored the late-night indulgence. Afterward, she stared across the table at Amos.

"I'd do anything to get out of this wedding in the morning." Naomi shook her head. "And that makes me a terrible person." They'd already talked about how neither of them wanted to go, but it lightened the load to say it out loud.

An eager look flashed in his eyes. Not a muscle on his face moved, not even a twitch. This man seemed to speak with his eyes. "Then let's don't go."

Naomi frowned. "What? I have to go. You might be able to get out of it since you don't really know the bride and groom."

He scratched his chin, a gesture she'd noticed him doing often when thinking something through. "*Ya*, true. But *mei mamm* would be pretty upset with me." He grinned, then took another bite of pie. After swallowing he said, "So, you see, we'd both be in trouble. We could just go ready the horse, get in the buggy, and take off." He pointed the fork at her. "We'd leave a note, of course. We wouldn't want everyone worrying about us. That would ruin the wedding. They'd be mad, but they'd get over it."

Naomi momentarily put a hand over her mouth, afraid she might burst out laughing. "I almost think you're serious."

Those eyes of his met hers again and twinkled with mischief. "I am."

She leaned back in the chair, slouching a little as she strummed her fingers on the table. "Very tempting." Then she shook her head and returned to her pie. "But I have to go."

His eyes found hers again. "I know."

They were quiet, each enjoying the pie, lost in their own thoughts. Naomi was anyway. She hadn't lied. She had to attend the wedding, even though she really didn't want to. Thomas was invited, but she had no idea if he was coming. Apparently there had been no RSVP one way or the other. Naomi wanted to despise and hate him, but she still loved him. She'd take him back if he asked her to. That kind of love only came along once in a lifetime. Surely, he'd only gotten cold feet. But every time her thoughts moved optimistically toward a reunion, she reminded herself that she hadn't heard from him.

Amos stood up and carried his dishes to the sink. "Four is

going to come early. If things get too hard for you tomorrow, come find me. We'll make our escape." Smiling, he said, "*Gut nacht*, Naomi. Try to sleep, and *Gott*'s peace be with you."

"And with you," she said in a whisper as he walked away.

                                       ⟢⟣

Amos was programmed to get up at four, no alarm needed, but he was slow moving the next day. The sense of dread hadn't vanished overnight. If anything, it had intensified. Would he see Sarah's face throughout the entire ceremony, picturing the two of them taking their vows?

Strangely, he had a growing curiosity about something else that he hoped might be a distraction. He wondered what Thomas looked like. Naomi was beautiful—one of the most beautiful women he'd ever met. Was her ex-fiancé a handsome and charming guy? He couldn't imagine anyone leaving Naomi, not anyone who truly loved her. He was wise enough to know that beauty ran far beneath the skin, but Naomi had an air of kindness, mixed with just enough humor to make her not only beautiful, but interesting. Even though he wasn't in the market for a relationship, he enjoyed conversation with her.

By the time he got downstairs, everyone was bustling about. Amos could tell an attempt was being made to be quiet. The new guests were still upstairs sleeping. But with five of them putting on jackets, capes, and bonnets, there was still a flurry of activity.

When they reached their destination, Amos would be prepared to help the men with any setup that needed to be done—tables, chairs, tents outside. The women would mostly be in the kitchen until the ceremony started. Some of the ladies would even continue with food preparations while the wedding was going on inside the house. After the ceremony everyone would gather to eat outside. Amos remembered the setup well, and he'd heard Amish weddings were mostly universal. He could still recall the anticipation and excitement he'd felt about his own wedding day, before Sarah got sick. It was unlike the tightness in his chest and temptation to flee he was feeling today.

Lizzie pointed to an ice chest on the floor. "Amos, can I trouble you to put that in Esther's buggy, the same one you took yesterday?"

"*Ya, ya.* Of course." Amos picked up the cooler, and Naomi opened the door for him. He wondered if his eyes were as telling as hers. *Let's get this day over with.*

After everyone had donned warm clothes that could be shed later when it warmed up, Lizzie announced that she, Esther, and Amos's mother would ride in one buggy, and Amos and Naomi could take Lizzie's buggy, following them to the wedding. He could tell by the way the two sisters and his mother grinned that this was a setup. But that was okay. He enjoyed Naomi's company, and they were in the same sinking boat until this event was behind them.

Naomi's teeth chattered in the darkness as Amos guided the buggy down the road to the bride's house, where Suzanne and Isaiah would be married. The drive was a straight shot but would take about ten minutes.

Amos looked over his shoulder. "I don't see a blanket, but you're shaking." He started to ease his jacket off his shoulders.

"*Nee*, don't do that. I'm fine." She turned to him, still shivering. "I don't know how much of my shaking is due to the cold. I'm incredibly nervous."

Amos nodded. "We need a code word."

Naomi chuckled lightly. "What?"

"A code word. If the situation becomes unbearable for either one of us, we can say the word, whether it's in conversation or we have to mouth it to each other across the room or from underneath the tent. Then we can meet up and get away."

Naomi laughed again, a nervous sound that she hoped didn't slip out at the wedding. "As silly as that sounds, I'm going to go along with it." She tapped a finger to her chin. "Hmm . . ." She twisted her mouth back and forth. "If we aren't close by, we can just raise a hand. If we're close enough to hear each other, let's make the word . . ." She thought about it some more, then shrugged, giggling. "I don't know."

Amos chuckled, turning to her briefly. "We're not very *gut* at this."

As Naomi pondered, Suzanne's house appeared in the distance, easy to see since it was lit up like the county fairground at night. People often joked that the highest propane bill they ever had was the day and night of a wedding, an all-day affair. "We better hurry." She pointed in front of her. "We're still a mile or so away, but we're failing miserably."

"Dancing shadows." Amos glanced at her before shifting his eyes back to the road.

Naomi frowned. "Dancing shadows? What in the world made you think of that?"

His eyes gleamed in the pale light of the moon as he slowed the horse's gait slightly. "The moonlight behind the trees has been casting little shadows across your face, like little people dancing."

She laughed. "Our people don't dance."

Amos chuckled too. "I know, but it was the first thing that came to mind."

Naomi shook her head. "Little people dancing on *mei* face? Really?" She paused and gave a taut nod of her head. "*Ach*, well, that's it then. Dancing shadows, even though that's two words." She playfully pointed a finger at him.

They were almost there, and she had to give Amos credit. He'd managed to keep her mind occupied during the short trip. Thomas hadn't crept into her head until now. She wanted to thank Amos, but any words she tried to form were wedged in her throat. As they turned into the driveway, a war of emotions raged within her.

She jumped when Amos gently touched her arm. "You're going to be okay. Remember . . . dancing shadows."

It sounded like an odd choice. How closely had Amos been watching her? Had he stolen glances when she wasn't looking? It didn't really matter. Naomi just stared straight ahead and nodded.

"Dancing shadows," she whispered.

❧

Esther's pockets were stuffed with tissues, and she'd already prayed several times that she wouldn't have another episode during the wedding. Or ever again. She hadn't slept much last night as she considered what might be ailing her. Cancer was the first thing that came to mind since her and Lizzie's mother had died of breast cancer. But Esther couldn't recall her mother ever coughing up blood. Gus was right. She was going to have to go to the doctor, no matter how terrifying the thought. She would go soon and get it over with. Then she'd know, and it would also mean fewer days she would have to take Gus a slice of pie. One of the women in their household was always making pies, so sharing wasn't the issue. Seeing Gus daily was the problem.

"Where is Naomi?" Lizzie was suddenly right next to her in the kitchen, which was filled with women preparing for the lavish meal to be served later.

"I don't know, but there are over two hundred people here. Some are out in the barn, and the men are still setting up tents outside." Esther's stomach rumbled, and without thinking, she put a hand across it.

"Are you still having trouble with your tummy?" Lizzie pointed a finger at her. "You need to go to—"

"Lizzie, where are your teeth?" Esther's eyes widened.

"Oops." She reached into her apron pocket and fumbled around until she had the dentures in her hand. Then she began the process of trying to get them situated in her mouth.

"I suggest you don't bother me about a doctor until you go back to the dentist." Esther shook her head. "What do you need Naomi for?"

"I don't need her." Lizzie opened her mouth, twisting it from side to side, and miraculously, the teeth seemed to find their place. "I just wanted to make sure she was all right. I haven't seen Thomas here. I asked around, but not even his closest kin know if he's coming today."

"I feel sure it's best for Naomi if he doesn't show up." Esther had worried about the possibility. "This has to be a hard day for her. Seeing Thomas would be very upsetting. That boy hurt Naomi badly, and I don't think a reconciliation would be a *gut* thing. I think he would hurt her again."

Lizzie's eyes had drifted away, and she was grinning. "You're right. And maybe there is another prospect on the horizon." She nodded to where Naomi and Amos were standing beside each other in the living room. The panels separating the den and dining room had already been removed and relocated. Most of the furniture had also been hauled to the bedrooms to make room for everyone in attendance. It was going to be a tight squeeze, likely with a few dozen folks standing. Some homes simply weren't big enough to hold the service, and weddings would be held in the barn or beneath the tents. Suzanne's house was just barely making an indoor wedding possible.

"They look cozy," Lizzie added, a perfectly straight smile lighting up her expression.

Esther smiled. "I have to agree with you. He's such a handsome man and seems so nice. But he doesn't live nearby, and he and Anna Mae are leaving Sunday."

"That's three days away." Lizzie nudged Esther and giggled. "Besides, there's always the basement."

Esther narrowed her eyebrows into a frown. "Don't you ever do anything like that again. What if there had been a fire? If I had been home, I never would have allowed you to lock Naomi and that man in the basement."

Lizzie waved her off. "I was in the kitchen reading a book the entire time. They were never in danger."

"Still, it was a line that shouldn't have been crossed. And from what I recall, there was no chance of them becoming romantically involved after you forced them to spend time together." She glanced at Naomi and Amos. "But those two do make a beautiful couple, don't they?"

Lizzie nodded. "*Ya*, and we've got to find a way for him and Anna Mae to stay longer than Sunday."

"I will think on it." Esther wanted romance for Naomi. The girl was still healing, though.

"Now let's just hope Thomas doesn't show up and mess everything up."

For once, Esther agreed with her sister.

SIX

AMOS SAT THROUGH THE ENTIRE CEREMONY FEELING LIKE he was drowning, gulping air as his throat started to close up, and widening his eyes when he thought he might cry. He was a fish flapping around, the life slowly being sucked out of him. By the time the bishop placed a holy kiss on Isaiah's forehead and the bishop's wife did the same on Suzanne's, Amos was spent. He wanted to leave. As he'd suspected, he couldn't stop imagining himself and Sarah taking their vows, and the image was overwhelming. The tightness in his chest made him want to scream the code words and rush away with Naomi.

He could barely see her. She was sitting behind a very large woman, but every now and then she peeked around the lady and locked eyes with him, a stoic expression on her face. Maybe she was tolerating the service better than he was. Or she just hid her emotions better than he did.

Finally, the ceremony was over. The men began to mosey out to the barn. If the after-party was like those he'd attended back home, a few men would tell jokes and even smoke cigars while the women scurried about to get the food on the tables. Amos didn't get in a hurry. He didn't have much of an appetite, and the wedding party would be served first. He felt a sort of obligation to check on Naomi but lost sight of her once everyone dispersed.

Outside, he wove in and out of the crowd under the tent, hoping and praying Naomi would find him and say she couldn't take it anymore. Amos still didn't know if Thomas was here.

After another thirty minutes of casually speaking to guests he didn't know, he found Naomi talking to a couple about their age, so he joined them.

"*Wie bischt*," he said as he looked back and forth between the couple. Naomi introduced them as Mary and John Lapp.

"They rent the *daadi haus* on Esther and Lizzie's property." Naomi smiled, but he could tell it was forced, and her thick eyelashes swept over dark circles beneath her eyes. Still beautiful, but she looked tired and miserable. *Say the words and we're out of here.*

"It's *gut* to meet you, Amos." John extended his hand. Mary echoed her husband, then asked, "Are you enjoying your visit to Montgomery?"

"*Ya*, it's different from where we live in Ohio, much smaller. I like the quaintness of the town." Amos glanced at Naomi, who looked a million miles away, her gaze drifting. Was Thomas here, or was she still looking for him?

The conversation turned to the weather and how it had warmed up to be a beautiful day. The sun had taken its highest place in the sky, and a gentle breeze swirled amid the crowd. An atmosphere any bride and groom would cherish on their special day.

Mary touched Naomi's arm. "I'm sure this hasn't been an easy day for you."

"*Ach*, I'm fine." Naomi glanced at Amos. "It was a lovely ceremony. I'm so happy for Suzanne and Isaiah." There was a tremble in her voice that fired a dagger of empathy straight into Amos's heart.

He knew she didn't need a gentle touch on the arm. She needed a hug, and the urge to embrace her was strong but would be inappropriate.

"Shadows . . ." she said a she scratched her head, her lip trembling.

Mary frowned. "What?"

Naomi shook her head. "I mean, maybe dancing . . . or . . ." She rubbed her forehead as Mary and John watched her with curiosity, waiting for her to make some sort of sense.

Amos met her eyes. "I saw that early this morning, the way the moon cast shadows from behind the trees. Is that what you mean, dancing shadows?" It sounded ridiculous, but when Naomi nodded, Amos rubbed his chin, trying to think of a reason for them to excuse themselves.

"Mary and John, again, it was nice to meet you, but we should probably go." He tipped his hat before turning to Naomi. "I almost forgot. *Mei mamm* was looking for you. I can take you to her." It was an outright lie but all he could come up with in the moment.

"*Ya*, okay." Naomi's expression fell. She obviously thought he was telling the truth. He started walking away, and Naomi followed. Before they reached the front porch, he veered left, gently taking hold of her elbow until they were behind the house.

"I'm sorry. I lied. *Mamm* isn't looking for you, but you seemed to be searching for our code words."

She had tears in her eyes. "Thomas isn't here. He is seeing someone in the community where he lives now and didn't think it would be appropriate to bring her. Mary had just told me when you walked up, and I got flustered, and . . ." She raised her shoulders, then dropped them slowly.

Without overthinking it, he pulled her into his arms and held her. He needed the hug as much as she did. After gently rubbing her back for a few seconds, Amos eased her away.

"How are we going to get out of here without causing a lot of unnecessary gossip? Everyone would see us leave in the buggy." Amos peeked around the corner of the house. "Any ideas? I'm assuming you're as ready to leave as I am."

She nodded. "Are you sure, though? I mean, do you really want to leave? You're bound to be hungry."

"Are you?"

"*Nee*."

"I'm not either." Amos's stomach grumbled in resistance, but he truly didn't think he could eat a thing. He glanced around, then noticed the fields of corn that normally would have been harvested by now. A local man had told him a lack of rain over the summer had delayed the farmers from bringing in some of the crops. Where the cornfields began about fifty feet away from them, a small path had been cleared and stretched as far as he could see with large stalks on either side.

"Where does that go?" He pointed to the opening.

"I don't know." Naomi gazed into the distance with a curious expression. He reached for her hand.

"Let's go."

They jogged to the entrance, not looking behind them to see if they'd been spotted. Leaves from the cornstalks as long as Amos was tall slapped them in the face as they ran, each holding an arm up in an attempt to avoid the whipping branches. When they finally stopped, Naomi burst out laughing.

"This is the silliest thing I've ever done." Smiling and winded, she took a deep breath, then blew it out slowly. "That felt *gut*. And I just couldn't take it anymore."

Amos gazed into her eyes, glad her tears had dried. He looked at her cheeks, red from running. But it was her smile, her lips, that drew in his focus. Slightly parted, full, and naturally pink. Amos hadn't kissed another woman since Sarah's death, but he wanted to kiss Naomi.

Instead, he gently brushed several loose strands of hair away from her face, causing her cheeks to turn even redder. Perhaps he'd overstepped.

∞

Naomi took a step closer to Amos, close enough to kiss him. As the wind blew through the cornstalks, sending the leaves in motion, the sunshine beamed down on them, on this beautiful, cloudless day. Amos was handsome, kind, and he was her hero today. But as she gazed into his eyes, all she saw was Thomas. She wondered if it would always be that way. Would she ever look at another man without thinking of Thomas? It didn't really matter, she supposed, since she wasn't willing to put her heart out there again.

She cleared her throat and backed away from Amos just enough to make her point without having to say, *"I can't kiss you because I see another man's face."* Maybe if she had kissed him, Thomas's face would have faded. But she couldn't do it. It would feel like a revenge kiss. She'd been praying for Thomas to come home since he left, but she had never considered he would become involved with someone else so quickly. The news had stabbed her heart, but she still believed Thomas would eventually realize Naomi was the one for him. He'd just gotten cold feet. And that's what she would hold on to in an attempt to soothe her soul.

She took deep breaths to collect herself, then recalled how Amos had no interest in a relationship. She realized she hadn't given him any room for his own grief today.

"How are you feeling?" She paused and bit her lip as she searched his eyes. "I mean, how did you do?"

He shrugged. "It was about like I thought it would be. I saw Sarah and me taking our vows, and I thought *mei* heart might crack."

"I'm so sorry." Naomi wanted to hug him. The first embrace had felt so good, but she was afraid. Her heart might be in shambles, but the rest of her body seemed to have a mind of its own.

"We both knew it would be like this. We just weren't ready to face a wedding." Amos's eyes captured hers, and an invitation seemed to appear in his sober expression as he edged closer to her. His dark eyes were probing her soul again, reaching into her thoughts. Then he cupped her cheek, and Naomi made no effort to stop him as she closed her eyes. "You won't always feel like you do now, Naomi," he said softly as he lowered his hand. "You're a beautiful woman, and you'll find love again."

She didn't think so, but she owed him a response that would encourage hope. "So will you." Her eyes melded into his again, and that feeling of oneness came over her. She'd only known him a couple days. Her attraction to him was tempting her to do things that would be inappropriate. Naomi's heart belonged to another man. "And *danki* for the compliment."

He looked past her. "Should we see how far this path goes?"

Naomi followed his gaze. "It looks like it goes on forever."

"Maybe it's like a rainbow and there will be a pot of gold at the end."

She laughed. "Then Suzanne's family has been hiding a big secret."

He motioned down the clearing between the cornstalks. "Shall we?"

Naomi smiled. "Why not?"

She followed Amos as he did his best to push away the leaves that hung in front of them, thicker in some areas than others. Naomi breathed in the sweet aroma of the corn and tried to let her thoughts drift to happy topics, like the blessings of the harvest, the fact that she had found a family with Esther and Lizzie, and that the Lord appeared to be blessing her with a new friend.

They walked quietly for a long while. It felt good just to *be*.

❧

Esther was clearing dishes from one of the tables when she saw Lizzie running toward her with the energy of a teenager. She huffed and puffed for several seconds when she finally stopped in front of Esther.

"It's happening!"

"What's happening?" Esther held four plates in her hands as she focused on Lizzie. "What are you talking about?"

"Naomi . . . and Amos." She struggled to catch her breath. "I watched them . . . go behind the *haus* together . . . and then . . . I saw them running through the cornfields on a path." Lizzie latched on to Esther's arm as her eyes grew moist. "Naomi was laughing, Esther. They both were."

Esther set the plates on the table and hugged Lizzie, her heart warm and full. "We can't let that boy leave Sunday." She leaned back and held her elbow with one hand, cupping her chin with the other and tapping her foot. "I have an idea."

76

Lizzie adjusted her teeth and bounced on her toes. "The basement?"

Esther groaned. "*Nee*. I told you not to do that again." She paused, still thinking out her plan. "Remember how Amos and Anna Mae said business was slow at his construction company?"

Lizzie's ears seemed to perk up as she grinned. "*Ya*."

"We have plenty of repairs that need to be done, enough to keep that boy around long enough to fall in *lieb*."

"I *lieb* that idea." Lizzie tapped a finger to her chin. "The back fence on the far pasture is falling over."

Esther's mind was reeling as well. "We're missing some shingles on the roof from the last storm, and we have two dead trees that need to be cut down. Then there's the barn door."

Lizzie named several other things that needed repairing. "This evening, we'll talk to Amos about staying on to do some work for us."

Esther had a tickle in her throat, similar to what she'd felt last night on Gus's porch. She hurried to grab a tissue from her apron pocket and quickly brought it to her face, pretending to dab at her nose while trailing it across her mouth. She was relieved when she pulled it back clear.

"Then that's the plan," she said smiling.

⌒∞⌒

"Do you hear that?" Amos stopped abruptly and raised a hand to his ear. He'd decided the path must go on for miles

77

and wondered if they should head back, but he thought he'd heard something.

Naomi stilled as Amos turned to face her. "Hear what?"

"Just listen." He lowered his hand but stayed perfectly still.

"*Ya*, I hear something." Naomi scooted closer to him as he tried to listen in the direction of the faint noise. "It sounds like a cat."

They inched toward the sound, then sped up when the meowing grew louder. It was certainly feline, and Amos hoped they weren't sneaking up on something bigger than they could handle. He'd already seen one bobcat scurry away when he'd been visiting relatives with his mother.

Naomi pushed her way between the cornstalks, her arms flailing. Amos stayed right behind her, dodging the leaves as best he could.

"Oh no!" She squatted and placed her hand on top of a closed box trap. "Most farmers set traps for raccoons. I imagine they are all over these cornfields. Maybe that's why the trails are here." She placed her hand on the bottom of the trap door, about to open it.

"Wait!" Amos went to his knees beside her. "That cat is probably feral and going to go crazy when you let it out."

"We can't just let him go. He'll die. Look at him. It's just a kitten, and he's starving. There's no telling how long he's been in there without water." Naomi lifted the cage, reached inside, and picked up the kitten by the scruff of its neck. Even if it was feral, it was too weak to put up a fight.

Amos had a soft spot for animals. He disliked trapping

them, but he'd heard stories about raccoons and other critters wiping out entire cornfields. So, he supposed it was necessary.

They stood, and Naomi lifted her black apron and draped it around the shivering cat. The temperature had warmed up throughout the day, but Amos wondered how the kitten survived however many nights it had been in that trap.

He reached down and gave it a gentle scratch behind the ears. "How old do you think he is?"

Grinning, Naomi said, "First of all, it's a *she*, and I would guess maybe a couple months. I'm going to take her back to Esther and Lizzie's, nurse her back to health, and then they will probably let her stay on in the barn to keep mice away. I've never had a cat." She glanced up at him and smiled.

"Really? We've always had cats—outside, but they're always around." Amos looked ahead at the path yet traveled. "I guess we aren't going to find out what's at the end of the path?"

"*Nee*, I think we better get this little girl some water."

Amos couldn't take his eyes off Naomi. For a split second, he pictured her as a mother. Her voice sounded so nurturing as she gazed at the solid black cat. "I guess you're not superstitious?"

"Because she's all black? *Nee*, I'm not. She's one of *Gott*'s creatures." She lowered her nose near the kitten. "Aren't you, sweet girl?"

That voice, so soft, so sweet. "Do you want me to carry her back?"

"*Nee*, I've got her." She started walking back toward the house, so Amos followed.

Surprisingly, they emerged from the cornfields in only a few minutes and returned to the festivities without anyone seeming to notice. Esther spotted them first.

"What have we here?" She leaned down to get a better look at the kitten.

"Well . . ." Naomi glanced at Amos, then back at Esther. "We heard a noise and went down the path in the cornfield, and we found her in a raccoon trap."

Amos stifled a grin. It was the truth, just not in the right order.

Esther straightened. "Best get her some water and see if she will eat something. Suzanne's *mudder* might have a can of tuna or salmon she could nibble on."

"If it's all right, I'd like to keep her in *mei* room until she's well enough to go outside." Naomi's face was aglow, and Amos was having trouble shaking the image of her as a mother.

"*I* don't mind at all." Esther frowned. "It's Lizzie you'll have to worry about. She's terrified of cats. That's why we've never had one." She raised an eyebrow. "And that's a black cat."

"She'll die outside this young and weak." Naomi held the animal closer.

Esther patted her back. "I'll handle Lizzie." She turned to Amos. "Amos, Lizzie and I would like to talk to you when we get back to the *haus*." She sighed. "Which will be soon for us. We are both tired."

Amos flinched. "Is anything wrong?"

Esther waved a hand and smiled. "*Nee, nee.* Nothing is wrong at all. We just have a bit of a proposition for you."

Amos rubbed his chin, wondering what the sisters had in mind.

SEVEN

NAOMI SAT IN THE ROCKING CHAIR IN THE LIVING ROOM. She'd snuck the kitten upstairs earlier when they returned from the wedding. It had been easy enough since the poor thing was too weak to object. But after Naomi set up a cat box and got her to eat something, the kitten began to meow. Lizzie didn't go upstairs much since she and Esther had bedrooms downstairs. Naomi had her fingers crossed that they wouldn't be able to hear the kitten, and hopefully Esther would smooth the way with Lizzie. Naomi was already trying to think of a name for the cat.

Amos sat on the couch with Esther beside him, and Lizzie was in the other rocking chair. Anna Mae had stayed at the wedding celebration to visit longer with relatives and had arranged for someone to bring her home later. Naomi was curious what the sisters were up to. What was the proposition Esther had mentioned?

Esther cleared her throat. "Amos, when you first arrived you mentioned that business was slow right now." He nodded. "Lizzie and I were wondering if you would mind staying here a little longer to do some repairs we've needed for a long time. We have quite a list and would pay your going rate. Naomi is a wonderful cook, as I'm sure you've come to realize, and meals and your room would be free."

Naomi swallowed hard as she began to twist the string of her prayer covering with her finger. "Esther, I'm sure Amos can't just leave his life in Ohio on a whim to stay here and work. He has a business to run." She was sure this must be one of the sisters' matchmaking attempts, and it was not going to work.

Amos opened his mouth to say something, then closed it as he glanced at Naomi and began rubbing his chin. "Hmm . . ."

Naomi's pulse picked up. Surely he wasn't considering their offer.

"Are you talking about general repairs or something specific."

Lizzie, shifting her teeth a bit, began to rattle off a list she'd obviously memorized—everything from fence repair to replacing shingles, and even the possibility of adding on to the barn.

"*Nee, nee.*" Naomi shook her head. "Amos, they are putting you on the spot, and they shouldn't do that. We know you have obligations at home." She spoke the truth, but she couldn't have Amos living under the same roof with her. He was so handsome and would be a constant temptation. How many times had she thought about kissing him today, a man she didn't love and barely knew?

Amos was still rubbing his chin, but his eyes were fixed on Naomi. "Hmm . . ." he said again.

"It would be a great help to us if you are able to work it out." Lizzie batted her eyes at Amos, and Naomi rolled hers.

"Amos . . ." Naomi paused, choosing her words carefully. "There are plenty of local carpenters Lizzie and Esther can hire. They are making an unrealistic request."

"Nonsense, dear." Esther sat taller. "We need a carpenter, and Amos needs work." She lifted her shoulders, dropped them slowly, and smiled. "I think it's a perfect fit."

Naomi couldn't believe he was considering the idea.

There was even a hint of amusement in his expression. "*Ya*, I'd have to say, it is a perfect fit. As long as *mei mamm* doesn't have a problem traveling home alone, I'll stay."

"Wonderful," Lizzie said as she stood up yawning. She'd taken about three steps when she came to an abrupt halt and cupped her ear to listen. "What's that?"

Naomi stood up. "I don't hear anything." *Forgive the lie*, Gott. But when the cries grew louder, she cringed. Everyone in the room heard the meowing.

"Is there a cat in this *haus*?" Lizzie slapped her hands to her hips as she glared at each of them.

"Calm down, Lizzie." Esther lifted herself from the couch. "Naomi and Amos found a kitten trapped in a raccoon cage. Naomi is just going to nurse it back to health, then it will make a *gut* barn cat."

"You won't even see her," Naomi said. "I'll keep *mei* bedroom door shut and take care of her."

Lizzie raised her chin. "Naomi, I *lieb* you, but I don't want to see that cat." She shook her head. "They hiss and claw and bare their teeth . . . dangerous little critters."

Esther covered her forehead with her palm. "Lizzie had a run-in with a cat when she was young." She glared at her sister. "Probably because she was dragging it around by the tail."

"That's not the way I remember it." Lizzie grimaced, waved her hand in the air, and headed to her bedroom. "It will probably attack *mei* in *mei* sleep or even if I go into the barn. I'll never be safe again."

After Lizzie closed her bedroom door—louder than normal—Naomi locked eyes with Esther, who was grinning. Then she looked at Amos, who said, "I don't think she likes cats very much."

They all laughed softly, but Naomi's thoughts shot back to the possibility of Amos living in the same house as her for longer than a few days.

⚬⚬⚬

Esther waited until Anna Mae had returned and all was quiet upstairs before she shuffled to the kitchen to get Gus a slice of pie. Luckily, there was one slice of pecan pie left. She wrapped it in foil, dressed in her cape and bonnet, then took the flashlight and walked to Gus's place. As usual, the lantern was lit. But Esther wasn't going to keep making this trek late at night. Gus probably didn't think nine was late, but Esther doubted he woke up early. She'd seen the glow from his lantern late into the evening on nights she couldn't sleep. Not to mention, it was getting colder in the evenings.

Gus opened the door, dropped his jaw, and feigned surprise. "Well, look who it is. That wouldn't happen to be pie, would it?"

Esther had never slapped anyone in her life, but the urge right now was overwhelming. She handed him the pie, spun on her heels, and didn't say a word.

"What's the matter? Cat got your tongue?"

Funny he should mention cats. "My visits don't include conversation," she said without turning around.

The door slammed. Esther sighed in relief. She wouldn't have to bring him pie much longer. Tomorrow she was going to make a doctor's appointment.

Amos climbed underneath the wedding quilt and stared at the intricate design and soft colors that should be calming. He shook his head and fluffed his pillow. Maybe a change of scenery would do him good and make room in his head to create some new memories. Right now, it was as if his remembrances were cataloged, and thoughts of Sarah dominated the file space in his mind. He'd almost said no to Esther and Lizzie since it was obvious Naomi didn't want him here.

Later in the evening his mother had encouraged him to

stay with way too much enthusiasm. She was obviously hopeful that something would spark between him and Naomi.

Amos had to admit that Naomi was the first woman since Sarah who brought to life a part of him he'd thought would never see the tiniest spark again. Still, no matter how much he enjoyed talking to her—and looking at her—neither was ready to move on. A friendship seemed to be forming, so he was a little curious why she was so adamant that he not accept Lizzie and Esther's offer. Then he recalled a moment out in the cornfield, the way they had looked at each other, the way he'd touched her face. He was still recalling the day when he heard a knock at the door.

"*Ya*, hang on." He was only wearing a white undershirt and briefs, so he scurried into the slacks he'd dropped on the floor by the bed, then turned up the lantern as he sat on the edge of the bed. "Come in."

Naomi stepped over the threshold wearing the maroon dress she'd had on earlier, but now a brown scarf was draped over her head. "Can I talk to you for a minute? I saw the light shining from under the door, so I knew you were still awake."

"*Ya*, sure." He pointed to the rocking chair. In Amos's community, this private interaction would be considered inappropriate. An unmarried woman was not supposed to come calling into a man's bedroom like this. When she closed the door, Amos tensed and waited until she was seated before he asked, "Is this okay? I mean, you being here like this. Would it upset Lizzie or Esther that we're alone together?" The moment with

Naomi was causing some unidentifiable emotion to bubble to the surface, and he feared it was lust. Maybe it wasn't a good idea for him to stay and work.

Naomi chuckled softly. "Upset them? Uh . . . *nee*. They might try to lock us in here together, though." Her face reddened. "They know me well enough to know that nothing inappropriate would happen."

"Why would they lock us in here?" Amos shifted his weight as an awkward curiosity scurried around in his head.

Naomi met his gaze, and for a few seconds, Amos felt that spark again, which took him back to second-guessing his decision to stay.

"Never mind," she said as she gave her head a quick shake. "You do see what's happening, right?"

Amos lifted an eyebrow as he shrugged. "I guess I'm not sure."

"Lizzie and Esther are playing matchmaker. They are hoping that if we are under the same roof together we'll fall madly in love." She threw her hands in the air in such a dramatic way that Amos couldn't help but smile. "But you and I know where we stand, and that's not what either of us is looking for."

She pointed a finger at him. "They're tricky too. Even Esther. Both of them had long and wonderful marriages, but after their spouses passed, they started occupying their time setting up couples. And right now, their focus is on me." She sat taller and tapped her hands on her knees once. "So, I've come to tell you that this isn't about the repairs. Granted, *ya*, there is work to be done, but that's not what is driving their offer."

Amos grinned. "Wow. You *really* don't want me here." He leaned back on his hands and locked eyes with her, raising his eyebrow again as he waited for her response. Her eyes shifted to his shoulders, and he couldn't help but swell with pride. In his line of work, it was almost impossible not to be muscular.

"Why do you say that?" Grimacing, she paused. "I'm just telling you that you are being manipulated."

Her voice held a hint of shakiness. "Do I make you nervous?" he asked, unable to keep from smiling.

She huffed. "Of course not. We've already discussed where we each are with our lives, so Lizzie and Esther will fail at their attempts to play matchmaker." She rose from the chair, one hand holding the scarf together beneath her chin. "I just wanted you to have the facts so you could make an informed decision." She drew her lips in a tight smile. "Those repairs can wait. Most of the things they mentioned have needed fixing for a long time."

Amos lifted himself off the bed. "I think *mei mamm* probably hopes we'll become more than friends, too, but I could use a change of scenery, and work *is* slow at home." He shrugged. "I'm clear about your feelings, and I think you understand mine. But we can be friends while I'm here. Or is there something you're not telling me?" He couldn't help but wonder if she was as physically attracted to him as he was to her. It was unexpected, but it had crept up on him.

She took a quick step forward. Amos waited. He was already uncomfortable being alone with her in the room.

"There's nothing I'm not telling you." Her voice had lost

the quiver, but now there was an edge to it. "I'm telling you what you didn't know, and now you can make an informed decision. There is no obligation to stay."

The more she fought for him to leave, the more he wanted to stay. It was childish, but he wondered how far she'd go to get him to leave. That would answer his question about whether or not he made her nervous. He'd have to lie if she fired the question back at him, because she did. But in a good way that he had no plans of admitting.

"I've already made up *mei* mind, since *mei mamm* doesn't mind traveling home alone."

Naomi raised her chin. "Very well. Don't say I didn't warn you when the shenanigans begin. It can be very disruptive to a person's life." Her eyes widened as she lowered her voice. "They actually locked me in the basement once with a man they thought was perfect for me."

Amos laughed.

"It's not funny." But she grinned before she turned to leave.

For some reason, Amos felt a glimmer of hope. Could he open his heart again? But even if he was capable, he was fairly certain Naomi wasn't. Then he thought about that moment in the cornfield again.

⨯

Naomi lowered the flame on her lantern and was just getting comfortable when the kitten jumped on the bed. She was more affectionate than Naomi would have thought. Her mother must have been a domestic cat, and somehow this little one had gotten away from the rest of the litter.

"You're one lucky little girl. I'm so glad we found you." She scratched the kitten behind the ears as she purred. "But I'm afraid you will be banned to the barn soon since a little food and water seemed to catapult your recovery."

She leaned back, and the kitten settled on her stomach. It was almost ten, and she needed to get to sleep, but thoughts of Amos down the hallway rattled her, and she couldn't put her finger on why. It had to be that he was handsome. She wouldn't be human if she didn't notice. His chiseled arms were certainly evidence of a man who worked hard.

But her heart wasn't up for grabs, and she hadn't realized until today how in love she still was with Thomas. She knew she still loved him, but hearing he had someone else and his not showing up at the wedding had affected her more than she expected. Maybe that's why she came so close to kissing Amos in the cornfield. But it would have been for the wrong reasons.

Yawning, she extinguished the lantern. She would just have to see Amos for what he was—a distraction who was easy on the eyes. Besides, a person couldn't have too many friends.

She rolled over and cuddled with the nameless kitten they'd saved, and a flood of tears overtook her. No matter how tightly she squeezed her eyes closed and tried to push away thoughts of Thomas, all she could see was him in another woman's arms.

I'll never fall in love again. It hurts too much.

⤬

Out in the barn Friday morning, Esther picked up the phone and made a doctor's appointment. Afterward, she took a few deep breaths, glad she'd forced herself to make the call. Then she checked the answering machine. When she heard the message, she hurried back into the house. Anna Mae and Amos were already seated at the table. Lizzie was slicing a loaf of bread fresh from the oven, and Naomi was filling Anna Mae's coffee cup.

"Company is coming." Esther pressed her palms together. They'd hoped business would pick up now that they were past the summer heat. If her stomach didn't act up too much, maybe this would provide a distraction from her medical woes, at least for the weekend. "An Amish woman from Shipshewana and her two *dochders* will be arriving this afternoon. I think she said they are on their way to visit relatives, although I don't remember where. They'll just be staying tonight."

Naomi finished frying the eggs, and when everyone was served and seated, she took her place next to Amos. Anna Mae had asked if they could all eat together when there weren't other guests, and the kitchen table had room for six. It was cozy compared to the formality of the dining room, and Esther was happy to oblige.

She hurried to finish her breakfast, which wasn't much. She could barely stomach anything lately. Lizzie had questioned her about it again, but Esther said she'd picked up a bug. In truth, she'd picked up something, but she also knew it wasn't a bug.

She pushed her chair back and excused herself. "Naomi, as always, the meal was very *gut*."

"*Danki*." Naomi barely smiled. The girl had dark circles under her eyes again, and Esther suspected she'd cried herself to sleep after hearing Thomas was with someone else. She glanced at Amos, hoping he might be the answer to their prayers.

She walked to the basket on the counter where they kept the mail. "Gus received mail, so I'm going to take it to him. I noticed the postmark is from Indianapolis, but there isn't a return address."

Lizzie cackled. "Who would write to that old grump?"

Esther chose not to tell Lizzie her teeth were protruding like a beaver's right now. "I don't know."

"Maybe his *dochder*, the one who never showed up," Naomi said as she moved her food around on her plate. She hadn't eaten much either.

"We may never know." Esther wished everyone a good day and started across the worn path to the cottage, waving to Mary who was sweeping the porch at the *daadi haus*. She and John kept to themselves. A sweet couple, but Esther sensed there was trouble in paradise over their inability to conceive a child. Several times she'd seen Mary on the front porch crying, but if Esther moved in her direction, Mary would slip inside. That was enough indication for Esther that the young woman didn't want to talk about whatever was ailing her. Esther had always thought Mary and Naomi might form a close relationship since they were close to the same age. But

Mary and John hadn't been here long, and Mary and Naomi were in very different places in their lives. Each woman seemed detached for dissimilar reasons.

As she neared Gus's cabin, Esther couldn't believe what she was about to do. It was going to take everything she had to make the request.

Gus answered the door right after she knocked. "Is it pie time?"

Their grumpy renter was allowing himself to fall back into disarray with his matted hair, sloppy unkept beard, and clothes that smelled like they belonged in the hamper.

"*Nee*. It is not pie time." She took a deep breath and let it out slowly. "I, um . . . need a favor from you." Cringing, Esther held her breath. Would Gus help her?

"Well, well, well . . . A favor, you say?" He rubbed his chin, grinning like a Cheshire cat.

Esther sighed. "*Ya*, a favor." *I can't believe I'm doing this.*

EIGHT

ESTHER'S CHEST TIGHTENED AS SHE WAITED FOR GUS'S RE-
sponse.

Still rubbing his chin, he said, "So, you want me to drive
you to the doctor? Why not hire one of those drivers like you
usually do?"

"Because people talk, especially the *Englisch* drivers who
know everyone's business. I don't want anyone to know, especially Lizzie. I would like to know what is wrong before I
tell her."

Gus shook his head. "I don't know." Shifting his weight to
one side, he squinted, drawing his bushy gray eyebrows into a
frown. "Once you get yourself fixed, then tell Lizzie, my pie
will stop coming."

Esther threw her hands up in disgust "Would you rather
I just stay sick? Even if *you* don't take me, I'll find a way to
the doctor and tell Lizzie. Can you do this for me on Monday

or not?" The thought of riding in Gus's rusty black truck, complete with obnoxious bumper stickers, caused Esther to feel sick. What if she vomited being in an enclosed vehicle with him? If he smelled anything like he did now, it was possible.

"Will my pie keep coming or not?"

Esther wanted to smack him, even though it went against everything she believed. "I promised to bring you pie in exchange for not mentioning my medical condition to anyone. Once I see a doctor, I will have to tell Lizzie what is wrong. So, no more daily pie after that. That was our agreement. Besides, I already bring you the occasional hot meal and desserts."

His water-balloon jowls jiggled as he shook his head. "I'm amending the agreement. I'd like pie every day from now on, and I'll happily take you to the doctor."

"What if I have follow-up appointments?" Esther despised having to negotiate with this man.

Gus nodded. "I'll agree to that. Unlimited rides to the doctor, and you keep the pie coming for the rest of my life."

Esther clenched her fists at her sides. "How is it, Gus, that you get people to commit to things for the rest of your life? How in the world did you manipulate our *mudder* into letting you live here for the rest of your life?" She stopped, reminding herself she needed the ride to Bedford. It was forty miles one way, too far for a horse and buggy.

Gus's expression fell into a look that was almost sorrowful. "I guess if your mother wanted you to know that information, she would have told you."

Esther and Lizzie had asked many times before their

mother passed, but she would only repeat that he needed a place to live, adding that he paid the rent and didn't cause trouble. The latter was debatable.

Lizzie and Esther had often wondered if Gus was keeping a secret about—or for—their mother, but there couldn't have been a kinder or more honest woman than Regina Yoder. Maybe *Mamm* had simply been pushed to rent the cottage to Gus the same way Esther found herself agreeing to a lifetime supply of pie.

She quivered just thinking about it—the ride with Gus to the doctor.

"Just keep the pie coming, and I'm at your beck and call." He waved his arm across his enlarged belly as he faked a bow.

Esther nodded and left. She prayed hard that whatever was wrong with her could be easily—and painlessly—cured.

∞

Naomi had just finished changing the sheets in Anna Mae's bedroom upstairs when she noticed movement out of the corner of her eye. She edged closer to the window. Every time Amos swung the ax and split the wood, his muscles rippled beneath his blue long-sleeve shirt.

She didn't have any tears left for Thomas, but even someone as nice looking as Amos couldn't distract her for long. Despite her tear ducts having dried up, her heart remained broken.

After she finished making the bed, she glanced around the

room to make sure everything was in order for when Anna Mae returned later. She was spending time with family again today. Deciding the room was fine, she checked the other guest rooms before she headed downstairs to the kitchen. She had two pies in the oven that should be done.

Amos was leaning against the counter guzzling a glass of water when she walked in. He ran a sleeve across his sweaty forehead.

"It's in the fifties out there, but I still managed to work up a sweat."

Naomi pulled open the oven door. The pies needed a few more minutes. "Chopping wood is hard work," she said as she closed the door.

"Have you ever split wood?" He grinned, which caused her to do the same.

"As a matter of fact, I have." She boldly met his gaze, challenging him to question her further.

"I'm impressed." He set the glass on the counter, winked at her, and went back outside, leaving her to ponder the gesture.

She walked to the window, wishing she hadn't since he looked over his shoulder and smiled at her. Stepping sideways out of view, she felt the flush working its way up her neck and filling her face. She hoped no one walked into the kitchen right then as she moved to the dining room to set the table for supper.

As she took out the moss rose china, she paused to eye the large oak table. Naomi loved everything about this room, from the big hutch that stored dishes and serving bowls, to the high-back chairs with white cushions on the seats. She set the dishes on the table, then gathered a stack of white lace doilies Esther had crocheted decades ago and began setting them out for their guests.

The dining room walls were painted a light shade of tan and met with wood floors of almost the same color. With so much white on the chairs and table, a simple elegance allowed the place settings to shine on their own with little fanfare. Naomi's favorite piece of furniture in the entire house was the grandfather clock in the corner. The lone window in the room permitted just enough light to make the atmosphere feel almost romantic, but still formal in a cozy sort of way. She wondered if she'd still be serving guests in this house when she was as old as Esther and Lizzie.

She glanced at the grandfather clock and saw that it was almost four. Remembering the pies, she shuffled back to the kitchen, pulled them both out, and set them on cooling racks. She turned off the oven, but placed the pork tenderloin, mashed potatoes, and glazed carrots inside to stay warm.

Everything was ready, so she sat on one of the kitchen chairs to think about Amos's wink. Was he just a charming guy? Or testing her resolve to see if she really was emotionally unavailable? Or just being a flirt for the fun of it?

Her thoughts were interrupted when she heard tires crunching against gravel. Their guests had arrived. Naomi crossed through the living room to the front door and waited to greet them. Esther and Lizzie emerged from their bedrooms at the same time. The sisters almost always took a late-afternoon nap.

"Oops." Lizzie stopped and flashed a toothless grin. She

went back in her room and returned with her teeth in her mouth—and in place for once.

"Welcome to The Peony Inn," Esther said as she held open the door for the woman and her two daughters. One of the girls was young, maybe twelve or thirteen. The other looked to be in her early twenties. She had blonde hair, blue eyes, and a flawless ivory complexion, as if she'd never seen a day in the sun. Naomi was envious right away. Her twenty-five-year-old skin was already showing the lines of time feathering from her eyes. She wondered if this was the type of woman Thomas had gone after.

Esther ushered the guests upstairs, and Naomi inspected the dining room a final time. Some bed-and-breakfast hostesses never joined the guests for meals, while others sometimes did. Esther usually waited for their guests to extend an invitation, as Anna Mae had. Esther enjoyed chatting with folks from other places, and the English seemed to enjoy conversations with Esther and Naomi. And sometimes with Lizzie, depending on her mood.

Lizzie didn't wait for an invitation and had decided they would all dine together this evening. She'd told Naomi to set out eight place settings. While Naomi went back to the kitchen to begin taking the food from the oven, Lizzie had apparently placed nametags on the plates for everyone. Amos's delegated spot was next to Naomi. She was tempted to switch the nametags around when Lizzie wasn't looking, just to spite her, but no sooner did she have the thought than Amos walked into the room.

Lizzie poured a glass of iced tea and handed it to him after he sat down.

"*Danki.*" He took a drink right away, and after he'd set the glass down, Lizzie squeezed the top of his arm.

"Construction work must keep you strong." Lizzie dropped her hand and grinned at Naomi. "Muscular fellow, *ya?*"

Here we go. Naomi glanced at Amos, who grinned. Lizzie turned to the window, and Naomi mouthed *I told you so* to Amos before excusing herself to the restroom.

When she returned, Anna Mae had joined them along with Esther and the new guests. Everyone was present and seated, except for Esther who was filling tea glasses. Lizzie's lips were thinned with displeasure. Naomi started toward her seat next to Amos, but the blonde woman was sitting in her place. Did Amos make the switch so he could sit by their new guest? Or did the beautiful blonde do it?

Naomi smiled, doing her best not to look affected by the change. As they bowed in prayer, she couldn't stop wondering who made the swap, then reminded herself it shouldn't matter.

After the prayer, Esther introduced everyone to the new guests.

"This pork is delicious." Catherine, the blonde, had her pinky extended as she held her fork. She wasn't like most Amish women Naomi knew. Even the younger daughter sat tall, poised, and with her little finger held at an elegant angle.

"Naomi is a very *gut* cook," Esther said. "We are lucky to have her."

"*Ach*, I didn't realize you were an employee, Naomi. I

thought maybe you were one of these ladies' *grossdochder*." She batted her eyes as she turned to Amos. "Do you work here also?"

Amos smiled, nodding, since he had just taken a bite of bread. After swallowing he said, "*Ya*, I'll be working here for a while. I live in Ohio, but I'm staying here for a bit to work."

Catherine smiled as she continued batting her eyes at Amos. "What type of work do you do?"

"I own a construction company." Amos held her gaze, and he was still holding it when Anna Mae spoke up a few seconds later.

"A very successful company." Amos's mother dabbed her mouth with her napkin, then shook her head. "He was engaged to a lovely woman who passed on before they were able to get married."

If Amos had been right about his mother also playing matchmaker between him and Naomi, she appeared to have jumped sides.

Catherine put her hand on Amos's arm. "I'm so sorry for your loss."

"*Danki*," he said before turning to his mother and shooting a much-deserved dirty look. That wasn't suppertime conversation, nor should Anna Mae have offered up the information to strangers, in Naomi's opinion.

Naomi forked a bite of meat and was chewing when Catherine asked, "Naomi, how long have you worked as a cook? Are you a housekeeper here too?"

Naomi couldn't answer due to her mouthful of food, so she

turned to Lizzie, whose expression was so taut she looked like steam might rise from her head at any moment.

"Naomi *isn't* a cook and she *isn't* a housekeeper." Lizzie smiled, teeth in place, but it wasn't her regular smile, and Naomi feared what might be coming. "So don't be getting all—"

"Naomi is like family to us." Esther cleared her throat. "That's what Lizzie was trying to say." She glared at her sister, but Catherine took the opportunity to ogle Amos. Again.

"Naomi, thank you for another fine meal." Amos wiped his mouth and stood. "And, ladies, it was *gut* to meet you all. *Gott's* blessings for safe travels." He left abruptly, and Naomi heard the front door shut behind him.

For reasons she couldn't explain, even to herself, the urge to run after him was strong. But she couldn't be rude, and she needed to clean the kitchen after everyone was done eating.

It was almost dark before she escaped the house and found Amos sitting on the bench by the lake. She was thankful it was hidden from view. Catherine surely would have found her way here otherwise.

Naomi sat down beside him. "Are you okay?"

"*Ya.*" His eyes were straight ahead as the sun slowly lowered into the stalks of dark green corn on the other side of the pond. "I just hate it when *Mamm* does that." He turned to Naomi. "She always brings up Sarah any time I meet an attractive woman. She has a prepared dialogue to gain sympathy. I don't want or need that."

Naomi lowered her gaze. "Catherine is very beautiful." She slowly lifted her eyes to his.

"Not my type." He shook his head. "I think the word Lizzie was probably about to blurt out before Esther stopped her was *uppity*."

Naomi chuckled. "I think so too."

They were quiet for what seemed like a long while.

"I-I can go . . . if you want to be alone. I just came to check on you." She folded her hands in her lap to keep herself from nervously tucking hair behind her ears, which she'd probably done five times since she sat down. Amos had guessed correctly the night before. He did make her nervous.

"*Nee*, stay." He turned to her, revealing a somber expression. Then his eyes drifted back to the sunset. "We will never have this day again."

"What?" The comment was a little jarring and out of the blue.

He turned back to her, the serious expression still present. "Think about it. This day, this minute, this second . . . We'll never have it back again. How old are you?"

"Twenty-five."

He took off his straw hat and placed it in his lap, then ran a hand through his hair and sighed. "So you've lived roughly around nine thousand days."

Keeping her eyes fused with his, she laughed a little. "I don't know how you figured that in your head so quickly, but *ya*, I guess so."

He smiled. "It's weird that I think about things like that, *ya*?"

"I don't think it's weird at all. It's about making each day count."

"Right." He faced straight ahead again as the crickets broke out in song and the sun continued its surrender to the moon. "And I don't think about it just because of Sarah's death. I've always recognized the fact that what we do with our time matters."

Naomi had no idea where he was going with this, but somehow, she understood. Whether it had anything to do with Sarah's death or not, life was short, and it was meant to be lived. "I haven't been making each day count. I don't feel like I've really been living at all since Thomas left."

He abruptly faced her, then studied her for a few seconds. "We should change that."

Naomi tensed. What was he suggesting?

"We both like to paint. We should paint." He pointed to the ground. "We should meet here in the evenings, much earlier than now, of course, when it's fully daylight, and we should paint."

He'd already said that you could tell a lot about a person by what and how they painted. Did he want to get to know her better? She was one step ahead of him. He just didn't know it yet. But he would see and understand soon enough.

"It's completely dark by about eight forty-five. We could plan to meet at six," she offered. "That would give me time to clean up the kitchen, gather supplies, and we could still attend devotions with everyone before we painted."

He gently popped his hand against his head. "Supplies. I didn't think about that."

"I have plenty of blank canvases, brushes, and paint in the basement."

"If you'll show me where, I can round it all up while you clear the dishes."

She felt a warm glow flow through her at the thought of painting again. She closed her eyes and inhaled a long breath of the fresh air. "Oh, how I've missed painting." Smiling, she opened her eyes and stared into his. "This will give me something to look forward to."

"Me too," he answered softly.

Amos moseyed up the stairs after he said goodnight to Naomi. It had been a long time since he'd spent any significant amount of time with a woman. And even longer since he'd painted. Naomi was easy to talk to. He was comfortable around her. They wanted the same thing, some sort of peace about the fact that their lives were moving in directions they hadn't chosen. They were also on the same page about not being in the market for love, which allowed Amos to relax around Naomi.

He walked into his bedroom but stopped right over the threshold and lifted his lantern to see better. He edged closer to the bed, toward the painting that rested against the headboard. Leaning down, he positioned the light so he could read the artist's signature, even though he already knew who painted the landscape. *Naomi Marie Byler.*

Amos adjusted the flame until the lantern was at its brightest, then placed it on the nightstand as he sat on the bed. He gingerly ran his hand along the top of the large canvas, honored that Naomi had chosen to share it with him.

He slipped his shoes off and tucked one leg under the other, eyeing everything about the brilliant colors and wishing he hadn't told her he'd paint with her. She was way better than he was. He had already learned something about her, even if it was a tiny blow to his ego.

He studied Naomi's work and wondered why she'd chosen to share the painting with him. Did she want him to know her better? Was she reaching out to him? Could they heal each other? He knew only God could do that, but he also believed He often worked through others.

Amos leaned closer to the vibrant colors. She'd painted this when she was happy, that was certain. Amos was no art critic. He'd visited a few museums and even attended some artists' events where they spoke about the use of color and what it means. If he was interpreting this painting correctly, he liked what he saw.

He gazed upon the reflection of Naomi's personality for another fifteen minutes before he carefully leaned it against the wall. He'd decide by tomorrow whether or not to share his thoughts with her. If he did, she'd know right away that he'd begun to feel something more than friendship toward her, which came as a complete surprise to Amos.

NINE

NAOMI WASN'T SORRY TO SEE THE WOMAN AND HER TWO daughters leave right after breakfast. Catherine had delivered another play for Amos's affections, and her actions had gotten under Naomi's skin more than she could have predicted. Her nametag had been moved again at breakfast, and she knew Amos didn't do it. She'd caught Catherine making the switch.

Naomi had to admit that what she felt was jealousy, but that didn't make sense. She was looking forward to spending time with Amos this evening too. And what did he think about the painting she'd left in his room? Since he had gone to the back pasture to work on the fence, she'd have to wait until this evening to find out, unless he brought it up at dinner or supper. She suspected he would wait until they were alone at the pond.

Suddenly, her stomach started to churn. She'd always been hesitant about letting anyone see her paintings, and it had taken a lot of courage to show Amos the one she treasured most.

What if he didn't like it? And to actually paint *with* someone . . .
Her stomach roiled again. *What was I thinking?* She'd been so
caught up in the thought of unveiling a creative part of herself
that she hadn't considered how personal it would feel to paint
side by side with Amos.

Naomi placed the last clean dish on the rack and was drying her hands when Lizzie walked into the kitchen. Usually
Lizzie helped her clear the breakfast dishes, but she'd been
quiet through the meal and disappeared upstairs without eating much.

Lizzie hung her head, her arms straight at her sides, shoulders slumped.

Naomi took a step closer and waited until Lizzie looked
up. "Are you okay?" She hoped this wasn't about Whiskers,
the name she'd given her kitten, who would soon be sent outside to live as a barn cat. Twice now Naomi hadn't closed her
bedroom door all the way, and Whiskers found her way out
and toured the upstairs area. Luckily Naomi found her before
Lizzie. Naomi hated leaving the cat in her bedroom all day. She
tried to spend as much time with her as she could. Whiskers
would probably be happier chasing mice in the barn than being
confined to Naomi's room.

"I've lost *mei* teeth." Lizzie pressed her thin lips together as
she clenched her fists at her sides. "Don't tell Esther."

Naomi fought hard not to smile. "I think she will notice."
Pausing, she leaned against the kitchen counter. "Is that why
you didn't eat much at breakfast?"

"*Ya.*" She raised an eyebrow. "Any eggs left?"

"*Nee*. Do you want me to cook you some oatmeal?"

Lizzie's eyes darted around the kitchen. "How much time do we have? Where's Esther?"

Now she couldn't stop herself from grinning. "Lizzie, you might as well just tell Esther you lost your teeth. You won't be able to hide it for long. And you'll starve yourself if you don't find them soon."

"They're here somewhere. I'll find them." She twisted to peek in the living room, then looked back at Naomi. "Where is Esther?" she asked again.

"She said Gus had more mail." She pointed to the kitchen window. "It looks like she's almost at the cottage."

"That old grump should get his own mail, but I guess if Esther can stomach being around him, it's better than him coming here." Lizzie pressed her palms together. "Child, if you would make me some oatmeal, I'd be grateful."

"Of course." Naomi took a pot from the cabinet.

"Please knock on *mei* bedroom door three times," she said in a whisper. "I'll know it's you. I've got to find *mei* teeth."

Naomi didn't know why a secret knock was needed, but she nodded. "I'll help you look for your dentures after I make the oatmeal. Have you been upstairs?"

Lizzie rubbed the back of her neck. "*Ya*, I had to go up there to find some quilting scraps I had stored in the linen closet." She spoke with an odd lisp. "But I didn't stay long. I heard that varmint running around in your room. Sounded like he was bouncing off the walls." She crossed her arms and hugged herself. "You brought a vicious creature under our roof."

Naomi laughed. "Lizzie, Whiskers—who is a *she*, by the way—is just a sweet, harmless little kitten. If you got to know her—"

"Stop." Lizzie held her arms out, both palms facing Naomi. "They scratch, they bite, they jump out and scare you for no reason, and I'm sure they are descendants of some prehistoric, aggressive creature."

Naomi chuckled.

"Go ahead and laugh." Lizzie pointed a finger at her. "But don't say I didn't warn you if that critter attacks you in the night."

"I'll remember that." Naomi took the oatmeal from the cupboard.

"Don't forget, knock three times." Lizzie scampered away like a child playing hide-and-seek.

Naomi shook her head, grinning. Hopefully they would find the dentures before Esther noticed. Naomi wasn't sure Lizzie could sit silently through another meal.

❦

Esther plodded up the steps to the cottage, and Gus opened the door before she knocked. She pushed a slice of key lime pie at him, along with two pieces of mail.

"Why are you bringing me pie this early in the morning?" Gus scratched his forehead as he yawned.

"It's not that early, and since I am also delivering mail, I decided to save myself a trip later. I also wanted to let you know that *mei* appointment with the doctor is at ten Monday morning, so I'd like to leave at nine."

Gus lifted the foil from the pie and sniffed. "I'm going to eat this, but just for future reference, I'm not real fond of key lime."

Esther took a deep breath, wanting to tell him that he'd have to accept whatever she brought him. But she might need more than one ride from him.

Thankfully, Gus stepped backward and closed the door. Early morning conversation with him was never a good way to start the day.

As she walked back to the main house, she made a mental to-do list of the things she wanted to tend to today. She liked to keep her agenda light on Saturdays. Naomi took care of most of the housework, but Esther liked to haul out the rugs, hang them over the clothesline, and give them an old-fashioned bashing with the broom. After that, she wanted to organize their preserves in the basement and make sure they were stocked up for winter. Then after a nap, she might treat herself to a good book.

She was almost back to the main house when she heard a faint whimpering. It was Mary. She was on her porch, sweeping. The leaves this time of year were a nuisance. Esther added another item to her list of things to do today, if Lizzie or Naomi didn't get to it first: sweep the porch.

Mary cried a lot, and since John wasn't home, Esther decided to see if she could help. In the past Mary rushed into the house when Esther veered in her direction. Esther had heard rumors that their inability to have a baby was taking a toll on the marriage. The girl quickly pulled a tissue from her apron pocket, dabbed at her eyes, and tried to smile.

"*Wie bischt*, Esther." Mary stilled the broom and waited for Esther to come up the steps to the *daadi haus*. All the houses had steps, and they became more of a challenge for Esther with each passing year.

"I see you're busy sweeping, but I thought maybe I could sit a spell." Esther wished she could do something to ease the young woman's suffering. She understood the anguish of an empty womb all too well. It was decades ago, but she could still remember a doctor telling her she wouldn't be able to have children. Lizzie was told the same thing within the same year. The reasons were different, and the doctor had said not to try to rationalize it, that it was the hand they'd each been dealt. Looking back, it seemed a cold delivery of such horrible news.

"If I spend a little time resting over here, Lizzie will have more time to find her teeth." Esther chuckled, hoping to lighten Mary's mood. "She thinks I don't know, but when Lizzie doesn't talk and barely eats during a meal, it's a sure sign she has misplaced her dentures again."

Mary offered a small smile. "Stay as long as you'd like." She pointed to one of the chairs. "We can sit outside, or if it's too cool for you, we can go inside and I'll put on a pot of *kaffi*."

Sunrays flooded the porch with morning light. "I always prefer to be outside when possible to enjoy these beautiful surroundings, if you're not too cold."

"Not at all." Mary's voice was a little shaky as she leaned the broom against the house and both women sat down. Her eyes drifted to the inn. "You grew up in the main *haus*, *ya*? I bet you have so many wonderful memories."

Esther shrugged. "Some *gut*, some not so *gut*. But I'm blessed that the *gut* outweigh the bad." She decided to get to the point. "Mary, are your tears because you and John haven't conceived a child?"

The color drained from the young woman's face. "You must think I don't do anything but cry all day." She hung her head.

"I think you probably cry more than most, but that you also have moments of joy." Esther hadn't meant to make Mary uncomfortable. They weren't all that close, after all. "But I do understand how hard it is to want a child and not be able to have one."

Mary still stared at her feet. "You must think I'm silly. I know there is a chance John and I can have a *boppli*, but I can't understand why it's taking so long." She looked at Esther, blinking back tears. "I know you and Lizzie couldn't have *kinner*, and that must have been devastating to hear."

"It was." Esther paused, reflecting on the good things in her life. "But we've been blessed in other ways. We both married men we loved and enjoyed many years with them. But I do understand the heartache, and Mary, I continue to pray that *Gott* will bless you with the family you long for. We never know why His time frame varies so much from our own expectations. I can only encourage you to hold tighter to the moments of joy, and . . ." Esther knew she was about to overstep, but she was going to do it anyway. "And don't let your grief become so great that other relationships suffer. John is a *gut* man." Esther wasn't close to Mary's husband, either, but she'd heard only good things about him from people in the community.

"He tries so hard to be patient with me." Mary's voice broke a little. "Sometimes I just want to lash out at *Gott*, tell Him that it's not fair to make us keep waiting. We've been trying to have a family for five years. And we've been to *Englisch* doctors. They said there isn't any notable reason we shouldn't be able to have a *boppli*."

Esther tipped her head to the side a bit, surprised Mary was confiding in her in such a personal way. She straightened and crossed one leg over the other. "I can't pretend to understand *Gott*'s timing, but Mary . . ." This next part would be hard for her to swallow. "I'm not telling you to give up your desire for a family, but I think you must also consider other ways to keep joy in your life, just in case it doesn't happen."

"Is that what you and Lizzie did?" Mary dabbed at her eyes with the tissue again.

Esther thought back for a moment. "I think Lizzie was more devastated than I was. She didn't get out of bed for days after she found out."

"You were okay with it, though?"

"*Nee*," Esther said, shaking her head. "I wasn't. It was a quite a blow. I wondered if anyone would ever want to marry me, knowing I couldn't have a family. We both found out before we married. *Mei* ovaries never matured, so *mei* chances of conceiving were very slim. It's been so many years, I honestly don't remember why Lizzie couldn't have *kinner*. And we don't speak of it much these days." She smiled. "Sometimes family is who we make it, and over the years, I've been blessed with relationships that have felt like family. Like Naomi. She's basically our *grossdochder*." Esther paused. "We would love to see more of you and John too."

"Is Gus your family too?" Mary actually grinned.

Esther chuckled. "I wouldn't go that far." Then she thought about it. "*Ach*, I guess in some ways he is. He's lived in the cottage for a long time. And doesn't every family have a black sheep?"

"I never talk to him." Mary shook her head. "He's miserable and never has anything nice to say. There is definitely no joy in his life." She locked eyes with Esther. "I don't want to be like that."

"Hon, I don't think you ever have to worry about that." She laughed again.

"Someone came looking for him the other day. She said her name was Heather and that she was Gus's *dochder*. I was shocked, but I told her Gus lived in the cottage across the way. She thanked me, then went back to her red car and just sat there for a long time, maybe thirty minutes. Then she drove away without ever going to Gus's door."

"So, he really does have a *dochder*," Esther whispered before looking at Mary. "We didn't know he had a child either. Gus asked me to cut his hair the other night, and he went to a lot of trouble to clean up the cottage. I admit, we watched out the window off and on all day, hoping to get a glimpse of her. Now that I think back, we did see a car in front of your *haus* once, but I thought it was an *Englisch* friend of yours. And I didn't realize the woman sat in the car for thirty minutes."

"I wonder why she didn't go see him." Mary's tears had dried up, and Esther was glad she'd provided a distraction from her struggles.

"Gus said he hadn't seen her since she was fifteen, and at the time, she apparently told him she never wanted to see him again." Esther's heart ached for him as she thought about how horrible that must have been, even for Gus.

"This woman was older, maybe in her fifties." Mary put a hand to her chest. "She hasn't seen her *daed* in a very long time."

"*Nee*, and even though it's Gus . . . I felt sorry for him when she didn't show up."

"She was pretty," Mary said. "And fancy. I mean, she had on pretty makeup and clothes and jewelry. And her car looked nice too." She pursed her lips. "Nothing like Gus. What makes a man turn out like Gus? I pray for him, but I've always wondered how he became the way he is."

"*Ya*, I think we all have. It also remains a mystery why *mei mamm* insisted on her death bed that Lizzie and I allow him to live in the cottage for the rest of his days."

Mary sighed. "Lizzie mentioned that to me one day."

Esther recalled the sullen expression on Gus's face when she asked him about it. It was the most vulnerable she'd ever seen him, even though he offered no explanation. He only said that if their mother had wanted them to know, she would have told them. But his response had offered a clue. There was a reason he'd been allowed to live there forever. Lizzie and Esther's mother had chosen not to tell them that reason. Gus must have something on their mother. That had to be it. But every time Esther rolled the thought over in her mind, it just didn't fit.

Mary and Esther both jumped from their chairs when they heard a loud scream coming from the main house that caused her heart to thump wildly in her chest.

"Lizzie!" Esther rushed from Mary's porch toward her house.

"I'm coming too!" Mary yelled as she caught up with Esther.

More screams followed, and Esther ran faster than she'd thought she was capable of these days. If anything happened to Lizzie . . .

TEN

NAOMI WAS COLLECTING EGGS WHEN SHE HEARD LIZZIE screaming from inside the house. She dropped the basket of six eggs and darted across the yard. When she flung open the front door, Lizzie was standing on the couch screeching at the top of her lungs.

"That cat thinks *mei* teeth are a toy!" Lizzie pointed at Whiskers who was playing hockey with her dentures across the wood floor. "I will never put those things in *mei* mouth again."

"Whiskers, *nee*!" Naomi yelled at the kitten as the animal scurried up the stairs with the teeth in her mouth. Naomi turned to Lizzie. "I'm so sorry! She must have gotten out of *mei* room again."

Esther and Mary were breathless as they burst through the front door.

"What's wrong?" Esther's face was red, and panic shone in her eyes. "Are you all right, Lizzie?"

"*Nee!* I was attacked by that cat who just ran off with *mei* teeth! And it's a black cat!" Lizzie collapsed onto the couch and threw a hand across her forehead. "Naomi, that critter has got to go."

Naomi nodded before she hurried upstairs. She found Whiskers under her bed guarding Lizzie's dentures like a dog guards a bone.

"Bad kitty," she said as she reached under the bed and wrangled the teeth out of the cat's mouth. Then she checked her bedroom door since she was sure she had closed it. When she pushed on it, it didn't lock into place, and apparently Whiskers had learned how to open it.

She didn't know how Lizzie typically cleaned her dentures, so she just ran them under cool water before she went back downstairs holding the teeth.

"You scared me to death!" Esther was still breathing hard and sat with her arms across her stomach. "I couldn't imagine what was happening."

Mary was still catching her breath too. "I'm glad you're okay."

Lizzie's eyes widened as she sat taller. "*Okay?* Do I look okay?" Her prayer covering had slipped to the side, but otherwise Naomi thought she looked fine. She offered Lizzie the dentures.

"I washed them off with water, but I'm sure they need a better cleaning." When Lizzie didn't take the teeth, Naomi set them on the coffee table.

"I'm not wearing those." Lizzie folded her arms across her chest.

"*Ach, ya*, you are," Esther said quickly as she dropped her arms to her sides, frowning. "Don't you remember how much those dentures cost? You just sanitize them, and you'll be fine."

Heavy footsteps pounded against the slats on the porch, then Gus crossed the threshold into the living room, his gray hair a matted mess spiking in every direction, like a worn gray mop.

"What the . . . ? Lizzie, have you finally lost the last of your marbles? I could hear you carrying on from my place. And I was taking a nap," he growled.

"She's fine, Gus. Just a little run-in with Naomi's new kitten." Esther sighed.

"I wish everyone would quit saying I'm fine." Lizzie laid her head against the back of the couch cushion, dramatically placing the top of her hand against her forehead again. "I could have been killed."

Naomi stifled a grin. She'd never known anyone so afraid of cats, especially a kitten as playful and affectionate as Whiskers.

Gus broke out in thunderous laughter. "All this over a stupid cat? You're afraid of a *cat*?"

Lizzie glared at Gus before turning to Esther. "Can you please tell that despicable man to get out of our *haus*?"

"Do you even know what that word means, you crazy old

broad?" Gus ran a hand through his hair, which made his disheveled appearance even worse.

"Gus, be quiet." Esther waved a dismissive hand in his direction. "And go home."

"With pleasure. This is a nut house." Gus shook his head and left. Mary followed a few minutes later.

Naomi was glad Amos's mother was gone visiting relatives again. It was a bit like a nut house this morning. Amos might not have heard the commotion since he was working on the back fence at the far end of the pasture.

Esther offered to make Lizzie some tea, and Naomi went upstairs to find Whiskers. He'd earned his place in the barn before he was really old enough to be on his own, but Naomi was a guest in this house, no matter how much Esther and Lizzie referred to her as family.

After everyone had settled down, Naomi went to fetch her eggs. Three were broken inside the wicker basket. Luckily there were a dozen more to be collected. After setting them in the kitchen she went to the barn and made Whiskers a bed out of hay and found two metal bowls she could use for food and water. She'd gotten used to cuddling with the cat at night, but after this incident, Whiskers would have to be a barn cat.

She was filling up the bowl with water at the pump outside when Amos walked up to her, breathing hard. "I ran across the pasture when I heard screaming, but it took me a while to get here. Is everyone okay?"

"*Ya, ya.*" Bowl filled, she started back to the barn, Amos following.

She placed the water next to the food bowl, then filled Amos in on the chaos from minutes earlier. "The kitten ran off with Lizzie's dentures, and since Lizzie is terrified of cats, Whiskers is going to have to stay outside now."

He chuckled. "I'm sorry. But I kind of wish I'd seen all that."

Naomi laughed too. "It was funny." She shook her head. "I wasn't ready to banish Whiskers to the barn just yet, but maybe she'll be happier out here."

"*Ya*, probably." Amos shifted his weight. "Um . . . *danki* for sharing your painting with me." He looped his thumbs beneath his suspenders. "It told me a lot about you."

Naomi sensed her face turning red. "*Gut* things, I hope." She hugged herself, wishing she had someone else to hug her sometimes.

"We can talk about it this evening. We're still on for painting that sunset, *ya?* Although I'm pretty sure I can't top what you already painted."

She avoided his eyes as she kicked at the dirt floor in the barn. "I painted it a long time ago."

"When you were happy," he said softly as one corner of his mouth lifted.

She looked up at him. "*Ya*, I guess so."

"Colors have meaning, and you captured the mood you were in." Now it was Amos who looked flushed.

"What do you mean, colors have meaning?" Naomi had never heard such a thing. Grinning, she said, "Are you secretly an art critic?"

He chuckled. "*Nee*. But a painting can reflect an artist's personality and reveal their state of mind."

Naomi gazed into his eyes, searching to know more about him, and leery for him to know more about her. "It's just a painting," she said softly.

"If you say so." He tipped the rim of his hat. "I better get back to work. See you after supper?"

"*Ya*." It had been a long time since Naomi had something to look forward to. The thought of painting with Amos made her nervous, but it was a thrilling sort of nervousness that seemed to be opening up that part of herself she'd closed off from the world.

◯◯◯

Amos took his time getting back to the fence work, his thoughts all over the place. There was more to Naomi Byler than she was letting him see. Amos supposed he was the same way—wary. Maybe letting his guard down would be a step toward a healing he hadn't cared to pursue before now. Maybe he and Naomi could help each other navigate the darkness and step back into the light of the living.

Even after he'd buried himself in his project again, his thoughts kept returning to her, and he wondered if he should tell her how much her painting meant to him. How it spoke to him. Amos wasn't a scholar. He'd had the same eighth grade education as every other Amish person. But he'd taken an interest in painting when he was young. His parents hadn't encouraged it, but they hadn't dissuaded it either, as long as he stuck to landscapes. Painting a portrait of a person wouldn't have been acceptable, although he'd always wanted to capture someone the way he saw them.

By suppertime he was even more anxious to put a brush to canvas. It had been so long. After the meal Naomi showed him where the supplies were, including two homemade easels, which caused him to wonder if she had painted with someone else at some point. Maybe Thomas. A niggling curiosity nipped at him as he wondered what Thomas would have painted. Would his choice of colors have indicated his future breakup with Naomi? He shook the thought away. Color perception was mostly in the eyes of the beholder and could probably be interpreted a hundred different ways.

Amos loaded everything into a small wagon he'd found in the barn. Naomi would meet him down by the pond after she cleared the dishes, and he planned to have things ready to go by the time she arrived.

❧

Esther, Lizzie, and Anna Mae peered out the window in the living room.

"Amos took painting supplies to the pond." Esther put a hand across her heart. "It's where Naomi used to paint, but she hasn't done that since she and her fiancé broke up."

"Amos has loved art since he was a young boy. It worried us at first, that he might become so taken with it that he'd choose to leave our community and pursue the craft in a more professional way." Anna Mae smiled. "But he never showed any indication that he wanted to leave the faith, or us. It was just something he enjoyed, and he was usually in a better mood when he had time to paint. It's been a long time since he's shown an interest—since Sarah died."

Lizzie clapped her hands as she bounced up on her toes. "They're going to fall in *lieb*."

"Slow down." Esther wanted a romance to bloom as much as Lizzie, but it was far too soon to tell if that would happen. "We must remember they are both nursing broken hearts."

"I see the way they look at each other." Lizzie sputtered without her teeth. All she'd eaten at supper was mashed potatoes. Esther didn't want to embarrass her sister in front of Anna Mae, but she'd speak with Lizzie later about wearing her dentures.

"I've always said I'd be crushed if one of *mei kinner* left our district in Ohio, but now I have to say I hope Amos finds *lieb* here. I've noticed the way they look at each other, too, and *mei sohn*'s happiness is worth more to me than having him physically close." Anna Mae paused as her eyes took on a faraway look. "He's been so filled with grief that I worried he would never get beyond losing Sarah. Seeing him with Naomi fills me with hope." She paused, seeming lost in her thoughts for a moment. "Anyway, I'll be leaving tomorrow. I wish I could stay, but *mei* family depends on me, and I miss them. It has been wonderful being here, seeing and meeting so many relatives, and spending time with you two and Naomi." She put a hand on Esther's arm. "I'm counting on you to write to me and let me know if romance begins to blossom."

"*Ach*, it is already," Lizzie said with the confidence of someone who could predict the future. Esther chose to revel in the possibility. Naomi was a lovely woman who deserved happiness. "They're wildly attracted to each other," Lizzie added.

"That's not appropriate talk, Lizzie. We both know there is more to love than physical attraction." Although, it was hard not to notice how handsome and charming Amos was.

"I'm off to bed." Anna Mae yawned. "But I'll be hoping and dreaming things go well for *mei* Amos and your Naomi."

Esther yawned, too, happy she could retire early this evening. She wouldn't have to wait until Lizzie was asleep to take Gus his pie. She'd handled that this morning.

But what about all the other days? The man got what he wanted through bribery, and eventually Esther would have to fess up to Lizzie about the deal she'd made with him—pie for life. It felt akin to making a deal with the devil. She'd have to lay eyes on that man every single day.

Heaviest on her heart right then was her impending doctor's appointment. She'd only had one other episode of coughing up blood since it happened in front of Gus, but something was definitely wrong. Even though she was terrified to find out what it was, she'd have no peace until she knew. After a diagnosis she'd tell Lizzie. Maybe she'd even break her bargain with Gus. What could he do if she didn't bring him pie every day, anyway?

For tonight she preferred to focus on Naomi and Amos.

Maybe God had sent the man Naomi was meant to be with. Esther had thought it was Thomas, although Lizzie doubted him from the beginning. She'd said it wasn't anything she could put her finger on, just that something about Thomas bothered her. It was odd since Lizzie was usually the head cheerleader when it came to love. But then Thomas left and never looked back.

∞

Naomi arrived at the pond about an hour before the sun would reach the trees. They would have just enough time to sketch the scene and then apply color during the last rays of sunset. Amos had everything set up. Each easel held a ten-by-thirteen canvas, and he'd laid out all the paints and brushes in the wagon between them. Naomi owned two color palettes, which were also in the wagon, along with a gallon of water and two cups for rinsing brushes.

"I feel weird painting in front of anyone." Amos scratched his cheek, but grinned.

Naomi smiled. And for once, she was smiling on the inside too. "I do too. *Danki* for admitting that."

"And I'm even more nervous after seeing your painting." He paused, his eyes locking with hers. "It says a lot about you."

"Probably that I'm not very *gut*." She laughed nervously.

Amos tipped back his hat, then rubbed his chin. "*Nee*, I think you're very *gut*. Like I said, much better than me. But you lack confidence."

She folded her arms across her chest. "Really? You could tell that from one painting?"

He raised an eyebrow, grinning again. "You just said you're probably not very *gut*. That sounds like a lack of confidence."

"How could you tell that from a painting?"

"I'll show you after we get started and get some color on the canvas." He picked up one of the color palettes and handed it to her, then grabbed the other one for himself.

"Now I'm really nervous." Naomi's stomach began to churn as she chewed on her bottom lip.

"Don't be. We both like to paint. We haven't done it in a long time." He shrugged. "Maybe we'll actually have some fun."

"Fun? What's that?" She let out another nervous chuckle.

"Exactly. Let's just enjoy ourselves and see how it goes."

Naomi nodded, then chose her colors and began to paint an outline of where the water met the shore on the other side, the towering cornstalks, and the twenty or so feet directly in front of them. She tried not to move her head, but occasionally she cut her eyes in Amos's direction. He was starting the same way, creating an outline of color.

They were both quiet for about fifteen minutes, until he said, "Did you know that colors have different meanings?"

Naomi finished painting the dark blue base of the water, where she'd later blend in hues of orange. If she did it right, the water would almost appear to be moving, glistening as day turned to night.

Lifting her brush from the canvas, she turned to face him. He was staring at her, and she instantly wondered how long he'd been watching her. "Colors are mentioned in the Bible, but I'm afraid I don't actually know what they mean or symbolize."

He looked back at his canvas. "I can't recall the meaning of colors in the Bible either."

She allowed herself a few seconds to watch his style, thinking she might take time to make the connection about colors and symbolism in the Bible. Even though she'd never painted with anyone, she had to assume everyone did it differently, and Amos's method was not the same as hers. He was . . . wilder with the paintbrush. Maybe that's what he meant about confidence, because he painted like he had all the confidence in the world, which made her wonder if he was like that in life. Perhaps that's what he meant about being able to tell things about a person from the way they paint. He'd picked up that she was underconfident, and to her, he appeared very self-assured.

When the sun met the horizon, they both stayed busily at work, not saying a word. There was only so much time to capture the beauty of a glowing sunset on a fall day. In the distance behind the corn, Naomi could see the orange-and-yellow leaves of the trees, which made for a lovely contrast against the dark green corn. Then there was the pond and the challenge to paint the reflections of both in all the right places.

Naomi finished before Amos, so she edged closer to have a better look at his work. He didn't seem to notice as he painted similar reflections against the water, but his painting looked nothing like hers.

"I don't know how you can say I'm a better painter than you, because it is absolutely not true." She gazed at his canvas with a sense of awe, and as she took in every detail, she realized it was indeed . . . telling. When he still hadn't responded or looked her way, she said, "You're a perfectionist."

Smiling, he slowly lifted his brush from the canvas. "What else do you see?"

She leaned closer, her arm brushing against his, which sent an unexpected tingle up her spine. "You . . ." Lifting her head to meet his eyes, she wasn't sure if she should say what was on her mind, but she took a deep breath and continued. "You hide things. I mean, not *things*. You hide your feelings."

He tilted his head to one side as if pondering her comment. "Maybe." He looked at his painting long and hard before he turned back to her. "How can you tell that from my painting?"

Careful not to touch the wet surface, she pointed to a spot in the forefront of his scene, where the weedy grass met the water's edge. "In reality the grass tapers down into the water, but in your painting, you don't show the gradual decline. It's like the weeds don't share space with the water, which hides the reality that they do."

He took off his hat, scratched his head, then put it back on. "Wow. You're right. I never would have noticed that. I guess it's impossible to be objective about your own work."

"I didn't mean it as an insult at all. You paint beautifully."

Grinning, he said, "Now let's have a look at yours."

She momentarily covered her face with her hands and spoke through her fingers. "Let's not."

He gently grabbed her wrists and eased her hands down. Then he walked behind her, his body pressed slightly against her.

"May I?" He didn't wait for an answer. Picking up her brush, he put it in her hand. With his arms coming around in front of her, he cupped one hand around hers and leaned over her shoulder. She could feel his breath warm against her neck as he guided her hand into the dark green paint. Then he dabbed a tiny amount of white on the end and moved toward the cornstalks.

"Here's why I said you're underconfident, not because of what you said." With perfect precision, he led the brush in her hand to the leafy part of a cornstalk, then pressed a soft swoosh upward.

She let out a small gasp as he pulled their hands away from the canvas, and when she turned to face him, he'd leaned down enough that they almost bumped noses.

"It looks so much better with that extra length, and it's so delicate. I'm always afraid of—" She stopped herself and grinned. "Underconfident." She nodded. "I guess you're right. I'm always afraid of the ripple effect that happens when I don't have enough paint on the brush."

"Look at all your other cornstalks. If you did this with all of them, it would show a sort of freedom, like they're endless and reaching for the clouds, growing in *Gott*'s grace." He smiled, but it quickly faded. "And I guess I need to quit hiding *mei* feelings."

Still facing him, she asked. "Was I right? Is that just the way you paint, or do you camouflage the way you feel also?"

He rubbed the side of his neck, avoiding her eyes. "*Ya*. I think I probably do."

"*Ach*, well, I guess we learned something about each other today." She took a small step away since they were clearly still in each other's personal space.

He backed up a few steps, putting more distance between him and the paintings. "Come stand beside me."

Naomi did and studied the paintings like he was.

"We're painting a fall sunset, so it's no surprise that we both used orange, brighter in the sky and softer as it reflects off of the water." He pointed to her painting. "You chose a base palette of brown for the grass and lightened up the blades with yellow to make it look plush. I did the same." Pulling back his hand, he lifted his hat and ran his other hand through his hair. "I'm not an art expert or anything"—he chuckled—"and everyone will always paint a different picture of the same thing." His expression sobered. "But you and I did one thing exactly the same."

Naomi glanced back and forth between the paintings a few times before she noticed it. "Wow," she said softly. "They both have an overall grayish tint, almost like we whitewashed a watercolor gray over the entire thing." She looked at him. "I didn't mean to do that. Did you?"

"*Nee*." He was quiet for a moment. "If I didn't say so before, *danki* for sharing your painting with me—the one you left in *mei* room."

She could feel herself blushing as she shrugged. "It's just unusual to find another Amish person who paints. Thomas thought it was a waste of time, but for me, it was the freedom to dream."

Amos frowned. "You were happy when you painted that picture. Hopeful."

Naomi managed a smile. "*Ya*, I was. I didn't know what it was like to have *mei* heart broken yet."

He looked back at both of their paintings as he pressed two fingers to his mouth, trying to hide a smile. "I know it's not funny, but there's no mistake that we both toned down what should have been a beautiful sunset filled with robust colors. It seems to symbolize our unhappiness and lack of hope."

"I don't want to be that person, but I feel stuck."

"That's how I feel too." He looped his thumbs beneath his suspenders and smiled at her. "I've enjoyed painting with you today. Maybe we can keep meeting in the evenings."

Naomi smiled, surprised at how much she'd enjoyed the evening and the discussion. "I'd like that. Do you want to keep painting this scene, or go somewhere else?"

"I think these paintings reflect our emotions. It wouldn't hurt either of us to see if we can cheer them. Maybe if we bring more color to the canvas, we'll bring more color to our lives."

Naomi locked eyes with him as butterflies swirled in her stomach. There was a small and recognizable hint of joy. She liked Amos. He was handsome and smart, and he shared her passion for painting. But he was emotionally unavailable, and Naomi needed to remember that and keep plenty of distance between them. Just the feel of his hand on hers earlier and his breath on her neck had filled her with pleasure. And that scared her a little.

ELEVEN

GUS WAS WAITING OUTSIDE THE COTTAGE AT NINE MONDAY morning. Esther met him at his truck and grimaced at the thought of riding around in the dingy truck with its tasteless bumper stickers. *Watch out for the idiot behind me. Honk if a kid falls out.* Several others weren't fit to take up space in her thoughts. She walked to the passenger side and waited for Gus to open her door the way their hired drivers did, then realized that was silly.

Gus pulled open his own door, the rusty hinges squeaking. The seat moaned when he sat down on the ripped cloth, springs bulging beneath his weight. Esther opened her door, happy to see her seat was intact, and hoisted herself into the truck. She pulled her black cape snug around her shoulders, tucked her chin as she pulled down on the front of her bonnet, then adjusted her sunglasses.

"Well, if you're trying to be incognito, I think you pulled it off." Gus laughed.

Esther didn't know what he meant, and his comment was overshadowed by her inability to ignore the odor in the truck.

"What is that smell?" She looked his way. He was wearing tattered blue jeans, worn-out brown boots, and a red-and-gray checkered shirt that he really should have left untucked. Instead, a brown belt accentuated his drooping belly. She tried to discern if the disgusting smell was coming from him or something in the truck.

"I don't smell anything." Gus's old truck wasn't automatic like most cars. He cranked it, then shifted gears from a throttle on the floorboard, and each time, a jerky action followed that caused Esther to bounce forward. She braced her palms against the dusty dashboard.

They were quiet as they drove away from the house to the main road until Gus finally spoke.

"So, what did you tell everyone about where I was taking you?" Gus turned to her briefly. Esther was still trying to get her seat belt fastened. After it finally clicked into place, she looked his way.

"I told Lizzie and Naomi you were taking me to the doctor for a checkup. Lizzie was surprised but glad I was going since she knows how much doctors scare me. And I told them none of our regular drivers were available."

"So you lied?" Gus grunted as he shook his head. "High and mighty, your people, always thinking you're better than everyone else, but you lie just like us regular folks."

"I will ask *Gott* to forgive the lie." She kept her eyes forward, wanting this day to be over.

"Yeah, so it's perfectly okay to tell a premeditated lie, as long as you ask your God for forgiveness later." He scoffed, which caused the hair on the back of Esther's neck to stand at attention.

"He's not my *Gott*, He's everyone's *Gott*."

"He ain't my God," Gus said with provocation, almost as if he was pushing for an argument. Esther had no plans to engage in a conversation about God with Gus. "Cuz if He was, I wouldn't be driving this old heap and living in a cottage run by a couple of cranky Amish widows." He paused, cutting his eyes at Esther. "Well, maybe not you, but your sister's a nut case."

Esther fought the urge to engage, but she just couldn't let it go. "There is a *Gott*, and maybe you should reach out to Him, but for reasons other than your living situation and the automobile you drive. Perhaps you should pray for things that are more important, like a relationship with Him. Maybe even pray about your *dochder*."

"I don't want to talk about her." Gus clamped his mouth shut.

Esther waited until he turned on a dirt road she knew was a shortcut to the clinic. "Your *dochder* came. Did you know that?"

He hit the break, then grinded the gears and turned to her. His bushy eyebrows were drawn into a frown. "She didn't come." He turned back to the road.

"*Ya*, she did. But she accidently went to Mary and John's *haus*. Mary pointed her to the cottage, but the woman went back to her car and just sat there a while. Then she left."

"Good riddance. I don't need some daughter I don't even know showing up after all these years."

Esther thought about the time and effort Gus had put into tidying up his house and appearance. "Were you married to the girl's *mudder*?"

"Yeah, I made an honest woman out of her since she was knocked up."

Esther cringed at his casual admission of something so important.

He shifted gears again and sped up once they were back on pavement. The truck managed to hit every pothole on the worn blacktop.

"And she ain't a girl anymore." He kept his eyes forward as he spoke. Esther tried holding her breath for short periods since the stench in the truck grew worse when Gus turned on the heater. She breathed a deep sigh of relief when they pulled into the clinic parking lot. Then she began to tremble as she fumbled to undo her seat belt with her arthritic hand that did not want to cooperate.

Her door flung open and before she knew it Gus's arm was across her, pressing against her stomach as he snapped the seat belt open. Then he stood back and waited for her to step out of the truck before he slammed the door closed.

"I don't need you coming inside with me." Her heart pounded. She was already worried about running into someone she knew since most of the people in the community used Dr. Elliot. And she certainly didn't want to be seen with Gus. That would cause more gossip than her being at the doctor.

"Yeah, I'm going in with you. What if you've got cancer or some other horrible disease that's going to kill you soon?" He paused, finding her eyes. "No one should have to hear that kind of news alone."

He could have chosen his words better, but there was something genuine in his eyes, a rarity for Gus. He actually sounded concerned. Shaking her head, she started walking across the parking lot toward the entrance, Gus by her side. When she reached the front door, she stopped, her feet rooted to the concrete pavement. She wasn't waiting for Gus to open the door for her. She simply didn't want to go in.

"You've come this far. Might as well get it over with." Gus reached for the door handle and slowly opened the door.

Esther stiffened, took a deep breath, then crossed over the threshold. The clinic housed several medical practices, including the dentist where Lizzie had gotten her dental work. When they reached Dr. Elliot's office, Esther's heart was racing so hard she worried her blood pressure might be off the chart. She briefly considered just going back to the truck, but for the second time today, Gus opened the door. Esther was happy to see that only two other people were in the waiting room—a mother with a small child on her lap.

Esther walked up to the window, told the woman her name, and was handed a clipboard with instructions to complete the forms. Gus had already sat down, and as much as she didn't want to sit next to him, she did. She wondered if she would have the courage to tell him on the way home that he smelled like a garbage dumpster. Or would she be so distraught about what Dr. Elliot said that Gus's odor wouldn't matter?

Her hands shook as she held the clipboard and tried to read the questions, which were blurring together. Her vision played tricks on her these days. She wasn't sure if it was due to glaucoma or some other ailment. The last time she'd been to the eye doctor was also seven or eight years ago. Lizzie put drops in her eyes daily for glaucoma. Her sister also took medications for high blood pressure and cholesterol. *There could be all kinds of things wrong with me.* As she had the thought, her hands trembled even more.

"Good grief. Give me that." Gus abruptly snatched the clipboard and took the pen from Esther's hand. "We're gonna be here all day."

He began filling out the paperwork. It was probably just her name, address, and other basic information. Then he turned to her and began asking her a series of questions. "Do you have a pacemaker?"

Esther shook her head.

"Ever had any surgeries?" Esther squeezed her eyes closed as vivid recollections flooded her mind, memories she'd tried to forget. She struggled to control her breathing.

"*Mei* appendix ruptured when I was a teenager." The pain had been unbearable, but it was the conversations that had taken place around her that lingered in her mind. *She might not make it. She has sepsis. Someone call the bishop.*

"And you lived to tell about it," Gus said casually without even looking at her.

He scanned the list, then stopped and scratched his head. "Uh, when . . ." He cleared his throat. "When did you have your last, uh . . . you know?"

Esther turned to look at him. "I'm not a mind reader, Gus."

"You know . . . your lady thing?" Gus's face turned bright red, and Esther's was bound to be the same color.

"Too long ago to remember," she finally said, wishing she'd just hired a driver and risked the gossip. But Gus didn't have anyone to tell about their trip—except Lizzie—and they'd made a deal about that. Gus didn't have any friends, for obvious reasons to everyone who crossed his path. It seemed surreal to have him here at the doctor with her, filling out her paperwork and asking her personal questions about her health.

After she returned the clipboard to the woman behind the glass, she only had to wait a few minutes before a nurse opened a door and called Esther's name. She slowly lifted herself up, but her feet didn't want to move. Gus stood.

"You are *not* coming with me." Esther was shaking from head to toe, but surely Gus knew he couldn't go in with her.

He groaned as a muscle flicked in his jaw. "I ain't going in with you, woman."

She decided to overlook the fact that he'd called her "woman."

"I-I just wanted to tell you that everything is gonna be okay." He cast his eyes down as he spoke, stuffing his hands into the pockets of his blue jeans. Esther was unexpectedly touched, and a tiny part of her wanted him to go with her. But she had no idea what kind of revealing tests might be performed, so she merely nodded and walked toward the nurse.

❦

Amos was glad when lunchtime finally rolled around. He'd overslept this morning, missed breakfast, and only grabbed a slice of toast and some bacon on his way out to finish working on the fence. No one had been around when he came downstairs, but a plate had been sitting on the counter with the food. He hoped he hadn't stolen someone else's breakfast.

If he kept up his pace he might finish the fence today and be ready to move on to the next project. He had a list but wasn't sure what he'd tackle next.

Inside the house he breathed in the aroma of something heavenly and recognized what he thought might be basil.

"I hope you like lasagna," Naomi said when he walked into the kitchen. "I know it's a bit heavy for lunch, but since you missed breakfast, I thought you might be starving." She nodded to a large casserole dish already on the kitchen table. It looked as wonderful as it smelled.

He put his hat on the pegs by the kitchen door. "*Ach*, I've never had lasagna. But it looks and smells delicious."

Naomi put her hands on her hips and grinned. "How could you have never had lasagna?" Then her smile faded. "Oh dear. Do you not care for pasta or tomato sauce?"

Amos closed his eyes and breathed in again before he

looked at her. "I love pasta and tomato sauce. *Mei mamm* only cooks traditional meat-and-potato meals."

"*Mei mamm* did too. But an *Englisch* friend taught me how to make this a long time ago. I've changed it up a bit and made it my own recipe. Lizzie and Esther love it, so I try to cook it every now and then, but usually for supper."

"Where are Lizzie and Esther?" Amos's mouth watered when Naomi placed a salad on the table next to the pasta dish.

"Lizzie is in the mudroom. She insisted she would run the clothes through the ringer, even though it's really *mei* job." She blew out a breath of frustration. "But it's hard to argue with Lizzie when she sets her mind on something. Esther actually went to the doctor for a checkup, which strikes me as suspicious."

"Why?" Amos was glad when Naomi finally sat down across from him. His stomach growled.

"She's terrified of doctors. I've seen her so sick with a cold that I thought it might turn into pneumonia, and she still wouldn't go to the doctor. I'm wondering if she suspects something is wrong."

Amos peeked out the kitchen window. "Her buggy is here."

"*Ya*, I know. Her appointment was in Bedford this morning. It's too far to travel by buggy." She sighed. "And she had Gus take her. She said all our drivers were busy, which is even more suspicious. None of us likes to spend any more time with Gus than we have to."

"I hope she's okay." Amos's eyes darted back and forth between Naomi and the lasagna. They bowed their heads in prayer, then she served him a large portion of the pasta.

After he'd swallowed the first bite, he said, "Please don't ever tell *mei mamm* this, but this is the best food I've ever eaten." He shook his head. "I'm going to have to marry someone who knows how to cook this." The moment the words slipped from his mouth, he found Naomi's wide eyes. He motioned back and forth between them with his hand. "I-I didn't mean, uh . . . you and me. I mean, I just meant . . ."

Smiling, she said, "I know what you meant, and that's a *gut* sign—that you can even make the statement, even joking. But I'm flattered you like it so much."

"'Like it' would be a big understatement." He was glad she hadn't taken his comment seriously. Sometimes when Naomi looked at him, he thought he saw longing in her eyes, but he wasn't sure how much of it was longing or grief. Amos confused his own emotions sometimes, so reading hers was only speculation. He was certain of one thing, though. He enjoyed being around her.

Amos said very little as he devoured his lunch. He even had seconds of the lasagna, wondering if he'd ever get enough.

"Did Lizzie already eat?" Over half the pan was still full, and Amos was pretty sure he could go another round, maybe a smaller one.

Naomi laughed. She'd had a small square of the casserole and some salad. "Why? Do you want to eat the entire pan?"

"Maybe." He smiled as she delivered a third helping to his plate.

"And, *ya*, Lizzie already ate some oatmeal. She still refuses to put in her teeth, since the cat played with them. I hope she changes her mind before Friday. We have a couple who booked a reservation for Friday and Saturday night."

About halfway through his third helping, Amos was sure he couldn't put one more bite in his mouth, but he didn't like to waste food, so he managed to clean his plate. He would just have to take it easier for the rest of the day. Naomi had been right. It was a heavy meal.

"How's your cat doing out in the barn?" He wiped his mouth, took a deep breath, and wished he could take a nap. Big midday meals made him sleepy.

Naomi bit her bottom lip. "I can't find her. I'm hoping she's just out exploring and returns soon."

Amos thought about all the raccoons and foxes in the area, not to mention the coyotes. "I'm sure that's it."

He stood up. "*Danki* for the best meal I've ever had in *mei* life."

Naomi rose, too, her cheeks taking on a rosy tint. "*Ach, danki*. I'm really, really flattered."

Amos moved toward the door and reached for his hat. "See you at supper." He put his hand across his stomach. "Although I might not eat as much as I usually do." He grinned. "But I'm looking forward to painting with you again."

"*Ya*, me too."

❧

Lizzie rushed into the kitchen carrying a load of wet laundry in a basket. She set it on the floor, scurried to Naomi, and clutched both of her shoulders. "He's the one, child. I can feel it in *mei* bones. And I've always said the way to a man's heart is through his stomach."

Naomi eased out of Lizzie's grasp and rested her hands on her hips. "Lizzie, were you eavesdropping?"

"Maybe a little." She flashed a toothless grin at Naomi.

"Amos is a very nice man, but neither of us is interested in pursuing a relationship. We both have a shared passion for painting." She pointed a finger at Lizzie. "No matchmaking. It won't work. Just let us enjoy the friendship we seem to be developing."

"That's how the best love stories start."

Naomi decided to change the subject. "Do you think Esther is okay? She never goes to the doctor, especially for a checkup. And for Gus to drive her to Bedford . . ."

Lizzie sat down at the table. "I wondered about that, too, since she has such a fear of doctors. But when I questioned her, she insisted it was just a checkup."

"It's *gut* she's going." Naomi suspected Esther might have several problems she wasn't telling them about because she didn't want to worry Lizzie. Esther seemed to have trouble with her eyes sometimes, and in addition to her stomach problems, her face turned red often. Naomi remembered a friend's father who became flushed when his blood pressure was high.

She picked up the basket of wet clothes. "I'm going to go hang these out on the line."

Lizzie nodded, but sad eyes and a frown indicated she was more concerned about her sister than she was letting on.

c❦ɔ

Esther listened in horror as Dr. Elliot told her about the tests she needed to have. She'd already made up her mind that she wasn't having any of them. She'd hoped whatever was wrong with her would be an easy fix and give her peace of mind. Instead, all her fears were turning into realities she wasn't ready to face. When the doctor told her about a procedure where they would put her in a large machine that spun around her, that was the final straw.

"It's important for you to have these tests, Mrs. Zook. You haven't had a checkup in a long time, and whatever is going on needs to be addressed." Dr. Elliot was about Esther's age. She wanted to tell him that maybe he should be retired and didn't know what he was talking about.

She nodded, even though her stomach churned.

"As I told you, this could be a minor thing. I suspect you have a stomach ulcer, but I wouldn't be doing my job well if we didn't rule out some other things too. And we need to run a blood panel to see where all your levels are, like cholesterol, blood sugar . . . things like that. Based on what you told me, I think you need to have your eyes checked as well."

She stood up on shaky legs, thanked the doctor, and walked down the hall. When she walked into the waiting room, anxious to leave, Gus rose to meet her.

"Let's go," she said as she moved faster toward the door.

"Wait, Mrs. Zook." The woman at the desk opened the glass window wider. "I need to give you the paperwork for the tests you need to schedule. They can all be done at the hospital here in Bedford."

Esther froze, didn't look at Gus, but turned around and accepted the papers from the woman, forcing a smile. She tucked them all in her purse and went to where Gus was actually holding open the exit door. Breezing by him, she stayed steadily ahead of him as she quickly walked to the truck. If he asked any questions, she'd tell him everything was fine. *Another lie. I'm sorry*, Gott.

"This ain't a marathon." Gus huffed and puffed to keep up with her, but she didn't slow or turn around. When she got to the truck, she opened her door, climbed in, slammed the door shut, and put her purse in her lap.

Gus opened his door and glared at her for a few seconds before he got in the seat. "You gonna tell me what the doc said?"

"It's personal, Gus." Esther raised her chin, hoping he didn't see her bottom lip trembling. "But I'm going to be fine."

He scratched his chin. "Then why all the tests?"

"Can you start the truck? I'm cold." Esther hugged herself, rubbing her shoulders.

Gus started the truck and adjusted the heater, but he didn't put the vehicle in gear. "I heard that woman say you gotta have tests. What tests?"

"Can you not respect *mei* privacy, please?" Esther's voice shook as she spoke, and her lip trembled even more when she thought about the test where they put you in a tube to take pictures.

Gus glared at her. "Put your seat belt on."

Esther pulled the strap across her chest, but once again she couldn't get her hands to cooperate.

Gus gently pushed her hand away and grabbed the strap, fastening the seat belt with ease. "What kind of tests?" he asked again.

Esther's blood pressure had been high in the doctor's office, and she was sure it was even higher now. She clenched her hands into fists around the strap of her small black purse. "Stop asking me! Please respect *mei* privacy!" She turned to Gus, blinking back tears. In all the years she'd known him, she'd never cried in front of him, not even at her mother's funeral. She'd managed to hold her emotions in until she was alone. But right now, she was unraveling right in front of him.

"You gonna die or what?" He asked the question as if he was asking if it was going to rain later. Esther had curse words on the tip of her tongue, words she'd only heard spoken by others, some she didn't even know the meaning of.

"You are a coldhearted man to ask me that." A tear slid down her cheek. "Do you have no compassion? Can't you see that I am upset?" She pointed her finger inches from his face. "You will keep your word and not say anything to Lizzie."

"You said you were gonna tell Lizzie." Gus's gruff voice didn't hold an ounce of compassion. "But I still get my pie."

"Gus Owens . . ." Esther's hands shook as she took a tissue out of her purse and dabbed at her eyes. "It's no wonder you have no friends! It's no wonder you have a *dochder* who doesn't want to see you. You are an unkind man who doesn't care about anyone but yourself."

Esther couldn't recall ever speaking to another human being the way she was speaking to Gus now, and the comment about his daughter was awful. "And you'll get your stupid pie." She held her face in her hands for a couple seconds before she wiped the tears from her eyes again.

"I'm sorry." She wasn't sure if she was or not, but it was a foul way to talk to a person. When she looked at him, her chest tightened. His eyes were moist, and it tugged at her heart more than she could have expected.

"I-I . . ." He locked eyes with her. "I kinda thought *you* were my friend. Maybe the only one, but . . ." He hung his head.

Esther reached into her purse, took out the papers the woman had given her, and handed them to Gus. Then she laid her head back against the seat and closed her eyes.

After reading them Gus cleared his throat, and Esther turned her head toward him, drained from crying, and resolved she was not going to have those tests. If it was the Lord's will to call her home, then so be it.

"Esther, now you listen to me." Gus spoke softly, in a way Esther had never heard from him. "None of these tests are painful. I've had them all. I know it can be scary but quit acting like a big ol' chicken. There's nothing to it. I'll bring you. It's up to you whether or not you tell that wacky sister of yours. But you have to have these tests done. They'll likely give you some pills afterward and you'll be all fixed up. There ain't nothing to an MRI either, if that's what you're all worked up about." He paused. "But ya gotta have it all done. It's just part of getting old."

Esther stared at him. She was worked up about all of it. "I don't have to do anything."

It was a long while before Gus responded. "Yeah, you do. And you know it. I know you're scared, but I'll be with you."

Esther blinked a few times as she tried to envision it. Grumpy Gus Owens by her side as she entered a world of medical mystery and strange tests that terrified her. But she couldn't tell Lizzie. Not yet.

"Okay," she said softly. She hadn't felt right in a long time. Perhaps enduring the tests was better than dying prematurely because of a medical phobia.

Gus finally put the truck in gear and neither one of them spoke on the way home.

Esther would take him his pie after supper. A deal was a deal.

TWELVE

NAOMI PUT THE JAMS, JELLIES, AND CHOW-CHOW ON THE table, then took a seat across from Amos at the small table in the kitchen. After the four of them prayed, she placed her napkin in her lap, hoping she wasn't about to overstep.

"How did your checkup go today?" She wasn't sure, but the circles under Esther's eyes seemed darker than usual. Naomi wondered if she'd been crying.

"Just fine." Esther dabbed butter on a slice of bread.

"You'll probably outlive us all," Lizzie said as she spooned mashed potatoes onto her plate. "But you cough a lot. What did the *Englisch* doctor say about that?"

So Lizzie had noticed the cough too.

"Probably just a bit of a cold." Esther wouldn't look at any of them. Naomi had never known Esther to lie, but she wondered if she was being completely truthful with them.

"Surely they're gonna do blood work since you haven't had

it done in so long." Lizzie sighed as she glanced back and forth between Naomi and Amos. "Esther's appendix burst when she was young, and it was a horrible ordeal for her." She looked back at her sister. "But having a little blood drawn isn't a big thing, Esther. Just a little pinprick. Nothing like what you went through as a teenager."

A flash of lightning turned their attention to the kitchen window, and a clap of thunder followed right behind, causing Naomi to flinch. She wasn't fond of storms.

"It's supposed to rain like this for days." Lizzie gummed her mashed potatoes, but at least she did it with her mouth closed.

Naomi's mood fell. *No painting tonight.*

"Uh . . ." Amos set his fork down. "All the projects on your list of repairs are outside. I'd like to earn my keep for these fine meals." He smiled at Naomi, which for some reason caused her heart to beat faster. "Are there any inside projects that you'd like me to do?"

"First of all, we're paying you, so the meals come free." Lizzie smiled as she looked back and forth between Naomi and Amos. "Just because you can't paint pictures, doesn't mean you two can't find something else fun to do." She shrugged. "It'll just have to be something indoors. And no, we don't have any inside projects."

Naomi wasn't sure about that as she thought about the leaky faucet upstairs, but she didn't say anything because she thought she might be blushing. Lizzie couldn't have been any more overt if she'd tried. Naomi was glad she'd told Amos about the sisters' matchmaking tactics. At least he knew what was going on, which made it less awkward.

After they'd eaten and Lizzie and Naomi had cleaned the kitchen, they all retired to the living room for devotions. A knock on the door interrupted them. Esther was closest and got up to answer it.

Gus was standing on the porch with an umbrella dangling at his side. He wasn't getting wet under the porch overhang, but he was soaked.

"Gus, what's wrong?" Esther asked, frowning.

"There was a black cat on my porch earlier. And if that's not bad luck, I don't know what is." He cringed. "Blasted thing even tried to run in the house."

"Whiskers!" Naomi stood up from where she'd been sitting on the couch. "Where is she?"

Lizzie groaned and laid her head back against the rocker.

"It had a flea collar on, so I wondered if it might be yours or Mary's." He waved a hand toward Lizzie. "I knew it wasn't hers. She's got some abnormal phobia about felines. But I didn't know if you or Esther were feeding the thing. Or Mary."

"Amos and I found her caught in a trap the day of Suzanne and Isaiah's wedding. I brought her home." Naomi sighed. "But she kept getting out of *mei* bedroom, and since Lizzie is afraid, I set her up a bed and put food and water in the barn. But then I didn't see her." Pausing, she was a bit surprised Gus made the trip in the weather. "*Danki* for coming over here in such bad weather to let us know."

"Yeah, whatever. She's on my porch. You can get her

tomorrow. Last thing I need is a black cat making my life any more miserable than it already is." He locked eyes with Esther. "Seems I've earned a piece of pie for trudging over here in the rain to inquire about a stupid cat."

Lizzie stood from the rocking chair, her fists balled at her sides. "You deserve a kick in the shin is what you deserve." She took a few steps forward and pushed her bottom lip out. "Just for being you."

Gus ran two fingers the length of his lips. "Zip it, crazy lady, and for heaven's sake, put your teeth in. You look like a fish out of water, smacking for air."

Lizzie moved closer to him, but Esther put a hand out to stop her. "I'll get you some pie, Gus. I know how much Naomi appreciates you coming in this weather to let her know about the cat."

"I want chocolate if you've got it." Gus stood dripping just on the other side of the threshold. Esther nodded and left for the kitchen. Gus stretched his neck into the living room, his eyes landing on Amos. "I don't know how you can live in this nut house with that one." He pointed to Lizzie.

Naomi braced herself, hoping Lizzie didn't go after him. Everyone in their district had been taught passiveness, but Lizzie didn't always adhere to that way of thinking. But she raised her chin, told everyone goodnight, and excused herself to her bedroom, slamming the door behind her. Something she'd been doing a lot of lately.

Before Amos could answer, Esther returned with a slice of pie she'd put in a plastic container. "Here, this should keep it from getting wet." She stepped onto the porch and closed the door behind her.

"What's she doing out there?" Amos asked.

Naomi shrugged. "I don't know." She had a niggling sense that all wasn't what it seemed.

∾

"I know you just wanted your pie, but it was nice of you to let Naomi know about the cat. I think the girl has been worried." She pushed the container toward Gus.

"I was afraid you'd try to bring me the pie in this weather since you're a woman of your word and wouldn't let a thunderstorm stop you." He paused. "And since you're all sick and everything, I figured I'd come collect it myself."

Esther folded her arms across her chest, shivering. "Well, I'm not the woman you think I am, then, because I wasn't going to venture out in this mess just to take you some pie."

Gus twisted his mouth back and forth, then shrugged. "I guess you could have brought me two slices tomorrow. So . . . if the weather is bad, I'll either come here, or—"

"*Nee.*" Esther held up a hand. "You can't come here every day for pie. I'll get it to you or save it up. You won't miss any." Closing her eyes, she sighed. "Anything else, Gus, because I have a lot on *mei* mind?"

"Nope." He handed her the pie while he opened the umbrella, then snatched back the container. "I've got my pie."

Esther watched him walk away. Today she'd seen a glimpse

of the man Gus could be. But no sooner did he appear to be a noble and caring person than he reverted to the grouch they'd always known.

She went back into the living room. Naomi was on one side of the room, sitting on the couch, and Amos was in a rocking chair. Esther sensed they might have been talking, but all was quiet when she walked in. She thought about how Joe used to love a good thunderstorm. They'd curl up on the couch, snuggling, thunder in the background. She'd miss that man until the day she died, which she feared might be coming sooner rather than later. She needed a distraction, and she had just the thing.

"I have something for you two." She smiled as she looked back and forth between Amos and Naomi. She held up a finger. "Wait right here."

She returned from her bedroom with a book she'd found at a yard sale years ago. She'd only bought it for the pretty pictures and because it was only a nickel. But it might come in handy now.

Esther sat beside Naomi on the couch. "Come join us, Amos."

He rose from the rocking chair and sat on the other side of Naomi. Esther put the book on Naomi's lap, and Amos leaned closer.

"I bought this a long time ago because I liked the pictures of the landscapes. But it's actually a book about how to paint landscapes. I'm not saying either of you need a book to teach you, but I thought you might enjoy looking at it."

Naomi opened the book, then eased it to her right so it was also in Amos's lap.

Perfect.

After they both thanked her, she excused herself, wanting to give the young people some time alone. At least the book got them on the couch next to each other. She trusted Naomi not to let anything get inappropriate if things moved in a romantic direction, which she hoped would happen.

Esther had a lot to think about. But first she just wanted to have a good, private cry in her room. She'd prayed and prayed for strength, but despite her belief that God heard her prayers, the urge to release some stored-up emotion still overwhelmed her.

~∞~

Naomi eyed the mountainous landscape in the book, but she was very aware of Amos's leg touching hers on the couch. His nearness made her senses alert in an unfamiliar way.

"Someday I'd like to go see mountains like this." Naomi gingerly ran her hand along the full-color photo of mountains covered in snow with a stunning blue sky in the background. "I don't think I could ever paint as well as this artist, though."

"He was probably professionally trained and has been doing it for a long time." Amos was holding one side of the book, Naomi the other. As he leaned even closer and eyed the painting, she breathed in his scent. He'd showered before supper, and the hint of musk filled her senses as her pulse quickened. Esther kept a basket of assorted soaps in the guest bathrooms, but Naomi couldn't recall anything that smelled the way Amos did now. She waited until her heartbeat got back to normal before she said anything.

"When I used to paint before, sometimes I felt like it was a waste of time, that I should be doing something more productive, like tackling the mending or ironing, cleaning areas I'd been putting off, or tending to other chores that needed to be done."

He looked at her, his eyes twinkling in the light of the lantern, shadows from the flames dancing above their heads. "I think it's okay to just have fun sometimes."

There was no mistaking the seductiveness in his voice. Naomi couldn't pull her gaze from his. A knot rose in her throat as blood coursed through her veins like an awakened river. She felt drugged by his clean, manly scent, along with the way he was looking at her, studying her. When he reached up and tucked a strand of loose hair behind her ear, the gentle touch of his hand was almost unbearable with tenderness. Her lips parted, and she waited, longing for the feel of his lips against hers.

But he retreated, eased away, and cleared his throat. "I-I guess I should go to bed."

Naomi wanted to tell him to stay, to hold her in his arms, to remind her what it was like to be loved and protected. But the sting of rejection prickled her skin, even though neither of them had made an actual advance.

"*Ya*, sure." When she abruptly stood up, the book fell to the floor. They both leaned down to pick it up and bumped heads.

Amos straightened with the book in his hand, and Naomi raised a hand to her forehead, wondering if his head hurt half as much as hers. They'd bumped hard enough that a goose egg was already forming on Naomi's forehead.

He eased her hand away, gently lifted her chin with his hand, and peered at her forehead. "*Ach*, wow. I'm sorry."

She shook her head and his hand dropped. "*Nee*, it was just as much *mei* fault as yours."

"You need some ice on it." He picked up the lantern and rushed to the kitchen, returning with some ice cubes wrapped in a kitchen towel. Gently, he pressed it against her head, and she flinched.

"You might need some ice on yours too." She eased the towel and ice from his hand and tenderly reached up to hold it against the knot on his head. Surprisingly, he winced a little, too, but eventually took the ice from her hand and handed it back.

"Here, take it with you to bed. *Mei* head is okay." But he didn't move, and neither did Naomi. Gazing into each other's eyes, the heady sensation returned, the prequel to a kiss, something neither of them was ready for. Or maybe they were. Perhaps it would help push them past the darkness they both seemed to be stuck in. But he'd withdrawn from the moment earlier.

Amos slowly lifted his hands and cupped her cheeks. Naomi dropped the towel she was holding, ice cubes tumbling across the wood floor, but even the noise wasn't enough to break the trance.

"Are you sure you're okay?" he whispered, still holding her face.

"*Ya.*" It was all she could manage as she stared into his eyes, again anticipating the feel of his lips on hers. An undeniable magnetism had snuck up on them, but was it right?

He leaned down, his breath warm against her mouth as he pulled her closer to him. Just before his lips met hers, he dropped his hands and stepped back.

"I'm sorry." He wound around the coffee table and headed toward the staircase, taking the steps two at a time.

Naomi stood with her arms at her sides as the ice cubes puddled on the floor. She waited until her knees stopped shaking, then she picked up the lantern and went to get a mop. She would likely spend the next few hours analyzing what he meant when he said he was sorry. Sorry that he still loved Sarah too much to kiss another woman? Sorry that he bumped her head? Sorry that he didn't want to lead her on since he had no desire to have a relationship? Or was it something else?

Whatever his reason, the exchange had left Naomi longing for passion more than ever. But there was a difference between passion and love, and the love should come first. She barely knew Amos.

Her thoughts shifted to Thomas. Prior to his hasty departure, she'd thought she had it all with him. He was handsome, and they had a lot in common. Thomas loved animals as much as Naomi, and they planned to have a big farm. And even though gardening was mostly women's work, Thomas had loved to work alongside Naomi. They often laid on a blanket outside when the sky was clear, wishing on shooting stars and stealing kisses.

What happened? She could still recall with painful clarity Thomas's words when he ended their relationship outside his parents' house. "I love you, Naomi, but I'm not ready to get married." After asking him repeatedly through her tears why he wasn't ready, he turned and walked away.

They'd both been baptized and begun preparing for a life together. He left town two days later, before Naomi could question him further. Did he not love her enough? If she'd had more answers, would she have been able to move on? She'd likely never know. All she knew for sure was that romantic love caused unbearable pain when it didn't work out.

No matter her attraction to Amos, she was going to need to keep some distance between them.

∞

Amos sat on the side of his bed, resting his elbows on his knees as he held his head in his hands. His head was splitting, but not from the bump on his noggin. He'd come close to kissing Naomi. Twice. A combination of longing and guilt consumed him. Even though he wasn't interested in a relationship, he couldn't deny his attraction to her. If he continued to live here with her, he wasn't sure he could harness his temptation. Sarah had been his entire world. How could he be so desirous of a woman he barely knew?

Lightning lit up the night sky, followed by claps of thunder that were becoming less frequent. The storm was moving out. Maybe Lizzie was wrong about it raining for days.

He slipped out of his slacks, took off his shirt, and got into bed. Closing his eyes, he pictured Sarah, her bright blue eyes, the way her cheeks dimpled when she laughed—which had been often—and every curve of her body in just the right place. He was caught off guard when the image began to fade, something that had never happened before. He couldn't visualize Sarah as clearly. As Naomi crept into his mind, he could see her brown doe eyes longing for him to kiss her. Shaking his head, he tried to clear the vision, but as he tried to sleep, she was all he could see.

Groaning, he got out of bed and paced in the darkness of the bedroom, barely lit now by the occasional flash of lightning. He walked to the window and, from the light of the propane lamp in the yard, he could see that it was still misting rain. A movement caught his attention.

Peering out past the lamppost, he saw a man standing in the yard. Amos couldn't make out any details, just that the person was wearing pants. It looked like he might have on a straw hat, but Amos couldn't tell for sure. Was the man a threat? Or an elderly fellow who might be lost? He recalled a neighbor back home who suffered from Alzheimer's disease. He was often found wandering the streets, unable to find his way home.

Without lighting the lantern, Amos put his clothes back on and went to check it out.

Thirteen

NAOMI PICKED AT HER BREAKFAST. SHE LOVED PANCAKES, but she didn't have much of an appetite this morning. She'd stayed awake until after midnight pondering what had happened between her and Amos last night. She'd thought for sure he was going to kiss her. And, right or wrong, she would have let him. But now she wondered if maybe she'd exaggerated or misinterpreted his gestures.

Then why can't I look at him? They'd bumped heads, and he comforted her. She reached up and touched her forehead, but the bump on her head was gone, as if it was never there in the first place.

"Um . . ." Naomi looked up, and Amos wiped his mouth with his napkin before continuing. But he was looking at Esther. "Last night, there was a man in the yard. It had mostly stopped raining, and I thought I better go see if he was okay or needed something."

"Did he tell you his name? Was he Amish?" Esther set her fork on her plate.

"I didn't see him, except from the bedroom window." Amos scratched his forehead. "He was gone by the time I got outside. I looked around for a while, but I never found anyone. There wasn't a car or buggy, so he'd traveled on foot. From the window it looked like he had on a straw hat, but I'm not sure."

"That was probably Ben, Marie's husband. At the last quilting party, she said he's getting all *ab im kopp*." Lizzie pointed to her head and twirled her finger, then cleared her throat and flashed everyone a big smile.

"*Ya*," Esther said. "Your teeth look lovely, Lizzie."

"I'll probably die from some rare disease." She stopped smiling and looked at Naomi. "I scrubbed these dentures, but I hope I don't end up with cat-scratch fever."

Naomi chuckled and glanced at Amos to see him smiling too. "Lizzie, I think the cat would have to scratch you to give you that."

"Back to this man." Esther tipped her head slightly to one side. "I don't think that could have been Ben. Their farm is two miles down the road."

"*Ach*, well, who else would be silly enough to roam around at night in the rain?" Lizzie smiled again, even though there wasn't really anything to smile about.

Esther put her napkin across her plate, then got up and carried it to the sink. When she turned around she said, "I know we don't usually lock the doors at night, but let's do so for a few evenings, just to be safe."

Naomi nodded before lifting her eyes to Amos, who was staring at her. She lowered her gaze, wondering what was going on in his mind and still trying to decide if she'd misread him.

"Look at that." Lizzie pointed to the kitchen window. "The sun's coming up, and there are only a few clouds in the sky. Doesn't look like rain to me. Those fellas in the newspaper don't know what they're talking about. They made it sound like we'd be homebound for days." Lizzie rolled her eyes and showed her teeth again.

Naomi pressed her lips together to avoid grinning. She was happy Lizzie finally seemed to be getting used to her teeth and that she'd gotten over the cat incident—at least enough to wear the dentures again.

"So, it looks like you two can resume your painting." Lizzie flashed her pearly whites again.

Naomi looked across the table at Amos and forced a smile, waiting to see if he would say anything.

"I'm looking forward to it," he said before he winked at Naomi.

What is he doing? She glanced at Esther, then Lizzie. They were both wide-eyed as they exchanged all-knowing looks. The wink would only fuel their matchmaking efforts. Things were already awkward enough. *Why did he do that?*

Naomi was sure her face was red, but she nodded. "*Ya,* me too."

"I-I guess I'll get back to work while it isn't raining," Amos said to Esther before he turned to Naomi. "And I guess I'll see you for painting tonight, weather permitting."

There was no mistaking the blush on Amos's cheeks. *So, he feels awkward too? Then why wink at me?*

Naomi grinned. "So, you aren't planning on having dinner or supper?"

"Well, uh . . . *ya*. Of course." He stood up. "I'm not going to miss any of your wonderful meals."

Naomi prepared herself for the sisters, and when the front door shut behind Amos, Lizzie started.

"I saw it!" She pointed a finger at Naomi, a huge smile on her face. "He winked at you, and he's flirting with you."

Before Naomi could think of a response, Esther pressed her palms together and said, "And did you see him blushing? He's nervous. That's so sweet."

Naomi didn't know what to say. The wink had surprised her too. She pushed her chair back and began clearing the table, shaking her head. After she placed the dishes in soapy water, she turned around and leaned against the counter.

"I have already explained to Amos that I am not interested in a romantic relationship. And he is still recovering from the death of his fiancée and feels the same way about not wanting to get involved in anything romantic. We are just friends. So, please don't make a big deal out of a little wink." She folded her arms across her chest and raised her chin.

"Whatever you say, dear." Esther nodded, but she was still grinning as she left the kitchen.

Lizzie followed her sister, giggling like a schoolgirl. "He's sweet on her," she said before she looked over her shoulder and gave Naomi an exaggerated wink.

Naomi held back a grin. She was looking forward to painting with Amos tonight more than she cared to admit, even to herself.

∞

Amos shook his head as he marched to the back fence. Maybe if he tossed his head around enough, he'd clear the loose marbles having a party in his mind. *What in the world am I doing?* He had clearly and intentionally flirted with Naomi. And he'd done it in front of Esther and Lizzie.

By the time he reached the back fence, he had a headache from overanalyzing his actions. Or maybe his head ached from bumping hers the night before. He touched his forehead. Nothing was there, not even a bruise.

Then it hit him. He'd flirted with her because it felt good. It was nice to be attracted to someone and to act on it. Besides, feeling good about anything hadn't been a part of Amos's life until recently.

But were his actions going to be like taking a step back? Would he scare off Naomi completely? He enjoyed having a friend he was comfortable around. If she wasn't so gorgeous, the friendship would be easier to maintain without the temptations that went along with Naomi's looks. He'd thought he was clear on his position about relationships and no desire to have one. He'd also thought he was clear about Naomi's position and lack of desire to be anything more than friends. But he was sure she'd wanted him to kiss her last night. They seemed to be sending each other mixed signals. *Why?*

He spent another ten minutes remembering the moment in the living room. Part of him wished he had kissed her, for his own selfish reasons. But he knew they both would have regretted it afterward. He didn't want to lose her as a friend. They would have crossed a line they'd clearly set for themselves.

Amos's chest tightened. He hadn't thought about Sarah even once all day. And that left him engulfed in guilt, but strangely, entangled in his mind with the marbles and guilt . . . there was hope.

❦

Esther was happy things might be moving in a romantic direction with Naomi and Amos, but thoughts about her health weighed heavily on her mind. She'd decided not to go with Lizzie and Naomi to the Bargain Center in the late afternoon. She usually looked forward to the outings, but she was nauseated after breakfast and had skipped lunch, feigning a headache—which wasn't a lie.

Amos had finished the fence and was splitting wood they'd need for the winter. With Lizzie and Naomi gone, Esther decided to get her most dreaded task behind her. The rain had let up for today, but Indiana weather was unpredictable. She was going to take Gus an entire pie. Why hadn't she thought to do that before? It would make for fewer trips to his house.

She packed up a chocolate pie since that seemed to be his favorite. Maybe he wouldn't be in such a foul mood today. It was unlikely, but she'd stay hopeful. She wrapped her cape around her and was only a few steps into the yard when she noticed a car in front of Gus's cottage—a red car, like Mary said she'd seen.

Esther slowed and considered going back to the house, but she was too curious about the possibility of seeing Gus's daughter. She started walking again, glancing at the sky, thankful for the sunshine.

When she stepped onto the front porch and raised her hand to knock, she heard loud voices and lowered her arm, knowing she should leave. Instead, she leaned an ear closer to the door.

"Then why'd you even come here if you feel like that?" Gus's deep voice bellowed out the words. "Just to rub my nose in your troubles? They ain't my troubles, so I don't see how it can be my fault!"

"You are even worse than you were when I was a kid, and I never would have believed that possible. You were mean back then, and you still are. I guess I came just to see if growing older had changed you at all." There was a pause, and Esther held her breath, waiting. When the woman—who had to be Heather—finally spoke again, her language was worse than anything Esther had ever heard.

Esther covered her mouth with her hand, almost dropping

the pie. She knew she should set it on the table by the rocking chair, but she couldn't bring herself to leave.

"Oh, and by the way, Mom died three years ago, in case you might care one tiny little bit."

Silence.

The door suddenly swung open and hit Esther so hard she almost fell over. The pie wasn't so lucky as it toppled to the porch and landed upside down.

A nicely dressed lady, who looked to be in her fifties, gasped. "Are you all right? I'm so sorry." The woman leaned down and picked up the dilapidated pie with the meringue mashed against the plastic wrap that covered it. She handed it back to Esther, who found herself speechless.

"What are you doing here?" Gus's face was redder than red as he locked eyes with Esther.

His daughter shook her head. "Good luck with him. I'm done," she said to Esther before she rushed down the cottage steps, got in her car, and left.

"I decided to bring you an entire pie in case it rains. And it will be easier on me to bring you a whole pie even if it's not raining so I don't have to sneak over here every day." She was already wondering what she would tell Lizzie and Naomi about Gus carting her to the tests she was going to be having. She shivered at the thought of being poked and prodded by strangers. "But I'm sorry. I seem to have interrupted you and your *dochder*."

"She's no one to me." He paused as he lowered his head. Esther felt an odd urge to hug him, but she waited, and he finally lifted his eyes to hers. "That wasn't our deal. I don't want to eat the same pie all week." He glowered at her, shifting his gaze over her shoulder where his daughter's car had been. Sorrow filled Gus's expression, no matter how hard he tried to mask it with anger.

Esther took a deep breath.

"This pie is no longer fit to eat anyway." She wanted to ask Gus if he was okay, but she knew he would only lash out at her. "I will bring you a fresh slice of pie this evening. I think Naomi made an apple one this morning."

"This will be fine." Gus snatched the pie from her hands, then slammed the door closed behind him.

Esther peered in the window, half expecting Gus to throw the pie across the room. Or maybe he would save it and throw something else. Even she had been known to throw a small thing here and there out of anger. Instead, he slowly set the pie on the TV tray by the couch, then he sat down, putting his back to her.

His shoulders began to rise and fall, and she watched him cover his face with both hands. Esther's hand covered her mouth. *Is he crying?* A crack was forming in her heart for Grumpy Gus Owens, who had begun showing a more human side of himself lately.

She tiptoed to the front door and reached for the knob. Even if he didn't smell very good, she was going to pull him into a big hug. Everyone needed a hug sometimes, even those who might not deserve one. She couldn't imagine having a child, not seeing that child for decades, and then having a conversation as horrible as the one she'd just overheard. Her heart hurt for all involved.

When she heard Gus actually sobbing, she placed her hand flat on the door and closed her eyes. Esther couldn't cure Gus's pain with a hug, and the intrusion would likely embarrass or enrage him. So, she did the only thing she knew would help Gus. She prayed for him.

After she lowered her hand and tiptoed down the steps, she trudged home. Mary and John were on their front porch. Esther couldn't hear what they were saying, and she was glad. Mary's hands were on her hips, and John was leaning toward her—and not in a romantic way. They were fighting again.

Esther lifted her eyes to the sky. *Why can't there just be peace?*

∞

Naomi scurried to finish cleaning the kitchen after supper with Lizzie's help. Amos had already carried the painting supplies to the wagon and was halfway to their spot.

"That boy is sweet on you," Lizzie said as she climbed a step stool to put a casserole dish on a shelf.

"Don't start, Lizzie. We are just friends." Naomi recalled the way Amos had almost kissed her—twice—but recoiled both times.

Lizzie folded the stool and stashed it between the wall and refrigerator, then put her hands on her hips. "You'd have to be blind not to see the way Amos looks at you." She peered at Naomi. "And you're not blind."

Naomi had noticed the way Amos looked at her, especially the night before. "You're making too much of it."

Lizzie scooted toward Naomi and cupped her cheek. "*Mei* sweet *maedel*, it is okay to allow yourself to be happy. Thomas was a cad." She lowered her hand. "I never did think he was the one, but you were happy, and that's all we've ever wanted for you."

"He wasn't a cad." Naomi wanted to get to the pond, but she couldn't have Lizzie calling the man she loved a cad.

"Of course he was. He professed his love for you, asked you to marry him, then fled the district, leaving you embarrassed and heartbroken."

Naomi tried not to recall her feelings after Thomas had left, but Lizzie was making it feel raw again. "I am going to go paint with Amos, but you need to stop saying he's sweet on me." She glared at Lizzie. "And please stop calling Thomas a cad." Lizzie had used that word to describe Thomas more than once since the breakup.

She stormed out, regretting her harsh tone with Lizzie, but Naomi was having a hard enough time sorting out her feelings without Lizzie making her even more confused.

By the time she got to the pond, she was breathless from hurrying. A chill hung in the air, and she'd forgotten her cape.

"Do you want me to go back to the *haus* and get your cape? You're shivering." Amos already had a paintbrush and palette in his hand. He was wearing a light jacket over his long-sleeve blue shirt.

"*Nee*, I'll warm up." Naomi wasn't sure that was true, but she didn't want to waste any daylight. She rubbed her arms as Amos set the brush and palette in the wagon and slipped out of his coat. "*Nee*, don't do that. I'll be fine."

He draped it around her shoulders, gently pulled it snug around her, then grinned. "It's *kinda* big for you. But I'm warm without it."

Naomi was still shuddering, but it wasn't from the cool air. Amos had that seductive look in his eyes again, the expression that caused Naomi to wonder if she was misreading him. But when he didn't move and their eyes remained locked again, she waited.

He stepped back and cleared his throat before picking up his brush and palette. He stared out over the pond, his forehead wrinkling. "Do you think we should keep painting this same scene?"

Naomi took a deep breath and swallowed back the nervous knot in her throat. "Um, I don't know." She turned to him, but he was still staring out over the water. "I've painted this scene a lot. It's a beautiful spot, and each time I see it differently.

He turned to her and scratched his chin. "We both painted depressing pictures of this beautiful landscape. Maybe we should keep working on it until we come up with a happier and more accurate end result, without all the gray. Something cheerful, like your other picture."

She thought for a few moments. "Maybe you're right. It could be like therapy."

He laughed. "This view deserves our best effort."

Naomi gave a taut nod of her head. "Agreed."

They worked in silence, and Naomi tried to brighten up her picture and apply the technique Amos had shown her, extending the leaves on the cornstalks. She stepped back a couple feet and smiled. "I think the therapy must be working."

Amos set down his painting tools and scooted over to her side. "It's brighter." His eyes met hers. "I think it's probably more reflective of the real you."

She reveled in the compliment as she looked over at his painting. "Wow, yours is more colorful too. Maybe we just needed each other to point out the gray tints in order to see ourselves more clearly, or at least see who we want to be."

"Naomi." He gently placed his hands on her shoulders and turned her to face him. "I know we talked about just being friends, but I feel an overwhelming desire to kiss you, and I don't know if that's a *gut* thing for either of us." He paused as he dropped his arms to his sides. "I feel something for you, something I didn't expect." Shaking his head, he sighed. "Maybe I'm overanalyzing it. You're a beautiful woman, and I like you, and I want to kiss you."

Naomi went weak in the knees, her body shaking again but not from the cold. "I like you, too, and I admit I'm surprised that I feel . . ." She searched for a word to explain. "I'm surprised that I want you to kiss me. I didn't think I'd ever feel that way again."

"Well . . ." Amos grinned and tapped a finger to his chin. "That sounded kind of like permission." He tucked loose strands of hair behind her ears, the way he'd done before. And as he lowered his mouth to hers, Naomi knew she was crossing into an area she'd forbidden herself to go since Thomas. But she'd never met a man like Amos, and he made the risk feel worth it.

Just as she closed her eyes, someone called her name.

She backed away from Amos and turned to the voice she'd recognize anywhere. Her heart thumped wildly as she blinked to clear her vision, wondering if she was seeing things. But she wasn't.

"Thomas," she said softly as she watched him walking to-ward them.

FOURTEEN

AMOS SUDDENLY FELT INVISIBLE. NAOMI HAD MOVED TO-
ward her ex-fiancé without looking back at him.

The two exchanged a few words before Naomi led him
to where Amos stood. She handed him back his coat, which
seemed significant.

"Amos . . ." Her face had brightened in a way that caused a
huge lump to form in his throat. "This is Thomas." She glanced
at the man by her side, and there was no doubt how she was
feeling. He was shorter than Amos, a nice-looking fellow with
wavy brown hair, dark eyes, and a square jaw. Amos shouldn't
be surprised that such a guy had courted Naomi. She was
probably out of Amos's league anyway. But until he'd met her,
there hadn't been a league worth considering.

Amos took the man's hand when he extended his. "*Wie
bischt*, nice to meet you."

Thomas nodded before he turned to Naomi, whose smile seemed to keep growing. If she'd held any hostility toward her ex, it was gone.

"I came by last night, but it was late. I'm staying with *mei* parents, and I decided to take a walk." Thomas shrugged. "I ended up here, then I realized how silly it was to come calling at that time of night." Pausing, he reached for her hand. "I've missed you."

Naomi didn't hesitate. She took the offered hand and said, "I've missed you too."

Amos tried to imagine how he would feel if Sarah was alive and miraculously walked up to him. He supposed his reaction would have been similar to Naomi's. She loved Thomas the same way Amos had loved Sarah, who would never walk up to him again.

Naomi was still aglow, her smile stretched across her beautiful face. He needed to be happy for her, but she'd nicked the armor around his heart, opened the dark place a tiny bit, enough for the sting of Thomas showing up to nip at his emotions. *Stupid, stupid.* Thankfully, he hadn't kissed her. How much had Thomas seen? Had he seen how close Amos had been to Naomi? Did he even consider that she might have moved on?

Still holding Naomi's hand, he edged closer to the paintings. "Still painting, *ya?*"

She nodded and finally glanced at Amos. "But not until recently."

Finally, Thomas seemed to recognize that a situation might

be in front of him. "Did I, uh . . . interrupt something?" He glanced back and forth between Naomi and Amos.

"Not at all. We just both like to paint and decided to try our hands at it since it had been a while for both of us." Amos forced a smile but avoided looking at Naomi, afraid she'd see the regret in his expression, maybe feel it vibrating from his heart.

"Do you live near here?" Thomas let go of Naomi's hand and stood taller.

"I'm staying at the inn for a while. *Mei* and *mei mamm* came from Ohio to attend a wedding and visit family. *Mamm* went back home Sunday, but Lizzie and Esther asked me to stay on for a while and take care of some repairs. I agreed since business is slow for me back home this time of year."

"Ah . . ." Thomas looped his thumbs beneath his suspenders. "So you're staying at the main *haus*?" He lifted an eyebrow as any hint of a smile disappeared.

"*Ya*." He turned to Naomi. "I'm sure you two have lots to talk about. I'll probably paint for a while, then I'll haul all of this inside." He motioned toward the wagon.

"So you know who I am?" Thomas's voice might have been considered confrontational by some people, but Amos was trying to put himself in the man's shoes. Even though he was sure nothing ever could have made him leave Sarah.

"*Ya*, Naomi told me about you." Amos heard the edge in his voice.

"Thomas, do you want to take a walk?" Naomi wasn't smiling anymore. Maybe she sensed the tension building.

"Uh, *ya*." Thomas glanced her way. "Sure."

Finally, Naomi looked Amos in the eye. "Are you sure you don't mind taking all of this back later?"

He'd done the heavy lifting the night before, but she'd helped by carrying one of the easels. "*Nee*, I don't mind. But I'm going to finish what I started."

She lowered her gaze and nodded. He was pretty sure she picked up on his meaning.

As he watched Naomi walk off with the man she loved, Amos silently chastised himself for opening his heart to her. He barely knew Naomi, but the ache in his chest grew with each step she took.

He began packing up the painting supplies. He'd lost interest for tonight.

❧

Naomi held Thomas's hand after he draped his jacket around her as they headed toward the barn, where he said it would be warmer and private.

They were both quiet, and Naomi was tempted to look over her shoulder, but she didn't want Thomas to see her do that and question her. If he had walked up on them five seconds later, he would have caught Naomi kissing Amos, and her chance of reconciling with Thomas probably would have been gone. Thomas's tone had tensed when he learned Amos was staying under the same roof as Naomi. Maybe it would do him good to be a little jealous after what he'd put her through.

She quickly shook the thought from her mind, refusing to

let anger and resentment get in the way of them resuming their relationship. She'd always known she'd take him back, given the opportunity. *And now he's here.*

He opened the barn door, and a couple chickens squawked and scampered to the corner of the barn. "Those two are escape artists. They keep finding a way out of the chicken coop."

Thomas pulled her close to him, and his mouth was on hers before she had time to catch a breath. She savored the familiarity and the passion even though her emotions swirled and skidded in different directions. His hands began to travel to forbidden areas, and she forced him away. She loved him and longed for his touch, but Thomas had always pushed the boundaries. Naomi had wondered if her resistance to his physical advances was one of the reasons he'd left her. She'd never shared her suspicions with anyone, but she believed some things were reserved for marriage.

"I'm sorry," he said softly before he took her hand and pressed a kiss into it. "I've just missed you so much. I've been such a cad."

Naomi recalled Lizzie's use of the word, but shook her head. "*Nee,* don't say that. You're here now, and that's all the matters."

She knew others—especially Lizzie and Esther—would chide her for taking Thomas back without hesitation. Naomi knew she could play hard to get and make him fight for a place back in her life, but that wasn't who she was. Those tactics would only be playing games. She was glad Thomas had shown up before Amos kissed her. With him here now, she could see things clearer. Loneliness had fueled her attraction to Amos and made her receptive to his flirtatious gestures and advances.

"Is there still a future for us?" Thomas kissed her palm again, then lowered his arm and squeezed her hand. "Things looked cozy between you and Amos." He lowered his head and sighed, and when he looked back up at her, tears were in his eyes. "I don't deserve you, Naomi, but if you'll let me, I'll spend the rest of *mei* life making things up to you."

"I knew you'd come back." It wasn't true, but she threw her arms around his neck, and within seconds they were making out like teenagers in the barn. This time, Thomas kept his hands respectfully where they belonged.

"I love you, Naomi," he whispered in between kisses.

Naomi's heart filled like an empty vessel being replenished with everything she'd prayed for. "I love you too."

❧

Esther stared out the window, Lizzie by her side.

"Well, he's back," Esther said. "When I saw them walk into the barn, I assumed a reconciliation would follow."

Lizzie shook her head. "He's going to hurt her again."

"Maybe." Esther turned to her sister. "But it is not our place to interfere."

Lizzie chuckled. "We always interfere."

Esther sighed as she looked down and smoothed the

wrinkles in her apron. "We sometimes give a gentle push when we see the potential for love. It's not really interfering."

"She's going to give up that handsome Amos. Seems a shame." Lizzie pressed her lips together. She'd already taken out her teeth for the night, and they were both in their bed-clothes. Esther was proud that Lizzie continued to make an attempt with the dentures, especially after the cat ordeal.

"Amos hasn't been here long, so there hasn't been enough time for him and Naomi to get to know each other." A pain squeezed Esther's heart. She also thought that since Thomas left once, he might do it again. And Amos seemed like a good catch. He was hardworking, polite, and a looker for sure. Esther had seen the spark between them, the looks exchanged, and their eagerness to paint together. But whatever had been taking hold of them wouldn't have an opportunity to bloom now.

"Exactly. She needs more time with Amos." Lizzie looked over her shoulder at the basement door.

"Don't even think about it. You will not lock that poor girl in the basement with another man. She has the right to make her own decisions. Love is not something you can force." Even though she and Lizzie had tried and failed with many others besides Naomi, they'd also helped many couples find their way to each other. Sometimes folks just needed a nudge. But this was different.

Lizzie stuffed her hands in the pockets of her robe.

Esther could see her sister's wheels spinning.

∞

Naomi was relieved when Esther told her Amos had grabbed some bacon before he left this morning. He told them he wanted to get an early start on replacing the rotten slats on the barn.

She'd almost kissed Amos last night, and she dreaded having to face him today. But he'd surely come in for dinner, and she couldn't avoid him forever. For now, she would be alone with Lizzie and Esther. She wondered if they'd seen Thomas the night before.

After the three of them bowed in prayer, Lizzie picked up her fork and pointed it at Naomi. "You're making a mistake letting Amos slip away to go back to Thomas, if that's what you're doing." Then she whispered under her breath. "Because Thomas is a cad."

Esther huffed. "Lizzie, what did we talk about? This is not our concern."

"Well, he is." Lizzie was back to shifting her teeth around in her mouth, but she glowered at Naomi. "You deserve better."

Naomi put her fork on her plate and slouched into her chair. Placing a hand over her forehead, she said, "I've been miserable since Thomas left, and now he's back. Can't you be happy for me?" She was tempted to tell Lizzie—who was far worse than Esther—to stop meddling in her life, but she loved the woman too much to be that disrespectful.

Lizzie lifted her shoulders then dropped them slowly. "Did he at least offer an explanation for why he left in the first place? Or what brought him back?" She peered at Naomi in such a way that it caused her chest to tighten. Naomi remained silent.

"At the wedding we all heard he was seeing someone new. Is he only back now because that woman broke up with him? Are you his second choice? Naomi, did you have any conversation with Thomas, or did you just open your arms and let him waltz back into your life?"

Esther tapped her palm to the table. "Lizzie, stop!"

Naomi opened her mouth to respond, but her bottom lip was trembling so badly, she pushed back her chair and left the kitchen. As she ran upstairs, she heard Esther and Lizzie arguing. She closed her bedroom door and sat on the bed holding her head in her hands. She'd been so caught up in the moment that she'd barely considered any of the things Lizzie mentioned, especially about the other woman. Maybe she didn't want to hear the answers. But could she really get back together with Thomas without having that uncomfortable conversation?

As much as she wanted to put everything behind her and resume where they'd left off, she knew she couldn't. Even after the unpleasant talk, would Naomi always worry that Thomas would leave again? Was he settling for his second choice?

❧

Amos tried to stay focused as he held a level up against a board he'd replaced on the barn wall, but he couldn't stop thinking about Naomi. It was probably good Thomas had shown up, for Amos's sake. He'd let his guard down, and Naomi had punctured his resolve a little. But he'd get over it, even though he worried about her. She took the guy back so quickly, without the slightest hesitation. Would he leave her again? Amos didn't think her heart could take it.

He held a nail between his lips as he hammered another one into the wood. After taking his last swing and getting the nail flush with the board, he heard the door of the barn open. He hesitated before he turned around. Naomi might feel like she had to explain herself, but that was a conversation he didn't want to have. When he turned around, however, he saw Lizzie.

Amos took the nail from his mouth. "*Wie bischt.*"

Lizzie walked to the workbench and sat on the stool in front of it. "Do you have any feelings for Naomi?" She had her teeth in, but she wasn't smiling, and the lines running across her forehead deepened as she frowned. "I mean, more than just being friends?"

Amos pushed back the rim of his hat, searching for a response since Lizzie had caught him off guard. "I-I don't know Naomi very well."

She waved an arm in his direction, as if she were swatting at a fly. "*Ach*, I know that. And I know you will always miss your fiancée. But I thought I saw a spark between the two of you, and I want you to tell me if I was wrong."

Naomi had warned him about Lizzie and Esther and how they loved to play matchmaker, so he wasn't sure how much to say. The older woman's sad eyes and forlorn expression tugged at his heart.

"I guess I thought maybe there was a spark." He cringed, fearing his honesty might not be the way to go. "But her fiancé showed up last night while we were painting." He swallowed hard. "And it was pretty clear she wants to be with him."

"He's a cad, that Thomas." Lizzie pinched her lips together as she squinted her eyes. "He'll leave her again, no doubt about it."

Amos's pulse sped up, which was confusing. He'd already talked himself out of caring for this woman he barely knew. But when he thought about Thomas leaving again, he couldn't stand it.

"Why do you think he'll leave her again?" Amos had already had the thought, but he was curious to hear Lizzie's opinion.

"If you love someone the way I loved Reuben—that was *mei* husband—you don't leave that person." Lizzie blinked back tears. "Naomi is very upset with me right now. I told her how I felt, that Thomas isn't a *gut* man to do what he did to her, and that he'd do it again." She reached into her apron pocket and took out a tissue. After she dabbed at her eyes, she said, "Naomi ran to her bedroom and doesn't want to talk to me or Esther."

Amos took off his hat and ran a hand through his hair, sighing. "I'm sure Naomi wants everyone to share her happiness that Thomas is back."

Lizzie shook her head, frowning again. "I can't do that."

"What if you're wrong? What if they get married and live long, happy lives together like you and Reuben?" Amos didn't get a good feeling about Thomas, the way he'd reclaimed Naomi as if he hadn't ripped her heart to shreds. But

Amos had blamed the thought on his being a little jealous of Thomas.

"I hope I *am* wrong." Lizzie sniffled before she blew her nose. "Me and Esther love Naomi. We don't want to see her hurt again. But I went too far at breakfast this morning." A tear rolled down her cheek as she batted her eyes at Amos. "Could you talk to her?"

Amos's chest tightened. He wanted to do whatever he could for Lizzie so she wouldn't be so sad, but he wasn't the right person to talk to Naomi about this. "Uh . . . maybe one of her close friends should be the one to talk to her. What about Mary, the woman in the *daadi haus*?"

Lizzie shook her head. "*Nee*, Naomi and Mary aren't close. At least not close enough that Mary would feel comfortable talking to her."

"I'm sure she's a lot closer to Naomi than I am. What about other girlfriends?" Amos couldn't possibly have a conversation with Naomi about Thomas. It wasn't his business. He wanted to tell Lizzie that he just worked here and wasn't onboard to help with family problems.

"Naomi distanced herself from her friends after Thomas left. Most of them were already married, and I guess Naomi didn't feel like she fit in. Her closest friends had been involved in planning the wedding, and they all tried to be there for her after Thomas left, but Naomi closed herself off more and more." She paused, sniffling.

"Amos, I've seen Naomi smile more since you've been here than she has since Thomas left. I know you don't know each other very well, and maybe there was a spark or maybe not, but since you're not as emotionally involved as Esther and me, it would mean the world to us if you would talk to her."

He couldn't admit to Lizzie what he refused to admit to himself—that he was more emotionally involved than he cared to be. When another tear slipped down the older woman's cheek, Amos didn't think he could deny her request.

"Please," she said before dabbing at her eyes with the tissue.

Sighing, Amos said, "*Ya*, okay."

FIFTEEN

ESTHER PEERED OUT THE WINDOW, THEN HELD BOTH hands to her chest when Lizzie walked out of the barn grinning like she'd won a prize. Her sister gave her a thumbs-up as she paraded her way to the house. Amos must have agreed to talk to Naomi. Esther scurried to the door and tugged it open, pushing the screen wide so Lizzie could come in.

"He's going to talk to her." Lizzie bounced up on her toes after she'd crossed the threshold and Esther had closed the door. Esther wished she was as nimble as her much smaller and energetic sister. Maybe she would be when she found out what was wrong with her and got it taken care of. She forced away thoughts about her health since it always wrapped her in a blanket of fear.

Esther stepped closer to her sister and tipped her head to one side. "Have you been crying?" She raised her chin. "What exactly did you say to that boy?" Lifting an eyebrow, she said, "I hope you didn't lie."

"*Ya*, I have been crying. I'm upset about the way I talked to Naomi." She squeezed her eyes closed and flinched before she looked back at Esther. "Maybe I poured it on a little thick, but I didn't lie. Naomi doesn't want to talk to either of us."

"We haven't gone upstairs and tried yet." Esther had agreed to Lizzie's plan of asking if Amos would talk to Naomi. It seemed a good way to kill two birds with one stone. Hopefully he could smooth things over where Lizzie was concerned, since she had gone too far this morning. And it couldn't hurt for the two for them to spend a little alone time together and talk.

Lizzie waved a dismissive hand at Esther. "It doesn't matter. The boy said he will talk to her." She put a finger to her lips when they heard the barn door shut. Esther made a mental note to ask Amos if he could adjust the old door so it didn't slam so hard.

She felt a little sorry for Amos when he walked into the living room. He was fidgeting with his hands, and his expression reminded her of someone about to walk the plank on a ship.

"Is now a *gut* time?" Amos took off his hat and clutched the rim.

Lizzie pulled out a tissue and dabbed at her eyes, and Esther fought the urge to roll her eyes since Lizzie hadn't shed a tear since she'd walked in the house.

"*Ya*, I think the sooner the better." Lizzie lowered her head, sniffling.

Esther believed Lizzie was regretful about being so hard

on Naomi and knew the tears she'd shed earlier were probably real. But she also believed her sister had been correct about pouring it on a little thick. Either way, Amos walked to the stairs.

"In our day it wouldn't be proper for a man to go into a young woman's bedroom," Esther said when Amos was out of earshot. "But I trust Naomi. And strangely, I trust Amos too." Esther had never trusted Thomas. Something about him had always bothered her, even though she hadn't been able to put her finger on it.

She said a silent prayer that, at the very least, Amos would be able to lift Naomi's spirits and that she would be forgiving when it came to Lizzie. She couldn't help also asking the Lord to maybe give them a little push toward something more than friendship, if it was His will.

◈

Naomi was still crying when there was a knock at her bedroom door. "Can we please talk later?"

"Uh, it's me."

She sat up and swiped at her eyes. "Now isn't a *gut* time, Amos." She tried unsuccessfully to control the shakiness in her voice.

"Are you decent? I'm coming in."

A conversation with Amos was the last thing she wanted or needed, but before she could object, he opened the door and left it ajar as he entered her bedroom.

"I'm fine. I really am," she said through her tears as she reached for a tissue on her bedside table. "Lizzie and I had words, and . . ." She paused, sniffling. "Did she send you up here?"

Amos took off his hat, held it in front of him, and nervously turned it in circles. Naomi was sure this wasn't his idea.

"It doesn't matter if she did or not. Can I stay for a few minutes?" He sat in the rocking chair, still clutching his hat with both hands, before she could respond. "Lizzie and Esther love you. They're just worried about you."

This was proof enough that Lizzie had told Amos what happened, and she'd likely prodded him to do her bidding. "I love them, too, but they aren't happy that Thomas returned. They're convinced he will leave again." She avoided the intensity of his gaze, feeling like she'd shared too much already.

"What do you think?" His voice was so tender that Naomi wanted to run into his arms, mostly because she needed a friend and a hug.

She couldn't look at him. Lizzie's remarks had hit her hard and caused her to think about things she hadn't wanted to face. Finally, she looked at Amos.

"I think he got cold feet about getting married. I think he spent time with another woman and then realized he wants to spend the rest of his life with me. I owe us a second chance at love." She paused, dabbing at another tear that escaped down her cheek. "I just want someone to be happy for me."

Amos took a deep breath. If she didn't stop crying, he was going to have to go sit by her on the bed and hug her. She was breaking his heart in a whole new way. "I'm happy for you." It wasn't exactly a lie, but it wasn't completely truthful either.

She locked eyes with him and held his gaze for a long time. "Amos, you almost kissed me."

He nodded. "*Ya*, I did. I think you are a beautiful woman, and despite *mei* desire not to get involved with anyone, I like you. I surprised myself." Now he was telling the truth. "But things have changed, and I know that." He scratched his head. "I tried to put myself in your shoes and picture how I would feel if Sarah showed up the way Thomas did. I know that's not possible, but after thinking about it, I know I would have run to her without hesitation."

"But she didn't leave you voluntarily." Naomi's bottom lip trembled as she spoke.

As memories of Sarah flooded his mind, he reminded himself that he was here for Naomi. "*Nee*, she didn't. But I do believe in second chances." It was true, although he had doubts about Thomas staying. He couldn't tell her that and rub more salt in her wound.

"What if I'm his second choice?" She kept her eyes fused with his.

She was facing the hard questions without Amos having to pose them, and for that he was thankful. "Or your first scenario could be correct, that he got cold feet and has returned to the woman he wants to spend the rest of his life with." Amos had no plans to interfere with a reconciliation between Naomi and Thomas. He'd already made a mistake by almost kissing her and opening his heart to possibilities he hadn't considered before he met her.

"I want to believe I'm his first choice. But how do I know he won't leave me again?" Her eyes beckoned for an answer that would soothe her soul, but love can be complicated. Lying to her wouldn't help.

"You don't know. That's where trust comes in."

"I trusted him before," she responded right away, a hint of anger rising to the surface. "But I don't want to play games or pretend I don't love him. I don't want to make him jealous either."

"I think you already did last night." Amos grinned briefly as he recalled Thomas's attitude. "But your true feelings will show, and he'll get comfortable with the fact that I'm staying here for a while." Amos wondered if he'd get comfortable seeing her with Thomas, or even being around her and knowing she was off limits now. Later he'd calculate how much longer he'd have to stay to complete the list of jobs he'd committed to.

Naomi stared at him long and hard. "Are *you* comfortable staying here?"

Had she seen into his thoughts, felt the pang of regret in his heart? "*Ya*, absolutely," he lied. She didn't need anything else to worry about, and he didn't want things to be awkward between them. As much as he'd dreaded coming upstairs to have this conversation, maybe this was the best thing that could have happened.

"Lizzie is pretty upset and sorry for the way she talked to you," he said when her mind seemed to trail away. "I think you need to talk to her, maybe let her off the hook."

Naomi smiled a little, even though she was still sniffling and blotting her eyes with a tissue. "*Ya*, I know. Lizzie's heart is always in the right place, but sometimes she's too outspoken. And Thomas just arrived. I'm still trying to wrap *mei* mind around that."

They were quiet for a few seconds, and Amos knew her thoughts must be all over the place. "I'm still going to paint in the evenings. I'm determined to get that sunset right." Painting had always been calming to him. He hadn't realized how much he'd missed it until now. "You're welcome to join me tonight if it isn't raining. I heard Lizzie say the forecast had changed, less chance of rain for the next few days."

She cleared her throat and lowered her eyes. "Actually, I'm having supper with Thomas tonight. I'll prepare the meal for you, Lizzie, and Esther, but then Thomas is taking me to eat pizza." She began to blush with her eyes still cast down.

Amos winced as he struggled to hide his disappointment. "That's great." He stood up and put on his hat. Naomi lifted herself from the bed, and walked toward him, close enough that he caught a whiff of lavender, maybe her lotion.

"*Danki* for coming to talk to me. I'll say something to Lizzie and assure her I'm okay." Pausing, the hint of a smile crept onto her face. "And *danki* for not making things awkward between us."

"You're welcome. Enjoy your supper." He quickly turned

and left before his expression revealed the awkwardness he did feel.

∾∾

By the time the supper hour was upon them, Esther was glad she didn't have to take Gus any pie. He'd have to make do with the smooshed one. She'd spit up blood twice during the day and wasn't very hungry, but she struggled to eat some beans and rice so Lizzie wouldn't question her. Her sister had once told her she didn't think she could live if anything happened to Esther. It was a dramatic thing to say, even for Lizzie, but Esther knew it would be a huge blow to Lizzie if something was seriously wrong with her. Lizzie was as brave as a lion when it came to her own health, but she turned to mush when others were ill.

Esther could still recall the turmoil Lizzie went through during her husband's cancer and the months leading up to his death. Esther had grieved when she lost her beloved Joe, but they'd created a beautiful life filled with memories Esther clung to during those hard times. Lizzie's grief after Reuben died left her a different person for a while. She'd been the same when their father passed and years later when their mother died. Even though their people believed it was God's will when He took a person home, the loss was always extra hard on Lizzie. Each time, she eventually bounced back to her old self, but it was a long and slow process.

"Naomi allowed me to apologize about the way I talked to her." Lizzie mashed her beans and rice with the prongs of her fork, having opted not to wear her dentures. "And I bit *mei* tongue and didn't call Thomas a cad."

"We just want her to be happy," Esther said to Amos, who hadn't had much to say all evening, only nodding when Lizzie thanked him. He wasn't downstairs when Thomas came to the door to get Naomi. Sadness seemed to fill his expression. Or perhaps he was just tired after putting in a long day of work on the barn. Esther had firmly instructed Lizzie not to say or do anything to make Amos feel uncomfortable. They'd both politely thanked him for smoothing things over between Naomi and Lizzie, but Esther was as curious as Lizzie about what was said during that conversation.

Following the quiet supper, Amos excused himself and said he was going to go paint for a while.

Lizzie waited until he was outside, carrying only one easel while pulling the wagon.

"Did you see how sad he was during supper?" She spoke with an unwarranted sense of excitement. "He's lovesick!"

Esther shook her head, which was starting to throb. "We don't know that. He worked hard today and might just be exhausted."

"*Nee.*" Lizzie sat taller and raised her chin. "I know I'm right about this. If Thomas had returned two or three weeks later, I think he'd have found something more than friendship between Naomi and Amos."

"Maybe, but we'll never know." She paused, smiling. "And you must admit it was nice to see Naomi glowing again."

"*Ya, ya.*" Lizzie sighed. "But if Thomas hurts her again,

I'm going to hang him on the clothesline and beat him with a broom like a dirty rug."

Esther laughed and laid her fork across her plate.

"Are you losing weight? You haven't been eating much lately." Lizzie squinted at Esther. "I know you've had some stomach troubles."

"I don't think so." Esther suspected she'd lost a little weight, although she wasn't sure if it was due to her medical condition or her worry about what was wrong. She needed to change the subject so Lizzie wouldn't push her about it. "I hope Naomi is having a *gut* time this evening, and that's what you should hope too."

Lizzie leaned her head back and closed her eyes. "I know, I know."

❧

Naomi couldn't believe Thomas was sitting across the table from her. She'd dreamed of the scenario ever since he left. He had mentioned several times how sorry he was for leaving and how happy he was to be back.

Still, something was amiss. Naomi wanted her heart to stay full, but as questions somersaulted around in her mind, a slow leak seemed to have sprung in her heart. She had decided that for them to be able to move forward, they had to take a look backward, no matter how painful.

"You've been quiet." Thomas wiped his mouth with his napkin and captured her eyes with his own. He had beautiful blue eyes set against an olive complexion. When he smiled, he lit up a room.

"I-I just need to know why you came back." She pressed her lips together, afraid he might not be honest with her. "I know there was another woman."

Thomas hung his head, sighed, then looked back at her. "I knew I'd made a mistake when I left and that you were the only woman I'd ever love. But I didn't know how to come back. The longer I was gone, the harder it was to return and face everyone, especially you." He paused, his eyes glistening with moisture. "And I still have to have a hard conversation with the bishop and elders since I'd been baptized before I left. I will assure him that I will never leave *mei* faith again. And I won't leave this town or you ever again." He took a deep breath and stared into her eyes. "I promise you, Naomi, I will *never* leave you again. Never."

She wanted to believe him, but she couldn't help noticing he had swerved around her question. "What happened with the other woman?" She held her breath. It was a direct question, and he had to answer it.

"Does it matter? I'm back. I'm in love with you. And I'm promising you a lifetime of happiness."

She looked down at the slice of pizza on her plate that she hadn't touched. Slowly, she lifted her eyes to his. "*Ya*, it matters."

"I missed you so much, and I was terrified about coming back. I guess I fell into the first woman's arms who showed me a little attention." He shook his head. "I knew it was a mistake the first time I kissed her. Your face was all I saw."

Naomi could have done without that detail as she flinched,

picturing Thomas kissing someone else. But parallel in her thoughts was how close she had come to kissing Amos. Would she have seen Thomas in her mind while kissing Amos?

"Can we please just be happy together now that I'm back and put the past behind us?" Thomas's eyes pleaded with her.

She nodded. Thomas started talking about how he was going to resume working for his father at their lumberyard, and Naomi's mind began to drift. She wondered if Amos was painting.

∞

Amos stepped back and eyed his canvas, then cast his eyes toward the horizon. There couldn't have been a more beautiful sunset, and capturing the glory of it seemed impossible. He was determined to do better this time, and he was glad Naomi had a lot of blank canvases in the basement so he could start over. His initial plan was to fix the one he'd started with Naomi, but that had changed. Like any hope of pursuing more than friendship with her.

As his eyes darted back and forth between the beautiful landscape in front of him and his new painting, he still felt like something was missing. The painting was brighter, didn't have the grayish tint, and he'd replicated the reflection off the pond almost exactly as he saw it. Still, something was wrong.

Maybe it was the loss of his painting partner.

∞

As Thomas pulled into the driveway, Naomi ignored her desire to look and see if Amos was painting. Thomas might catch her, and she didn't want to upset him. He already appeared uncomfortable that Amos was staying in the house.

"I had a *gut* time," she said once they were on the porch.

He cupped her cheeks in his hands and gently pulled her toward him, kissing her with all the passion she remembered.

"I love you so much," he said before his mouth covered hers again.

After a few minutes she pulled back and thanked him for supper. "I love you too."

"I might not see you tomorrow." His shoulders slumped. "*Mei daed* wants to stay late with me at the lumberyard to show me the new inventory system he's using. I don't think it's necessary since it's similar to the one I was using while I was gone and working for my cousin." He kissed her tenderly on the cheek. "I'd much rather be with you."

"It's fine," she said, smiling. "We have a lifetime to spend together."

"*Ya*, things are going to be *gut*, Naomi." He grinned. "Tomorrow is Halloween. Don't let any of the *Englisch* ghosts and goblins get you."

Naomi laughed. "I don't think we'll have any goblins at the *haus*. Most everyone around here knows we don't celebrate Halloween."

"Well, be safe until I see you again." He kissed her one last time, then left.

Naomi waved until he turned onto the road that led to the

highway. Then she walked across the front yard, far enough to see if Amos was down by the pond. *He's there.* She ran back to the house. Lizzie and Esther were settled in for the night in their bedrooms, but there was probably an hour of daylight left.

She tiptoed across the living room and went upstairs to get the painting she'd been working on, then hurried to the basement to grab the other easel. With a bounce in her step, she carried both across the yard and started toward the pond.

Halfway there, she stopped. *What am I doing?*

Even though she and Amos had agreed to be friends, she couldn't deny the mutual attraction. Why put herself in a tempting situation? More concerning was that she even considered it a tempting situation.

Shoulders slumped, she slowly turned around and went back to the house. She'd lost the bounce in her step.

SIXTEEN

ESTHER WAVED TO NAOMI AND LIZZIE AS NAOMI MANEU-vered the buggy out of the driveway. She was glad Naomi had the reins. Lizzie had a tendency to go too fast. They would be gone for hours to Sister's Day, so when Gus carted her to her first medical test, she wouldn't have to explain why she didn't hire a driver. Amos had been quiet at breakfast and lunch, much like he'd been the past few days. With the exception of one night, Naomi had left with Thomas when he got off work each evening.

Amos had taken Esther's buggy to pick up more supplies he needed to work on the barn. The timing couldn't have been better as she made her way to Gus's cottage. If all went well, she'd be back home before anyone knew she was gone. Except maybe Amos, and she'd deal with him later if he saw her re-turning in Gus's truck.

They'd had guests in two of the bedrooms over the weekend—a young *Englisch* couple who gobbled down their breakfast both mornings, then didn't return until after dark each night. A woman had stayed only Saturday night, and she'd been very inquisitive. She was *Englisch* and in town doing research for a book about farming in different states.

Even though Naomi did most of the work, cleaning and preparing meals, Esther was exhausted today. She'd be glad to get this test behind her and get home to take a nap.

Gus was sitting in the rocking chair on the front porch. Esther put her hands on her hips and laughed. "I never would have pictured you as a cat person."

He shook his head, eased the black kitten off his lap, and set it on the porch. "I've taken this thing back to the barn a dozen times, but every morning when I get up, it's on my porch." Shaking his head and groaning, he stood up. "There ain't a white hair anywhere on that cat. Solid black. I've got enough bad luck to last the rest of my life." His eyes widened. "It whined and cried all night on Halloween. I wasn't going to get any sleep, so I had to let it in. And do you know what?"

Esther waited, grinning.

"It isn't funny. When I woke up the next morning, that cat was sleeping at the foot of my bed. I'm sure I'm cursed." He brushed past her when he was down the porch steps. "Let's go get this over with."

After they were in the truck, Esther wrapped an arm across her stomach, hoping she didn't have to ask Gus to pull over so she could vomit. Again, she wondered if some of her physical responses were due to whatever was ailing her, her nerves, or the stench in Gus's truck.

"What stinks in here?" She pinched her nostrils.

Gus scowled. "That ain't a very nice thing to say to the person who's hauling you around."

"It smells like something dead. Maybe a critter got underneath the hood and died."

"I don't smell anything." He glanced at her, frowning.

Esther decided to let it go. It didn't take much to get Gus wound up, and she had enough on her mind. Several minutes lapsed before Gus cleared his throat.

"I've already told you, an MRI doesn't hurt. Quit looking so scared." He shook his head, frowning.

What Esther wouldn't do for some compassion today. Perhaps that was Gus's idea of compassion. She chose not to answer him, fearful her voice would tremble and he'd say something to either infuriate her or make her cry. Esther rarely let her emotions get the best of her, but if the knot in her throat was any indication of how unstable her emotions were right now, tears weren't out of the question. She reminded herself she was a mature woman who should be able to handle this noninvasive procedure.

When they arrived at the hospital, she took in Gus's appearance. He'd cleaned himself up again, but more so than last time. His hair looked like maybe he'd run a brush through it. His beard was growing out, but it wasn't as scruffy as before. He wore black slacks with a blue long-sleeve shirt, and suspenders held his pants up, like always. He wasn't wearing a hat, but in every other way, he looked like an Amish man. Esther wondered if the people at the hospital would think he was her husband, a thought that caused her to shiver.

He opened the door and went in ahead of her but held the door until she was inside. She supposed that was as much gentlemanly behavior as he could muster up.

"Go over there." He pointed to a desk to their right. "They'll make you fill out a bunch of paperwork, like at the doctor's office."

Esther glanced around the large waiting room with lots of occupied chairs, tables filled with magazines, and fish tanks. There were also two desks and a closed window with a bell in front of it.

"How do you know that's the right place to go?" Her knees shook as she stood in the middle of the room.

"This ain't my first rodeo. Trust me. That's where you go."

Gus left her standing there as he walked to an empty seat.

Esther coaxed her feet to move, and when she arrived at the desk and told the woman her name, she handed her a clipboard, instructing her to read it and sign where indicated. Esther gulped back the growing knot in her throat and went to sit by Gus, who was picking up magazines, then tossing them back on a table in front of them rather recklessly.

She took her small reading glasses out of her black purse and started scanning the fine print, with a signature line at the bottom.

"You don't need to read all that. Just sign at the bottom." Gus had apparently found a magazine that was holding his interest. He didn't even look her way when he spoke. Esther started reading it anyway, and her heart about leapt out of her chest.

She elbowed Gus. "This says they aren't responsible if I die." Bringing a hand to her chest, she took a deep breath.

"Good grief. Just sign at the bottom. There's always something like that when you sign stuff for tests." He flipped the page in his magazine, still not looking at her, which was probably a good thing since she could feel her bottom lip trembling.

She took his advice and skipped over the small print, signing at the bottom. Her life was in God's hands anyway.

"If you're done, take it back to that lady at the desk." Gus pointed to the same person Esther had gotten the forms from.

She did as he said and leaned closer to the woman and whispered, "What will I be wearing for this test?"

"You should be fine wearing what you have on, but no metal zippers, buttons, fasteners, or bras with underwire."

Esther thought about the pins holding her dress together beneath her apron. She supposed she would have to remove those, but she'd still be covered.

"Thank you," she said before she went back to her seat.

Folding her hands in her lap, she fought the urge to get up and run out the door. "You're sure this procedure won't hurt?" She fidgeted like a child. Somehow she'd managed to avoid tests like this for seventy-two years.

"No. It won't hurt." His eyes were still on the pages of whatever he was reading. "It's just loud."

A few moments went by.

"How loud?" Esther kept her eyes straight ahead, sure Gus was giving her a disgusted look.

"Real loud." He closed the magazine and sighed. "Look, it'll be over before you know it. It doesn't hurt. It's loud, but they'll give you earplugs or let you listen to music." He paused, waved a dismissive hand. "Forget the music. I know your people don't listen to music."

Esther's breath seized in her lungs when a woman called her name.

"It'll be fine." Gus went back to his magazine.

Esther hoped she didn't faint as she stood and began walking toward the woman. She'd never passed out before. But she was so weak in the knees and trembling from head to toe, she feared this might be the day.

"Ma'am, are you all right?" The middle-aged woman dressed in blue put a hand on Esther's arm.

"I-I . . . am just a bit nervous." Esther tried to smile, but she was pretty sure it was a failed attempt.

"If you'd like to bring your husband with you, you can." The woman nodded past Esther to Gus. "I saw you two sitting together when I called the last person in. He's welcome to come inside. We have open-concept MRI machines, so he can sit right beside you."

Esther shook her head. "Oh, *nee* . . . I mean, no. I mean . . ." She held up her first finger. "I'll be right back." On shaky legs, she shuffled back to where Gus was seated, sure that Joe was rolling over in his grave.

"What's wrong? Why are you back?" Gus groaned as

he looked up from his magazine. "Please tell me you didn't chicken out, that we did all this for nothing?" His gray eyebrows came together above his crinkled nose.

"Will . . . um . . ." She leaned closer and whispered. "Will you come with me?"

His jaw dropped. "Are you kidding me, woman?" He held up his hand. "Sorry about the 'woman' thing."

"Never mind. I don't know why I even asked." She turned around and briskly walked back to the woman as her eyes filled with tears.

"Aw, don't worry. Everything is going to be fine." The lady in blue held the door open and when Esther stepped past her, she heard heavy footsteps behind her. She looked over her shoulder at Gus, who shrugged.

"I ain't ever seen anyone so scared of an MRI."

Esther had mixed emotions about Gus being with her, but the need for someone familiar outweighed whatever obnoxious words might come out of Gus's mouth. Apparently she'd been right. Even without a straw hat, Gus resembled an Amish man, and the woman had just assumed he was Esther's husband.

It wasn't ten minutes later when Esther found herself flat on her back on a hard surface. Gus was sitting on the other side of a window with the woman in blue. Esther had removed the pins from her dress but was able to keep her apron on. The room was sterile and cold and . . . awful. They'd given her a panic button to hold and said if she was uncomfortable at any time to push the button and they would stop the machine. The woman also told her if that happened, they would have to start the procedure over. Just the thought of having a panic button was enough to induce panic.

As the platform slowly moved her into the machine, a large round wheel began to spin around her. She was crying and trembling and not sure if the test had officially even started. Her chest tightened as she squeezed her eyes shut. When she opened them, the lady in blue was standing beside her and the machine was slowing down.

"Sweetie, we can't do this unless you are perfectly still."

"I-I'm so very sorry. So sorry." Esther winced with embarrassment as she asked God to help her be still and get through this with some sort of dignity. *I wish Lizzie were here.*

"It will be over before you know it." The woman left the room and the door clicked closed. The spinning circle started up again, growing louder and louder. Even with ear plugs, the noise was uncomfortable. She squeezed her eyes shut, held tightly to the panic button, and prayed she could stop crying long enough for whatever they needed to do. She jumped when someone took hold of her free hand, and her eyes widened in shock.

"You're gonna be all right, Esther." Gus yelled as he squeezed her hand. "They said I can sit here with you through the whole thing. So try to relax, okay?"

Tears poured down both cheeks but she nodded, then closed her eyes, squeezed Gus's hand, and stayed as still as she could.

When it was over, she opened her eyes, let go of Gus's

hand, and waited for him to make fun of her or say something horrible that the staff would hear. But as they walked out of the room together, he patted her on the back.

"You did good." Then he chuckled, his jowls jiggling. "*Woman.*"

Esther was so relieved to have the test over and done with, she laughed. She'd always believed there was good in everyone. Sometimes it was just buried a little deeper in certain people.

∞

Naomi kissed Thomas goodbye after they'd had supper, which had become the norm. Lizzie even insisted on doing some of the cooking so Naomi could spend more time with him. It was a very unselfish gesture, considering her feelings about Thomas.

They'd settled into a routine and were starting to talk about wedding plans, even though it was too late in the season to get married any time soon. Weddings were always held in October or November after the harvest, so it would be almost a year before they could marry. Naomi wished it could be sooner. In the back of her mind, she constantly wondered if Thomas would disappear again before they began their lives as husband and wife. It was a worry she struggled with and pushed aside when it bubbled to the surface.

When he was out of sight, she walked across the yard until she could see Amos down by the pond. He was out there painting every night when she got home, and as much as Naomi longed to feel a brush in her hand, she wondered if it would be a betrayal to Thomas to spend time alone with Amos. She and Amos were pleasant enough to each other during meals and devotions, but it was awkward, whether they wanted to admit it or not. Today she was going to break the pattern. She was curious about his painting. And she wanted to prove to herself that she could get past any temptation she'd felt where Amos was concerned. Thomas was back, but talking to a friend wasn't betrayal.

"*Wie bischt,*" she said as she came up behind him, pulling her cape tightly around her. They'd had their first frost, and the nights were almost cold enough for a heavy coat.

He finished a long, careful stroke before easing the brush away from the canvas and turning to her. "How was your date?"

Naomi hesitated, trying to decide if there was any mockery in the question. "*Gut.*" She pointed to his painting. "You started over."

He looked at her for a few seconds. "*Ya,* I did." Still holding his paint palette, he laid down his brush and refocused on the canvas. "Something's missing. I've been working on this same canvas for days, but I can't get it the way I want." He turned to her. "What do you think?"

Naomi moved closer to him and the painting before she backed up a few steps and eyed the artwork. "Amos, this is beautiful." And she meant it. "I-I can't get over how pretty it is."

A flush crept across his cheeks. "*Danki.*" Setting down the palette, he backed up until he was standing right next to her.

"Only *Gott* can see this landscape for the true beauty I'm trying to capture, but something is missing."

As beautiful as the painting was, Naomi had to agree. Whatever was missing was so subtle that if Amos hadn't mentioned it, she wouldn't have noticed.

"You're frowning," he said. "Be honest. There is something missing, *ya?*" His arm brushed against hers as he raised his arm and scratched his forehead.

Naomi had figured it out, but she didn't have the heart to tell him. One color would add the missing element. There wasn't a hint of red in the painting, and despite all the orange hues, lush green cornstalks in the background, and a reflection off the pond that was as close to perfection as she'd ever seen—red was a major color used to enhance the overall brilliance in a painting. She'd read that in the book Esther had given her. Red was also the color of love.

Naomi had found her love again. Amos hadn't. He also hadn't read any of the book because it was in Naomi's bedroom.

"I think it's perfect," she finally said.

"*Nee.*" He shook his head before he turned to her. "I'll replace the two canvases I've used before I leave."

"Leave?" Her heart did an unexpected flip. "When?"

"I'll stay another week to finish Esther's list, then I'm going home." His eyes locked with hers.

"Um . . . of course." She tried to smile. "You can't stay forever. I know you have a business to get back to."

"Not much going on this time of year, but it's time for me to go when I'm done."

He wasn't smiling, and his expression wasn't revealing much. Did he have any regret that he would be leaving soon? She supposed nothing was keeping him here.

"There's no reason for me to stay," he said, then he began packing up the painting supplies.

Naomi was confused why this bothered her so much. "Would you have stayed if Thomas hadn't come back?" It was a bold thing to ask, but the words slipped out before she had time to consider the consequences. What if he said yes?

He folded the easel, picked up the wagon handle, and with no emotion on his face, said, "I guess we'll never know."

She was trying to form a sentence that would make sense, but he began the trek to the house. The more she thought about him leaving in a week, the more it stung. *Why?* She loved Thomas.

But as the sun made its final descent, she surmised that she and Amos had become friends, and anytime you had to say goodbye to a friend, it was difficult. She wondered if they would stay in touch by writing letters to each other. Would that be a betrayal to Thomas? She didn't think Thomas would like that, and once they were married, he would be the head of the household.

Naomi was raised in a household where her mother had a say in everything, but ultimately her father had the final word. Her mother said that was the way things went in Amish families. It wasn't the kind of thing she'd ever questioned.

Why did she feel unsettled about Thomas being the head

of their household and having final decision-making power over her? Was this her version of cold feet?

She watched Amos walk into the house.

Or is it something else?

SEVENTEEN

Amos fluffed his pillow, settled into the covers, and stared at the ceiling. There was no doubt Naomi had a negative reaction when he told her he was leaving. Now he couldn't stop thinking about her question. Would he be leaving so soon if Thomas hadn't come back?

He'd answered truthfully by saying they'd never know. Amos had a family and a business in Ohio. But would he have stayed long enough to see if the feelings he had for Naomi escalated into more than friendship? As it was now, all he could think about was the kiss they'd almost had, and what it would have been like. Although it would have been worse if he'd kissed her, making it harder to part ways.

As he tried to turn off his mind about Naomi, guilt moved in. He hadn't thought about Sarah all day, maybe not even the day before, or the day before that. Amos had assumed he would think about her every day for the rest of his life. He would love her forever, but since he'd arrived in Indiana, she hadn't consumed his thoughts as she had over the past year. Was it because of Naomi? Had there been more brewing between them than he'd realized?

He rolled over on his side, deciding it didn't matter. Thomas was home.

⚭

Esther knocked on Gus's door around ten, after she was sure everyone was asleep.

"I still have chocolate pie," he said after he opened the door.

"*Ach, ya,* but I figured it was almost gone, and it did land upside down on your porch." She pushed a covered plate toward him. "I brought you a slice of apple, one of pecan, and two fresh slices of chocolate."

Gus actually smiled, but it was fleeting, and his signature scowl returned. "I'm already taking you to your medical tests. You aren't going to ask me for another favor, are you?"

Esther stared at the ground for a couple seconds before she looked back at him. "*Nee,* Gus. I was just returning a kindness, and a deal's a deal."

"What kindness?" He crinkled his nose. "You widows hate me."

"Gus . . ." Esther tried to choose her words carefully. He obviously didn't recognize the kindness he'd shown her during the MRI earlier that day. "We don't *hate* you."

"That wacky sister of yours does." He lifted the plastic wrap on one side of the plate, pulled out the slice of pecan pie, and took a big bite.

"Lizzie doesn't hate you either." Esther didn't think Lizzie was capable of hating anyone, even though her feelings about Gus could definitely be described as a strong dislike.

"Thanks for the pie." He closed the door in Esther's face, but instead of being mad, she smiled. Gus could keep on pretending he was a horrible man, and maybe he had been, based on the comments she'd overheard from his daughter and her own prior experiences with him. But Esther had once again been given a glimpse of the man Gus could be.

All the way back to the house, she prayed that the Lord would open Gus's heart so he could recognize the good in himself, then apply that goodness in his life. Then she recalled a comment Gus had made about God. Maybe Gus wasn't a believer, but God believed in him. Over time, Esther hoped Gus would come to realize the current of love that flowed both ways.

❧

Naomi stayed out of sight as Esther came up the porch steps, but she'd watched from the window when Esther came back from Gus's house. She'd carried a lantern that lit the space around her just enough to see her expression when she got near the main house. In Naomi's experience, there wasn't much to smile about when it came to Gus. Esther had always been more tolerant of him than Lizzie was, but Naomi had heard her complaining about the man plenty of times.

She reached for her brush in the drawer of her nightstand and began running it through her brown hair, which reached well past her waist. Thomas had never seen her hair down. She'd always worn her prayer covering, even though lots of women she knew admitted that their husbands saw their hair down before they were married. Naomi wanted to keep with tradition. She pictured their wedding night—Thomas easing off her prayer covering, removing the pins that held her hair, and running his hands through it as it fell past her shoulders. She'd had the vision a hundred times, but tonight it didn't hold the allure it once had. *Why?*

Amos. She couldn't help but wonder what would have happened if Thomas hadn't returned. Would she and Amos have broken their own rule and fallen in love? He was right when he said they'd never know. She wondered if he regretted not having the opportunity. Naomi questioned why she was even considering it when it would never happen now, but she couldn't corral her thoughts. What would have happened if Amos had kissed her?

As her mind drifted in another direction, she cringed when she thought about Thomas kissing another woman. She wondered if that was all they'd done. Thomas's hands had always tried to drift to places they shouldn't.

She climbed into bed, much later than normal, and somehow anger had latched on to her like a hungry tick, feeding on her until she festered. As she closed her eyes to try to sleep, she prayed for God to remove this delayed resentment from her heart.

She'd told Thomas they needed to look backward before they could move forward, and they'd done that, even if he had avoided some of her questions. Carrying the weight of the past wasn't going to help them build a future together. She tried to push past her bitterness and sleep, but she tossed and turned for a long time.

⁕

Naomi yawned on and off during breakfast.

"Someone must not have slept well." Lizzie smiled wide, which cheered Naomi up. Lizzie was always proud when she had her dentures in correctly, and she smiled at everything.

"*Nee*, I tossed and turned a lot." Without being overt, she couldn't look at Amos sitting next to her. She had a strong urge to have a conversation with him, even though she had no idea what she wanted to say, which sounded silly in her mind.

He pushed back his chair, stood up, and looked at Naomi. "*Danki* for another *gut* meal. *Mei mamm* is a wonderful cook, but I think you've outdone her." He grinned. "But let's don't ever tell her that." He chuckled, as if going home didn't hold any consequences or regrets for him. "I'll miss these great meals when I leave."

"Miss them? Leave?" Lizzie glanced at Esther, then back at Amos. "There's still a lot to do here. I hope you aren't leaving soon."

"In a week," he said, still seemingly unaffected. "I will have completed everything on the list, and by the time I get home, Thanksgiving will only be a couple weeks away." Looking directly at Naomi, he said, "But I've enjoyed *mei* time here very much, and I've gotten reacquainted with painting and plan to keep doing it when I get home."

Naomi hadn't even thought about Thanksgiving. Of course he'd want to spend the holiday with his family.

Lizzie didn't say anything. Neither did Esther. How could they argue with him for wanting to be home at Thanksgiving?

After he left, Lizzie groaned softly. Esther remained quiet.

"You know I'm with Thomas now, and we're planning our wedding for next fall. There is no hope of pushing Amos and me together." She glanced back and forth between Esther and Lizzie, pointing a finger. "So no trickery. No locking us in the basement or any other crazy thing to make him stay. Surely you understand that he wants to be with his family for Thanksgiving."

Esther sighed. "Of course, dear."

Lizzie raised her chin and sat taller. "With a little more time, I think you'd realize that Amos is a much better fit for you than Thomas."

"I'm a grown woman, Lizzie. I'm quite capable of choosing who is the best fit for me, and I'd like to spend the rest of *mei* life with Thomas." Naomi's voice had risen as she spoke, a surprise even to her. Was she trying to convince herself she'd made the right decision? She wasn't even sure there was a decision on the table.

They were quiet, and then they all cleaned the kitchen together. When they were done, Naomi waited until Esther and Lizzie were occupied before she walked out to the barn. She pulled the door open and noticed it didn't stick or squeak anymore.

"You fixed the barn door," she said as she came inside, shivering.

"And you forgot your cape again." Amos slipped out of his jacket and put it around her shoulders, lingering close to her for longer than was necessary before he moved back to the workbench.

Naomi pulled the coat around her and eased her way next to him. "What are you working on?"

He stretched some chicken wire taut, securing it to a frame. "I found where your chickens are getting out, so I'm adding some reinforcement."

"Oh." She folded her hands in front of her. "I'd like to paint with you tonight, if that's okay."

"*Ya*, sure." He glanced at her. "Why wouldn't it be?"

Naomi shrugged. She wished he had been a tad more excited, or even just happy to have company, but he sounded nonchalant, like he didn't care one way or the other.

"What about Thomas? You've been with him every night but one since he came back." He tugged on the wire and then reached for a hammer.

Ah, maybe he cares a little. "He doesn't tell me what to do. He won't mind." Naomi wondered where this attitude was coming from.

"You sure about that?" Grinning, Amos cut his eyes at her briefly. "I'm not sure he was happy about us staying under the same roof."

Naomi waved a hand in the air. "*Ach*, he got over that. He knows there is nothing between us." She'd intentionally not mentioned Amos's name around Thomas, based on his initial reaction to him.

"Then I guess I'll see you at dinner, supper, and then down by the pond."

It sounded like he was dismissing her. "Um . . . okay." She handed him back his coat, then slowly walked to the exit, but he never said anything else as she closed the repaired barn door behind her.

∽∾

Amos waited a few minutes then put down the hammer, sat on the stool, and held his head in his hands. Naomi's presence was starting to unravel him, and now he'd be alone with her tonight. Maybe he should leave before the week was up.

"*Wie bischt*, Amos."

He spun around. "Esther. Everything okay?"

"*Ya, ya.*" She walked his way and stopped directly in front of him, fully dressed in her cape and bonnet. "Lizzie and I will be going to town for a while. I just wanted to let you know."

Esther and Lizzie weren't in the habit of sharing their itineraries with him.

"Do you need anything while we're out?" Esther fumbled with the straps of her small black purse.

"*Nee*, I don't think so, but *danki* for asking."

Esther cleared her throat. "It's not too late, you know." She waited until Amos locked eyes with her.

"Not too late for what?"

Esther sighed. "Lizzie and I are two silly old women. We know that." She paused. "And we meddle sometimes when we shouldn't. But it's always with the best of intentions. And I don't think I can let you leave without telling you that . . . it's not too late." She winked at him. "Now, I'm off to the market."

She was gone before Amos could respond, which was probably a good thing since he had no idea what to say.

∞

Naomi didn't feel like herself, and she'd tried all day to figure out what exactly was bothering her. Was it the delayed anger about Thomas being with another woman, or something—or some*one*—else?

She'd slipped out of the house before the noon meal and left Amos a note that his dinner was keeping warm in the oven. Then she'd gone to the lumberyard at a time when she knew Thomas would be eating out somewhere. She left a note with the woman at the front desk, telling Thomas she couldn't meet for supper this evening. She didn't give an excuse, just said she'd see him the next night.

Now her stomach was churning almost as much as the confusing thoughts swirling around in her mind.

By suppertime her nerves still hadn't settled, nor had she regained her appetite. There was something she needed to know. Hopefully after she had her answer she could settle down.

She did her best to engage in polite conversation at supper, but her thoughts remained elsewhere. After the meal, Amos gathered up the painting supplies from the basement. He'd barely loaded everything in the wagon on the porch when Esther smiled.

"He's got two easels," Lizzie said as she pressed her palms together and grinned.

Naomi scurried to clear the dishes, pretending to ignore Lizzie's comment.

"Hmm . . ." Esther chimed in.

Naomi faced the women with her hands on her hips. "I like to paint. Amos likes to paint."

Esther stood, and Lizzie practically jumped up. "Go take advantage of all the daylight you can," Esther said as she stacked dishes on the table. "Lizzie and I can finish up in here."

"I always used to clean up, and I've already been shirking *mei* responsibilities by letting Lizzie do the dishes so I could go to supper with Thomas."

"*Mei maedel*, we've got this." Esther put a hand on Naomi's arm. "He's leaving in a week, so go enjoy having a painting partner."

Naomi opened her mouth to argue, but decided it wasn't

worth it. Lizzie and Esther would probably pound her with questions if she stayed.

"*Ya*, okay." She was anxious to get to the pond, and she didn't feel like putting up more of a fight.

By the time she reached him, Amos had everything set up.

"I brought the painting you'd been working on and a new canvas." He handed her a palette. "I didn't know if you wanted to keep working on the other one or . . ." He paused, any emotion he might be feeling suppressed behind a stoic expression. "Or start over."

Silence lengthened between them until it became awkward. "I'd like to start over." Naomi picked up the blank canvas and positioned it on the empty easel.

"Sometimes a fresh start is the best way to move forward."

She couldn't read his expression, but his eyes gave him away. They were filled with a longing Naomi understood. As his mouth became the focus of her attention, she forced herself to look away.

"And sometimes fixing what is broken is worth it." He nodded to her partially completed painting in the wagon, then at her blank canvas, which suddenly seemed to represent her life, her entire future.

"I guess you have to decide." His voice was level and without emotion, but his eyes beckoned her in a way that caused a tingling in the pit of her stomach.

Naomi wanted to look away, to pull her gaze from the temptation he posed. She'd worn a heavy coat this evening, and the air was still. The shivers down her spine couldn't be blamed on the weather. As he moved closer to her, she dropped the paint palette but barely noticed as his steady gaze bore into her.

She had her answer—there *was* a decision on the table, after all. Her knees trembled and her heart pounded as if it would burst from her chest.

"Tell me to stop," Amos said softly, his eyes never leaving hers as his broad shoulders blocked the setting sun.

She'd never kissed anyone besides Thomas, nor had she ever wanted to.

Until now.

EIGHTEEN

"TELL ME TO STOP," AMOS WHISPERED AGAIN AS HE MOVED closer. He'd never stepped into another man's territory, but he had to know if Naomi felt what seemed to have snuck up on both of them.

Her full lips parted, but she was silent, her eyes searching his as he tenderly cupped her cheek in one hand.

"Last chance," he breathed as his mouth grew closer to hers.

She stood on her toes and her lips brushed against his like a whisper of what was to come. Her kiss was slow, soft, and torturous, but Amos did his best to let her control what was sending his stomach into a wild swirl.

Finally, he gave in and pulled her to him kissing her with all the passion he'd kept bottled up since he first saw her. She responded with the same affection and intensity, and they fell in sync in a way that was natural, yet new at the same time.

"What am I doing?" she asked after she eased away, her eyes fearful and blinking as if she might cry. "I'm engaged."

"Are you?" He tried to sound as sensitive as he could, but Naomi's eyes only widened with fear. Amos wasn't a home-wrecker, but he also wasn't the kind of man who would have left the woman he loved. Esther and Lizzie seemed sure Thomas would leave Naomi again. Amos had no way of knowing. Maybe he was trying to justify what he'd just done.

Naomi put a hand to her forehead as she began to pace. "*Ya*, of course I am."

Amos flinched as her words kicked him in the gut. He shouldn't have expected a kiss to change her status, but . . . He blew out a breath of frustration.

"You initiated the kiss."

She stopped pacing and turned to face off with him, only a couple feet away. As blood siphoned from her face, she pointed a finger at him. "You knew exactly what you were doing, com-ing at me with that"—she wagged her finger at him—"that sensual voice."

Amos rubbed his chin, grinning, but when her nostrils started to flair, he pressed his lips together. "Who are you mad at? Me or yourself?"

"Both!" she spat as tears welled in the corners of her eyes.

"Naomi . . ." He inched closer to her as she covered her face with her hands. Gingerly, he put a hand on the small of her back and eased her into his arms until her head was bur-ied in his chest. "Please don't cry. I think we have both been thinking about that kiss for a while, and I'm sorry I blamed it on you. This is *mei* fault, so don't shoulder any guilt."

"*Nee*, it's *mei* fault." She pulled out of the hug, sniffling. "I'm just so confused."

He waited, but when she didn't elaborate, he said, "I guess I can understand that. I'm probably not helping your situation with Thomas." His chest tightened. "Did you kiss me to get even with him for being with another woman?"

She took a final swipe at her eyes and chewed her bottom lip for a few seconds. "I don't know."

It was probably an honest answer, but it stung. "*Ach*, well, I'm glad I could help you." He heard the heavy dose of sarcasm in his voice, but he hadn't expected such a forthcoming—and probably honest—response.

A glazed look of despair spread across her beautiful face. "I'm sorry." She took off in a sprint to the house.

Amos called after her, but she only ran faster. He went to his painting and stared at it for several seconds, then he picked up his palette, dipped his brush in black, and drew an *X* across the canvas.

∞

Naomi was breathless when she reached the house, but she stood on the porch and tried to gather herself before she went in. It wasn't even close to dark, and even though she didn't see Lizzie or Esther through the window, she doubted they were in their bedrooms yet. Although Esther had been retiring earlier and earlier. Lizzie might be in her room with her nose in a romance novel. Naomi had found three of them beneath Lizzie's mattress when she'd changed the sheets. Naomi was sure they all had a happily-ever-after ending, something she was starting to think she'd never have.

She wished Amos had never stayed here. Eventually, she would have to shed the anger that she'd unknowingly bottled up against Thomas. Now that the bottle was uncorked, she didn't know what to do with her emotions. Had she kissed Amos only to get back at Thomas?

She'd been so caught up in her thoughts that she didn't hear Amos pulling the wagon and toting the easels until he was nearing the house. She folded her hands in front of her, raised her chin, and waited.

He tucked the easels under his arm, lifted the wagon onto the porch, and took out the painting supplies that he'd already bagged up, all but the canvases. He moved past her and into the house without even glancing at her. When she saw the *X* across his painting, she gasped. He'd worked every day on that painting.

Naomi was on his heels as he clicked the flashlight on and started down the basement stairs carrying the bag of supplies in his other hand with the easels still tucked under his arm.

"Why did you do that? Why did you draw an *X* across your painting?" She stayed close behind him, following the beams from the flashlight. "It's beautiful, and you shouldn't have done that!"

"Sometimes beautiful things don't turn out the way you planned." He paused. "I'll start over when I get home."

Naomi's emotions were spiraling. After he wound his way around some stacked chairs, he set the bag on an old desk and leaned the easels against the wall. He spun around and shone the flashlight in her face, enough that she had to put a hand up to block the light.

"Can you please get that thing out of *mei* face?" She was yelling, which wasn't in her nature.

He lowered the light and shone it on the concrete floor between them. Shaking, Naomi pulled her coat snug around her and hugged herself.

"It hurts me that you did that to your painting."

Amos shrugged. "It's not that big of a deal."

Naomi was fuming and trembling and sure he was referring to her as much as the painting. "Fine." She put her hands on her hips. "I guess I thought maybe it was a big deal."

He lunged forward, keeping the flashlight pointed at the floor. "What do you want me to say, Naomi? What is it you want to hear?" He scratched his head, glaring at her. "Because I'm having a hard time figuring you out."

She gritted her teeth. "I'm just telling you how disappointed I am that you ruined your painting!" Her voice had risen again.

"Really? This is about *mei* painting?" His voice deepened, and in the darkness of the basement, his broad shoulders, height, and overall presence should have frightened her, but she knew without a doubt that Amos would never hurt her. Except maybe with his words, which were cutting into her heart, and she couldn't seem to stop shaking.

He was close enough to kiss her again, but she couldn't let that happen, even though every inch of her longed to be back in his arms. She took a step backward. "*Ya*, it's about the painting," she finally said as her bottom lip trembled.

"*Nee*, it's not." He looked at the ceiling, sighed, and then his eyes homed in on her lips, reminding her of the emotion attached to their kiss. "You're having doubts about Thomas. I understand that. But don't you think I felt what was inside of you through that kiss?" He gently pounded a fist against his chest. "It wasn't just a revenge kiss, and you should at least be able to admit that."

Naomi pressed her lips together and was quiet, swallowing the growing knot in her throat as she held her position, arms folded in front of her, shaking.

"I have fallen for you." He chuckled nervously. "And believe me, no one is more surprised than me. I didn't think I'd ever care about anyone like this again. I'm admitting how I feel, honestly, and maybe you could do the same."

But she couldn't. Admitting she'd fallen for him would only make things more complicated than they were. She'd known Thomas for years. He'd made a mistake, but he'd returned home to make things right. But she'd hurt Amos, and she didn't want him leaving with a hole in his heart. He'd worked as hard as she had to get out of the dark place they'd both been hiding. God had given her a second chance with Thomas. She didn't want Amos to lose hope that he would find that same kind of happiness again. Naomi had no choice but to ignore her feelings for Amos and work through her anger about what Thomas had done and put her trust in him again.

"I love Thomas," she said softly. "But you will find someone again, Amos, someone you will love as much as you loved Sarah." She lowered her gaze. "It just can't be me."

He edged closer, causing her to back up against the wall.

"Tell me again how much you love Thomas." He pointed to his face. "And look me in the eye this time."

Naomi finally looked into his eyes. Her voice trembled as she said it again. "I love Thomas."

"You love him so much that you kissed another man." He raised his shoulders and lowered them slowly as he stared at her. "If I thought the kiss was for revenge, I'd walk away. But you felt something. You're just scared to upset a situation that isn't right for you."

He was correct. She'd felt something far more than friendship. But even though this unleashed anger at Thomas wasn't going to vanish overnight, she owed it to her fiancé to give him the second chance God was offering them. It seemed kinder to Amos to keep her feelings to herself. "We're physically attracted to each other, and we irresponsibly acted on it."

"You're lying." He was so close to her, she could feel his breath on her face, the magnetism of his lips moving toward hers.

She shuddered and turned her head to the side. He practically had her pinned against the wall.

"I'm not lying!" she yelled as he braced one arm on either

side of her. She let her tears flow, knowing she'd let him kiss her when she faced him.

"Naomi . . ." he said softly. "I'm not going to force myself on you. I think you're beautiful inside and out. I feel like our love for painting isn't the only thing we have in common. We haven't known each other that long, and we're both vulnerable. I'm able to admit all of that. But you are the first woman since Sarah died who makes me want to live again, the way I used to, enjoying life, praising *Gott*, and looking forward to the blessings of each new day." He paused, and when she looked at him another tear rolled down her cheek.

"I'm just confused," she said softly. "I need to sort out *mei* feelings, and I'm not being fair to Thomas by kissing you." Lowering her gaze, she finally admitted the truth. "I know it's more than physical attraction, but I am suffocating in guilt even though I want nothing more than for you to kiss me again."

He leaned closer and she closed her eyes, but he gently kissed her on the forehead, lingering before he eased away. "Now you are being honest, and you need to sort through your feelings. My being here doesn't make that any easier for you. I will leave here a better man for having spent time with you. I know there's hope for me to find someone else too."

She wanted to blurt out that she didn't want him to find anyone else. The thought stung as much as envisioning Thomas with another woman—maybe more. But telling him that would only make things worse.

A noise at the top of the stairs caught her attention, then

the door closed. With both hands, Naomi pushed Amos out of the way and felt her way around the chairs and back to the entrance. Amos followed with the flashlight.

"Nee, nee, nee!" She rushed up the basement steps. On the top one was a tray with two small plates, napkins, crackers, cheese spread, salami, and some pickles. Next to the platter was a small pot of coffee, along with two cups. Naomi turned the doorknob, yanking on it before she pounded on the door. It wouldn't budge.

"Lizzie, you open this door right now!" She looked over her shoulder at Amos, who was shining the light on the tray. "I told you! She does this sort of thing." She took a deep breath.

"Lizzie, you open this door right now! Do you hear me?"

∽∾

Esther poured herself a cup of coffee, knowing it would be a long night. She couldn't leave them locked in the basement and unattended. They might light the lantern down there. What if there was a mishap? She'd have to stay up long enough for them to sort things out.

Lizzie shuffled into the kitchen yawning and rubbing her eyes. "I must have dozed off while I was reading." She glanced at the clock on the wall. "It's too early for bed, even for me. What's all the ruckus?"

Esther cleared her throat. "The *kinner* were having a spat. I think they need some time to work through it." She nodded toward the basement door.

Lizzie was suddenly fully awake, eyes wide. "Esther Ann Zook! What have you done?"

"It's only for a while. I was around the corner and when I heard yelling, I came closer and listened. Those two need to realize they are already in *lieb*. They're both fighting their feelings. They just need a little time."

Lizzie covered her mouth with both hands and giggled softly. "I seem to recall that when I locked Naomi in the basement with that other fellow, you hollered at me and told me repeatedly how inappropriate and wrong it was."

"That young man wasn't right for Naomi." She picked up her coffee and took a sip. "Amos is perfect for her."

Lizzie clapped her hands together softly and slid into the kitchen chair across from Esther. "How long are you going to keep them in there?"

"However long it takes." Esther couldn't believe she had stooped to Lizzie's antics, but emotions were ebbing and flowing in all directions with the young couple. Naomi and Amos needed to sort things out, one way or the other. Esther was praying they'd talk enough to realize and admit their feelings for each other.

"How will you know how long it's going to take?" Lizzie placed her palms on the table and raised her eyebrows.

"*Gott* will give us a sign." Esther pointed to the kitchen drawer where they kept odds and ends. "You might as well get the cards. When's the last time we played a game of Spades?"

Lizzie quietly rose from her chair and tiptoed to the drawer, returning with the cards, softly chuckling.

"I already feel like a criminal, Lizzie. Maybe harness some of your excitement." Esther rolled her eyes.

"Ha!" She pointed a finger at Esther. "This one is on you, *mei schweschder*." She covered her mouth again and laughed.

Esther shuffled the cards as best she could without making too much noise. "Keep your voice down," she whispered. She'd had a coughing spell earlier, which had resulted in some blood again. She silently prayed it wouldn't happen in front of Lizzie. She had more dreaded tests next week, but then maybe she would get some answers. Mostly she was going to pray that Naomi and Amos would recognize and admit how they felt about each other.

She cringed when Naomi screamed Lizzie's name again.

Lizzie groaned, then leaned across the table and whispered, "Why does she assume I'm the one who locked them in there?"

Esther shook her head and sighed. "Because Naomi would never expect me to stoop to something like this. But I'd like to see her happy before I leave this earth."

Lizzie smiled. "You'll outlive us all. I've already told you I can't make it without you."

Esther dealt the cards as her chest tightened. "*Ya*, you could if you had to."

Naomi pounded on the door, yelling Lizzie's name again, and Esther stopped dealing the cards, frowning. "Maybe we should let them out."

"Nah. She'll settle down in about five minutes. That's how long it took last time."

"And last time it didn't work out. This might not either."
Esther shook her head.

"*Nee*, it'll work out. I just know it." Lizzie gave a taut nod
of her head as she picked up her set of cards.

Esther believed that, too, or she never would have locked
Amos and Naomi in the basement.

NINETEEN

AMOS SHONE THE LIGHT ON THE TRAY, THEN REACHED PAST Naomi and jiggled the doorknob. His gaze met hers as he held the flashlight at the ceiling and his jaw dropped. *This is crazy.* "Are they seriously not going to let us out of here?"

"*Nee*, not any time soon." She pounded on the door again. "Lizzie! You open this door right now!"

Amos handed her the flashlight and leaned down to pick up the tray. "At least they left us food and coffee." He chuckled. "Hold the light on the steps and I'll carry this down."

"Aren't you upset?" she asked from behind him.

He waited until they were at the bottom of the stairs and he'd set the tray on the old desk. "A little shocked." He grinned. "But hungry."

"Men. Food is always the first thing you think of in any situation." She set the flashlight on the table, lighting up the ceiling, then put her hands on her hips and eyed the items on

242

the tray. "Lizzie knows I love her cheese spread with crackers and salami. I guess she sent *mei* favorites to try to make up for locking us in." She threw her hands up. "See what I mean? Lizzie will go to any extreme she sees fit if she believes two people should be together. And it's not just *mei* love life she meddles with—there are others in the community."

Amos picked up a cracker and spread some cheese on it, topped it with salami, and handed it to her, then did the same for himself. "Are they ever successful?" he asked before he took a bite.

Naomi laughed. "*Ya*, actually. Believe it or not, sometimes they are."

Amos ate another cracker before he walked over to the stacked chairs. He carried two around the desk. They sat down and he asked, "Isn't Lizzie afraid we might freeze down here?"

Naomi pointed to her coat, then to his. "She probably saw us coming across the yard and noticed we didn't leave our coats on the rack." She snickered like a child with a secret, which was cute and made him smile. "But"—she picked up the flashlight and shone it on a cedar chest against the wall—"from *mei* last experience down here, I know there are blankets in that trunk."

Amos grinned. "So, who was the other poor soul she forced to stay down here with you?"

She playfully slapped him on the arm. "There are worse people to be stuck with."

He gazed into her eyes. "I'm not going to argue with that."

If she blushed, he couldn't tell, but she tucked her chin as she brushed strands of hair away from her face.

"It was a man staying here, but not a stranger. I don't think Lizzie would put me in harm's way. She's sitting at the kitchen table right now, probably reading her book and being as quiet as a church mouse." She reached for another cracker. "He was a close friend's *sohn*, and he'd come for a wedding."

Amos clicked his tongue and shook his head. "It's just not safe to come here for a wedding."

Naomi threw a hand over her mouth to avoid spewing the remains of the cracker from her mouth as she laughed.

"Don't spit on me." Amos put his hands up to block his face.

"Stop!" She said as she tried to swallow, her hand still hiding her mouth. "You're making me laugh."

Amos thought he could listen to her laugh for the rest of his life. "Okay, I'll be quiet. Go on. Tell me about this poor fellow."

Smiling, she shook her head. "Anyway, he was a very nice man, about five years older than me. I actually liked him, and it might not have been so terrible if he hadn't gone completely bonkers when he realized we were locked in. I asked him if he was claustrophobic, and he said he wasn't. He paced the entire time, screamed at Lizzie, and basically behaved like a five-year-old. All qualities I might not have seen if she hadn't forced us to stay down here. It was still a terrible thing to do, but I knew without a doubt by the time she let us out that he was *not* the man for me."

"Um, out of curiosity, exactly how long were you held

prisoners?" He rubbed his chin and tilted his head, searching her eyes.

"Four hours." She put a hand over her stomach, bent at the waist, and laughed so hard she couldn't catch her breath. "Looking back," she finally said, "it's rather funny."

Amos laughed, too, then quieted. "Naomi, it's nice to hear you laugh. Why don't we make the best of our imprisonment, enjoy the food, and try not to analyze anything right now." He leaned his head back against the wall behind his chair and yawned. "It's exhausting."

She nodded and smiled. "Deal."

Naomi had to give Lizzie credit for this little shenanigan. She'd seen glimpses of Amos's sense of humor before, but nothing like this. Had she ever laughed much with Thomas? She wrapped her arms around herself, shivering. Amos was quick to fumble his way to the cedar chest without grabbing the flashlight.

"Ouch." She wasn't sure what he bumped into, but he returned a moment later with a thick blanket.

"Why didn't you take the flashlight?" She grinned.

"I didn't know if you were afraid of the dark." He held up the blanket. "Please tell me this isn't the same blanket you cuddled in with your last guy."

She chuckled. "I assure you, there was no cuddling. He was much too frantic."

"Stand up."

She did and Amos slid her chair against the wall next to his, then patted the seat. "I promise. No funny stuff. Not even a kiss on the cheek."

She shuffled to the chair and sat, thinking a kiss on the cheek didn't sound so bad right now. Amos sat, then wrapped the blanket around both of them and pulled her a little closer.

"Strictly for body heat." He gently poked her in the ribs and she jumped. "Ha! You're ticklish." He poked her again in the same place.

"Stop." She looked up at him. "Behave."

"Always." He winked at her and, although they had a lot to talk about, for right now, she'd be happy in his arms. When she started yawning, he gently eased her head onto his shoulder. It couldn't be very late, but Amos was right. All the analyzing was exhausting.

"Sweet dreams," he whispered. "Unless you want to try to dig our way out."

Naomi giggled. She didn't want to go anywhere.

∞

Esther jerked her head up from the kitchen table in total darkness. She slammed her hands around the table until she found the flashlight. *Dead batteries.* Lizzie was snoring on the other side of the table. Esther stood and edged over to the drawer where they kept the matches and lit the lantern on the counter.

"Lizzie, wake up." She nudged her sister, who bolted upright.

"What? What? Where are we?" Lizzie stood and looked around the kitchen. "*Ach*, that's right. You locked Amos and Naomi in the basement." She rubbed her eyes. "What time is it?"

Esther held the lantern up to see the clock. "Oh dear, oh dear, oh dear! It's three in the morning! What have we done?"

"*You* locked them in the basement. None of this *we* stuff." Lizzie puckered her lips. "Do you think they're okay?"

"Probably freezing." Esther eased open the door to the basement. "Naomi? Amos?" She started down the steps, slow and clutching the handrail. Lizzie was right behind her. When they were about halfway down, Esther held up the lantern. "Look, Lizzie." She whispered and scooted to the side of the stairway so her sister could see.

"Isn't that the sweetest thing you've ever seen?" Esther sighed with relief.

"Look how he's got his arm around her, and her head's on his shoulder." Lizzie whispered. "All cuddled up in that blanket and sleeping." She grinned. "He's a snorer."

"So are you." Esther took another step down, but Lizzie tugged on her robe.

"Let's leave them. We can leave the door open and go to bed." Lizzie yawned, and Esther nodded as they turned and carefully went back up the steps.

"You know in most communities, what we've done would be considered highly inappropriate," Esther whispered as she raised an eyebrow at Lizzie. "Especially forcing them to be alone the way we did."

Lizzie stepped up the last step, then waited until Esther was in the kitchen before she folded her arms across her chest. "There is no *we* in this situation."

"You sat right there across from me the whole time, knowing they were down there. That makes you guilty too." Esther set the lantern on the table and began gathering up the scattered cards. "The open door should allow some heat to flow down there." Suddenly, she startled, gasped, and dropped some of the cards. "Someone's coming up the steps."

"Good morning, ladies."

Esther twisted around and glanced at Lizzie, who was flashing a toothless smile at Amos.

"I, uh . . ." Esther searched for the words to explain herself, but there were none.

Amos had a flashlight he was pointing at the floor as he walked over to the cabinet and took out a glass. He lifted his arms, stretched, then moseyed to the refrigerator.

"Our girl is thirsty." He set the flashlight on the counter before he took out the carton of milk and poured it in the glass. "We were wondering if breakfast might be a little later than normal?"

Esther nodded, as did Lizzie, both wide-eyed. "*Ya*, of course. *Ya*," they answered in unison.

Amos winked. "*Danki*." He put the milk away, then grabbed the flashlight and walked back to the basement door. He closed it behind him. Then they heard the deadbolt thump. Esther's heart pounded. There was a lock on the outside of the basement door and an old deadbolt inside.

Lizzie lifted both hands to her chest. "What have *you* done? You practically forced them to sin, right here in our own basement." She couldn't have looked more indignant if she'd tried, with her bottom lip pushed out in a pout as the wrinkles on her forehead crinkled even more than normal.

Esther's stomach twisted into a knot.

∞

"How did Lizzie act when she saw you?" Naomi was still wrapped in the blanket when Amos handed her the glass of milk. "*Danki.*" She took a drink and set it on the desk. "Did you play it up good?"

He sat next to her and she offered him the other half of the blanket. She felt comfortable next to him.

"For good measure, I locked the deadbolt from the inside." Amos chuckled.

Naomi raised her hand to her mouth to suppress her laughter. "I bet Lizzie is having a fit!"

"Actually, it was Lizzie *and* Esther when I walked in." He shook his head but his eyes crinkled at the corners as one side of his mouth curled upward. "They looked a mess. Most of their hair had fallen from beneath the scarves on their heads, and they had dark circles under their eyes. Cards were spread out on the table. I think they must have fallen asleep there." He pointed to the top of the steps. "Why is there a lock from the inside?"

"Esther said Lizzie's husband put it in because when they

were first married, they had the basement fixed up and lived here for a while as they finished building a *haus*. If the door was locked, everyone knew not to come down here."

"Well, their minds are awhirl now." Amos yawned. "But I guess we will have to emerge soon enough." He gazed at her in the dim glow of the flashlight. Naomi wasn't sure when they fell asleep, and she was surprised they had since they were sitting up. She recalled both of them admitting that analyzing things was exhausting. This morning, reality slapped her in the face. She would have to confront her feelings about Thomas. And Amos.

"Well, this should teach Lizzie, and apparently Esther, that they can't force love." Naomi thought her heart stopped for a second. "I-I didn't mean . . ."

"I know what you meant." He offered her his hand and pulled her to her feet. This time he picked up the flashlight and took it with him to return the blanket to the chest. "For the next prisoner locked down here," he said, grinning, when he was back in front of her.

"I doubt there will be any more hostages." Naomi giggled, but with each step up the stairs in front of Amos, the reality of her situation became more real. They walked through the kitchen, which was empty, then tiptoed through the living room and went up the stairs.

When they reached Naomi's bedroom door, Amos stopped beside her. "Your mind is already spinning with worry, isn't it?"

She nodded, wondering if he would kiss her, but after a few seconds of staring into her eyes he took a step back. "Good night." He rolled his eyes. "Or I guess, good morning. I asked if breakfast could be a little later so maybe we could get a few hours' sleep. I know we both woke up on and off in those chairs." Pausing, his expression sobered. "See you in a little while."

Naomi grinned. "Let's have some fun with Esther and Lizzie at breakfast."

"*Ya*, they have that coming, I reckon." He winked at her and walked down the hallway to his room.

Naomi snuggled into her covers, needing sleep, but knowing she had a lot to think about.

⁂

Esther and Lizzie started breakfast before Naomi joined them. Guilt was eating up Esther as she flipped the bacon. Lizzie was unusually quiet as she whisked eggs in a bowl. What if Naomi and Amos had really hit it off after spending time together? That was what they wanted, after all. But what if Amos wasn't the wholesome fellow he appeared to be? Had he seduced Naomi? Questions raced through Esther's mind, and she didn't know how to get answers without embarrassing them. She couldn't live with herself if she had coerced them into doing something reserved for married couples.

"*Wie bischt.*" Naomi walked into the kitchen smiling, possibly even glowing. "*Danki* for starting breakfast, but I can finish now."

"*Nee*, dear. You just sit and rest." Esther smiled over her shoulder as Naomi poured herself a cup of coffee. Amos walked in grinning a few minutes later, eased up next to Naomi, and got himself a cup of coffee.

"Good morning, ladies," he said with a bounce in his step as he followed Naomi to the kitchen table and sat in the chair beside her.

Are their chairs closer together than normal? Esther couldn't stand it anymore. She turned, twisting her hands together, and shook her head.

"We are so sorry for locking you in the basement. We heard you quarreling, and we wanted you to work things out. We never meant to fall asleep and leave you, and—"

"Stop!" Lizzie faced Esther with her palm raised. "Quit saying *we*." She turned to Amos and Naomi. "I was sleeping soundly in *mei* room, and when I came into the kitchen, Esther said she had locked you in the basement."

"You could have let them out," Esther said as she faced Lizzie. "You are as guilty as I am."

"It's fine," Amos said. He looked at Naomi and winked. "We're not upset at all."

Naomi smiled dreamily as she batted her eyes at him. "Not at all."

Amos put his arm around Naomi, and Esther went weak in the knees. But what could she say? Glancing at Lizzie, she prayed her sister would stay quiet, but she knew better.

Lizzie walked to the table with the whisk still in her hand, drizzling the wood floor with egg. "Naomi, you are a *gut* girl." She turned to Amos. "I don't know about you anymore."

"But, Lizzie, didn't you lock us down there so we could sort through our feelings and realize we were in *lieb*?" Naomi tilted her head to the side, her expression innocent.

Lizzie jumped up and down, slinging egg everywhere. "How many times do I have to say this? Are you people hard of hearing? *Esther* is the one who locked you in!"

Amos leaned over and kissed Naomi on the cheek, right there in front of Esther and Lizzie, who gasped.

"And we're glad you did," he said with an air of pride that seemed to confirm their fears.

"Dear Lord, what have we done?" Esther hung her head, shaking it.

Lizzie stomped her foot. "*We, we, we!* I guess you *are* hard of hearing."

"Lizzie, Esther." Naomi spoke softly and waited until they looked at her. "Nothing happened. Nothing at all."

Esther's pulse started to return to normal as she took a deep breath.

"But let this be a lesson to both of you not to meddle in other people's lives. It could have gone differently if Amos wasn't such a gentleman." She turned to him, and Esther saw the true admiration in her eyes. Maybe she hadn't done such a bad thing after all. She couldn't help but wonder if Amos and Naomi had admitted their feelings to each other. She wasn't about to ask. Instead, she'd wait, watch, and thank God she hadn't pushed the couple into sin.

Breakfast and dinner were uneventful, but Naomi had a hard task in front of her this evening. Supper with Thomas. He would surely ask what she'd done the night before, and she had to decide how much to tell him. She didn't want to lie, but the full version would surely hurt him.

She still hadn't decided what to do when he picked her up at the usual time, and her stomach was rolling with nerves.

"I got your note yesterday. Were you sick?" Thomas asked as soon as she got in the buggy. "Or you just needed a night away from me?" Grinning, he backed the horse out of the driveway and down the road.

"*Nee*, I wasn't sick." She tried to force her confused emotions into some sort of order, but her hesitation to explain further caused Thomas to pull back on the reins, slowing the horse to a walk.

"What then?" His expression grew tight with strain.

"I wanted to paint. I missed it." She stared straight ahead and took a deep breath before she looked at him.

"Um, that's fine." After a few seconds, he frowned, his eyes leveling off beneath slanted eyebrows. "Did you paint with Amos?"

Facing forward again, she nodded. "*Ya*, I did." Even though she hadn't even gotten her paintbrush wet, she'd been there.

"Uh, okay." Thomas sounded as confused as she felt. "Naomi, you're living under the same roof with this man, sharing meals with him, and now painting with him. Should I be worried?"

The moment of truth was upon her. Why hadn't she

planned better? "Can you pull off the road, maybe up on the left, at the school?"

"I guess I should be." There was an edge to his voice, and they were silent as he turned into the school parking lot and stopped. He twisted in his seat to face her. "What's going on?"

"I know you think painting for pleasure is a waste of time, but it's something I enjoy. I especially like painting the sunset. And it just so happens, Amos likes to paint too." She shrugged, trying to seem nonchalant as she gazed into his eyes, flashes of Amos's face obstructing her view. It was well after the fact and strange timing, but in that moment she realized that when she'd kissed Amos, she hadn't seen Thomas's face. She hadn't even thought about him until afterward, when the guilt settled in.

"We didn't need to pull over for you to tell me that, Naomi. I'm fine with you painting until we're married. I just wanted to make sure that you hadn't developed a romantic interest in him." His tone held a degree of warmth and concern, but his eyes revealed his unspoken fear.

Naomi pushed Amos to the back of her mind. "What do you mean, you're fine with *mei* painting 'until we're married'?"

He reached for her hand and squeezed it. "Once you're *mei fraa*, you'll have enough to occupy your time running our household." Smiling, he said, "And we can enjoy our free time by starting our family."

Naomi faced forward and clenched her jaw, trying to kill the sob coming up in her throat. "I kissed Amos," she said as her voice trembled.

Thomas let go of her hand as if her touch burned him. "What?" When she finally looked at him, his face was filled with loathing. "Last night while you were painting?"

"*Ya.*" Her heart ached, even though she knew this was something she had to do.

They were both silent and looking down for a while.

"Do you love him?" Thomas's voice was shaky as he posed the question.

Naomi didn't look up. "I barely know him." She wasn't answering the question, and she hoped Thomas didn't ask her again. Was it really possible to fall in love with someone that quickly anyway? Since last night, a warmth was in her heart, and she wanted to savor it, and possibly explore it.

"Look at me, Naomi." Thomas spoke softly, his voice still unsteady. "Did you do that . . . Did you kiss him to get back at me?" As he gazed into her eyes, she remembered the wonderful moments they'd had together. But for the first time, she was feeling a lack of emotional connection. That connection was part of what drew her to Amos. The more she compared the two men, the more confused she became.

She chose to avoid the question. "I guess the more I think about you leaving me and getting involved with someone else, the angrier I get. Do you know what I went through after you left? It wasn't just that my heart was broken. It was the humiliation and embarrassment. And to be honest, I'm having trouble getting past it, more than I realized."

"You have to forgive me, Naomi, because I am so sorry. You are who I want to be with. I'm not settling. I'm choosing

you, always and forever. I will never, ever leave you again."
He paused, sighing. "I can understand your need to hurt me
by kissing Amos. And believe me, it hurts. I know it's not even
a taste of what I put you through, but . . ."

Kissing Amos didn't have anything to do with hurting
Thomas. Amos had been right. It wasn't a revenge kiss. But
Naomi knew she had to forgive Thomas in order to move on,
whichever direction that might be.

"I forgive you, Thomas. I just need a little time."

He lifted her hand to his mouth and kissed her palm. "I
love you."

Her eyes watered instantly as she opened her mouth to
speak, but the words wouldn't come.

"I need time," she said again.

Thomas nodded as a tear slid down his cheek. Naomi
leaned into his arms, and they clung to each other and cried.

TWENTY

NAOMI DIDN'T WANT TO EAT SUPPER WITH THOMAS AFTER
they talked. She wanted to go home. When they pulled into
the driveway, Naomi leaned over and kissed him on the cheek.

"I need time to think," she said again.

Thomas nodded at the house. "I have to say, Amos has an
unfair advantage, living with you."

"He's leaving within a week." Naomi wasn't sure how she
felt about Amos leaving. She needed to be away from both men
if she was going to truly sort out her feelings. But she couldn't
imagine not seeing Amos's face throughout the day. Already,
she was looking forward to getting inside and hoped he was still
downstairs. It was about the time they gathered for devotions.

"I guess I can survive a week of him living in the same *haus*
as you." Thomas cupped her cheek. "You don't have to say it
back, but I have to tell you again that I love you."

Naomi pressed her hand over his. She wanted to tell him

that a part of her would love him forever, no matter what the future held. But she worried that might give him false hope.

"Good night," she said before she got out of the buggy.

She tried not to rush as she walked to the porch, then she turned and waved to Thomas. As disappointed as she was that Amos had ruined his painting, she wondered if it signified a new beginning for both of them, however things turned out. She was going to start fresh on a new painting tonight. She'd baked a chicken casserole before she left with Thomas. Maybe there were leftovers. Mostly, she wanted to be around Amos and try to identify what she was feeling. If he kept true to what he said, he would be gone in less than a week. That didn't give her much time.

When she walked into the living room, she shed her cape and bonnet. Esther and Lizzie were on the couch, each reading a book.

"Why are you back so early?" Esther took off her reading glasses.

Naomi shrugged. "It's a long and confusing story, but we decided not to go eat." Pausing, she didn't hear movement anywhere else in the house. "Where is Amos?"

Lizzie and Esther exchanged glances, then Esther stood.

"He's gone, Naomi. He packed up and left right after you left with Thomas. He thanked us for allowing him to work here during his slow time back home, and he asked us to give you this." Esther reached for something on the coffee table and handed Naomi an envelope with her name on it.

Naomi's hand shook as she accepted it. "No goodbye?" She folded the envelope in half and slipped it in her apron pocket. A new kind of anguish seared her heart, similar to how she'd felt when Thomas left her. Maybe worse.

"We tried to talk him out of leaving without seeing you." Esther sighed. "But he insisted it would be easier this way."

"A strong indication of how much he cares for you." Lizzie closed her book and folded her hands. "Aren't you going to read the letter?"

"*Ya*, I will." Even though Lizzie and Esther were stiff, quiet, and looked like they might burst from curiosity, Naomi wanted to read the letter in private. She tried to smile. "Couldn't you have locked him in the basement or something?"

Esther cringed. "*Nee*, dear. We are done meddling with your love life. We learned our lesson."

Naomi doubted that, and this was the one time she wished they had acted in character. For Amos not to say goodbye seemed harsh, but deep down, she understood. She was anxious, if not a little fearful, to read his note. Was it goodbye forever? Or was he just giving her space, just as she'd asked Thomas to give her time?

"Excuse me." She turned and went upstairs, closed her bedroom door behind her, and sat on the bed, trembling. It took her a minute to pull the envelope from her pocket. She slid her finger along the crease and eased out a yellow piece of lined paper. Slowly she unfolded it and read.

Dear Naomi,

Forgive me for not saying goodbye. I think you know why I didn't. I feel like putting some distance between us might help you open your heart to your true feelings. Perhaps Thomas is the man for you and deserves another chance. That is a choice only you can make.

You changed my life, Naomi. I'm smiling as I write this because it sounds so dramatic. But it's true. I've been so closed off since Sarah died and refused to open *mei* heart to anyone. Then I met you, and little by little, you chipped away at the wall around *mei* heart. I still have a lot of love to share with the right person.

I'll think of you every time I paint. There is a creek that borders our property at home. I used to love to go there and paint. Sarah didn't paint, but she knew how much I loved it and that the creek was my special place where I felt closest to *Gott*. After she was gone, I'd go there sometimes, but never to paint. I went to talk to *Gott*.

When I return, I plan to paint again, in that spot. I hope to keep the gray shadow out of *mei* work and replace it with the red that was missing. In case you didn't know, red is the color of love. And to paint a picture of love, you have to feel love in your heart before you can show it on canvas.

Naomi smiled through her tears. He had recognized, or finally figured out, what was missing from their paintings.

I'm leaving you with love in *mei* heart, something that's been missing for way too long. I'll miss you and forever remember our night in the basement.

To sum it up, you brought joy back into mei life,

showed me how to laugh again, and helped me recapture a part of myself I thought was gone forever. I will always be grateful to you for that.

I will pray for you. I will miss you. But mostly, I hope you find the peace in your heart I know you are searching for.

Fondly,
Amos

Naomi reread the letter two more times, trying to decide the level of finality it represented. He didn't ask her to write him back, nor did he mention ever seeing her again. As tears trailed down her face and dropped onto the paper, she supposed he was right. God had orchestrated a plan for them to help each other recover from their grief. The Lord had opened their hearts to the possibility of second chances, just not with each other.

Then why am I hurting so much, Gott? She threw her head back and stared at the ceiling, fighting the urge to be angry with God. What would have happened if Amos had stayed?

"We'll never know," she quoted his words aloud as she curled up on the bed and let the loss wash over her.

❧

"What are we going to do?" Lizzie twisted on the couch to face Esther, her expression as grim as Esther felt.

"We aren't going to do anything." She squeezed her eyes closed as her stomach clenched. "Every time I think about us leaving them in that basement for so long, I cringe. I only wanted to leave them down there long enough to face their feelings and stop fighting. Had they not both been ethical, God-fearing people, things could have gone badly. It was wrong of us to shove temptation at them the way we did."

Lizzie shook her head. "*You*, not *we*."

"*Ach*, Lizzie, stop it. You were right there at the kitchen table with me." She pointed at her sister. "No more matchmaking or meddling for us."

Lizzie wrinkled her nose and shook her head. "I think Amos was the one for Naomi, and we let him get away."

"They are adults, and we certainly couldn't keep him here. I think we can only hope that distance will make the heart grow fonder, for both of them." Esther set her book on the coffee table. "I need to go to Walmart tomorrow, and I couldn't find a driver, so I'm going to see if Gus will take me."

Lizzie disliked Walmart, and disliked Gus even more. It was a safe bet she wouldn't want to go. Esther didn't feel good about lying to her sister, but she had two final tests to endure tomorrow, then a meeting with her doctor to go over everything. Whatever the findings, she'd tell Lizzie when she knew what was wrong.

"I'd walk before I let that pompous grouch take me anywhere." Lizzie puckered her lips. "And I can't think of anything at Walmart that would make me go there. It's big and confusing and cold in that store."

"Even though the harvest was plentiful, we need more than corn to live on. The locals don't have the variety of vegetables

Walmart has brought in from other states." Esther was digging herself deeper into the lie. Maybe she'd beg Gus to stop at Walmart so she wouldn't be fibbing to Lizzie.

"*Ach*, I almost forgot to tell you, there were messages on the machine in the barn." Lizzie shuffled her teeth, and Esther prayed her doctor hadn't left a message for her. She'd instructed him not to do that.

"We're going to have a full *haus* for the next two weeks." Lizzie reached up and straightened her prayer covering. "Not every day, but a lot of folks made reservations."

"That might be a *gut* distraction for Naomi. It will keep her busy."

Esther hoped it might be a good distraction for her, too, depending on what the doctor said tomorrow. Her stomach churned just thinking about it.

∽

After a long bus ride, Amos was glad to be home. His family welcomed him back in a grand style. His mother served a fine meal, and his brothers and father had cleaned the workshop, a task Amos had been putting off for months. His brothers dabbled in the shop, but it was mostly where Amos ran his business. He'd let it become a mess before he went to Indiana.

"*Gut* to have you home, *bruder*." Amos's youngest brother, Daniel, shook his hand as they sat down for supper. His middle brother, Rudy, did the same.

"*Gut* to be home." Amos loved his family, but he had

started missing Naomi the moment he walked out the door of The Peony Inn. He wondered what her reaction was to his letter, and if she would write him back. Or was a clean split the best way, so she could focus on rebuilding her relationship with Thomas? The thought caused his stomach to twist, but he knew giving her time was the best thing to do.

"You have three jobs lined up this week," his father said. "Perfect timing, now that you're home."

"There were two small projects while you were gone." Rudy reached for a slice of bread, only to have his mother slap his hand away, reminding him they would say grace before putting anything on their plates. "I handled them, and I'll fill you in later," he said before they bowed their heads.

After the blessing, everyone filled him in on things he'd missed, which wasn't all that much. A couple they'd known since they were children had published their engagement. Levi Hostetler had been in a buggy accident, but he was going to be all right. Amos half listened, but he was distracted with thoughts of Naomi.

His brothers were anxious to finish eating and get out the door. They were both courting women in the community. After his father retired to the living room, Amos stayed seated in the kitchen, knowing his mother would have questions. He didn't want to talk about Naomi, but he doubted he could avoid a conversation about his time in Indiana.

"I thought you'd stay longer," she said as she cleared the table. "It sounded like Esther and Lizzie had so much work for you to do."

"*Ya*, and I got most of it done." He regretted leaving a few projects uncompleted, but the timing had been perfect, and if he stayed one more day, he was afraid he would beg Naomi not to marry Thomas and to give him a chance. But she had a history with Thomas and deserved the time to see if she could get past her anger.

When his mother had piled the dishes in soapy water, she sat down across from Amos at the table. "Esther wrote to me. She told me there was definitely a spark between you and Naomi." *Mamm* smiled. "Such a kind *maedel*, and I saw a hint of something between you before I left to come home. Were we all wrong?"

"*Nee*, there was something." Amos told his mother about Thomas's return and Naomi's history with him. "She needs to work things out without a distraction from me."

His mother's eyes drooped as she frowned but stayed quiet. Amos decided to throw her a bone.

"But, *Mamm*, spending time with Naomi helped *mei* to open *mei* heart to the possibility of love again. Maybe *Gott* has someone else for me and will see fit to give me a second chance." In his heart, though, he couldn't imagine a second chance with anyone but Naomi.

His mother offered a weak smile. "I'm happy about that, *sohn*. I really am."

Amos scratched his cheek. "Then why do you look so glum?"

His mother sighed. "Because I haven't seen that look in your eyes since Sarah. I would miss you very much if you left our community, but I don't want geography to dictate your decisions." Smiling, she stood and walked around the table, then kissed Amos on the forehead. "Love is a tricky business."

Amos remained at the table for a while longer, recalling the time he'd spent with Naomi, hoping and praying she'd write him back.

❧

Esther prayed for strength Wednesday morning, then put on her cape and bonnet and marched to Gus's cottage. He was waiting by the truck for her. When he opened his door to get in, she tugged on hers and slid onto the seat. No matter what this day should bring, Esther was determined not to fall apart the way she had during the MRI. She was a grown woman, and if she had cancer or some other dreadful disease, she would face it with bravery.

"Put your seat belt on." Gus pumped the gas several times before the old pickup started.

"Maybe you should wear yours too." Esther raised her chin and faced forward.

Gus glared at her, but he pulled the belt across his belly, groaning as he snapped it in place.

She turned and pointed a finger at him. "I do not want to hear anything foul from you today. You are to mind your manners and not upset me in any way."

They weren't even out of the driveway when Gus hit the brake abruptly.

Esther threw both hands against the dash so she wouldn't bang her head.

"If it's gonna be like this all day, maybe you better find another ride." Gus looked at her and raised an eyebrow.

"Just drive." Esther sighed.

After they were on the highway, Gus cut his eyes in her direction when he should have been watching the road. "This ain't a pretty side of you, Esther, all this hostility." He shook his head.

She coughed out a nervous laugh, covering her mouth in case any blood surfaced, but it didn't. "Gus Owens, I don't think you, of all people, should be telling me how to act. Do you ever listen to the way you talk to people? You are abrasive, often very rude, and I've never heard you pay anyone a compliment. You complain all the time and are generally a miserable person to be around. If I seem to be having one bad day, I'd appreciate it if you'd cut me some slack."

Gus grinned. "Cut you some slack? Ain't that kind of an English thing to say? Sounds funny coming from you."

"I probably heard it from you." She cut her eyes toward him. "And now that you've pointed it out, I won't be saying it again."

"Woman—yeah, *woman*—it's a good thing we're already on the highway, or I would have dropped you on the road back there. You wanna talk to me about being 'foul'? Maybe you can lose the attitude or find another ride back home."

Esther took a deep breath and released it slowly. "I'm sorry." She paused, thinking how poorly she'd treated Gus.

Most folks would say he had it coming, but it wasn't Esther's way to be so nasty.

"They are going to poke and prod me with more tests today, and then I have to wait to meet with the doctor so he can tell me if I'm going to die."

They were perfectly quiet for at least five minutes, the rumble of the truck not enough to drown out Esther's worries. She rolled the possibilities over, then tried to imagine how she would tell Lizzie that the Lord would be calling her home soon. Everything was God's will. Esther knew that. But she was terrified, which made her question how strong her faith really was.

"You're real pretty." Gus didn't look at her when he spoke.

Esther snapped her head to the left. "What?"

"You heard me. I shouldn't have to repeat it." He grumbled as he shifted the gear on the floorboard.

Esther realized her mouth was hanging open and snapped it closed. "What?" she asked again.

"Woman, you might be dying, but you're not hard of hearing. I said you're real pretty."

Esther closed her eyes and gave her head a quick shake. Maybe her mind was already taking a turn for the worse. "Gus, I'm a seventy-two-year-old, gray-haired, large woman with a roadmap of wrinkles, so I'm not sure what would make you say that. But I suppose a thank you is in order, so *danki*."

"You said you'd never heard me give anyone a compliment. I give you one, and this is how you act." He clicked his tongue.

"Sorry." She squeezed the handles of her purse and kept her eyes forward.

"You're pretty on the inside, too, and always real nice to people."

Esther threw her head back against the headrest. "The Lord is already preparing to take me home, because I am losing *mei* mind." With her head still pressed back, she turned to look at Gus. "Did I really just hear you give me a second compliment? Two in one day, in less than an hour?"

He wrinkled his nose but didn't answer. After a few minutes, she said, "Thank you, Gus, I appreciate that."

"You're welcome." He paused to grin at her. "Woman."

Esther smiled back at him. God never ceased to amaze her. Sometimes a good thing could come from the least expected person.

She sniffed the air. "That dreadful smell is gone." Pausing, she drew in another breath. "It smells like . . ." She thought for a moment. "Like apples and cinnamon."

"I wondered when you were gonna notice." Gus grimaced as he shoved the stick shift into place, grinding another gear. "You were right. There was a dead mouse under the hood."

"Well, whatever you sprayed inside the truck smells very nice."

He shrugged. "Yeah, I guess I had gotten used to it stinking. But I found some air freshener under the sink. I always buy the apple cinnamon kind. It was Heather's favorite when she was little."

Esther held her breath, debating what to say. It was Gus's

270

first mention of his daughter. She stayed quiet, fearing anything she said would send him into a tailspin, and today—of all days—she wanted to stay calm. And for Gus to do the same.

"I don't know how much you heard when Heather came to see me." Gus kept his eyes straight ahead with no readable expression on his face.

"I heard enough." Esther swallowed hard, then forced herself to take a deep breath.

After another minute, he said, "I had it coming, I guess—all the names she called me and stuff. But I guess I had hoped things would be different." Then he turned to Esther. "She ain't coming back. I'm pretty sure of that."

Esther decided to take a chance and jump into the conversation. "What prompted her visit after all this time?"

He burst out laughing. "Who knows. Maybe she thought she might need a kidney one day." He glared at Esther. "I don't want to talk about this anymore."

And just like that, Grumpy Gus returned full force. He'd shared more than he ever had, so Esther wasn't going to push. At least not today.

"I understand," she said softly. *Baby steps.*

They arrived at the hospital and parked, then Esther began walking toward the building. Gus patted her on the back.

"Esther, I feel like this God of yours still has plans for you. He ain't gonna take you home just yet."

"He's your *Gott*, too, Gus." Esther glanced up in time to see him crinkle his nose.

"Nah. There was a time when I thought so." He paused. "But God left me hung out to dry a long time ago."

Esther's people didn't minister by nature, but she couldn't help wondering if Gus's disposition was due to his lack of faith. Or maybe the world had kicked him hard one too many times, and he was kicking back twice as hard. Either way, Esther was convinced there was another man hiding inside Gus. A person who sometimes revealed his true self and wanted to escape the person he'd become.

As she walked up to the desk at the hospital, all thoughts of Gus fled, replaced with needles and tubes and . . . her results afterward.

TWENTY-ONE

ESTHER SUBMITTED TO THE WILL OF GOD, ENDURED HER final tests—mostly lab work and one X-ray—then she and Gus went to the building next to the hospital. Esther trembled on the inside, but outwardly, she presented herself to be the brave person she was not. She'd come up with a dozen different ways to tell Lizzie she was sick, possibly dying. The biggest and hardest part of the conversation would be convincing Lizzie that she could go on without her.

When the nurse opened the door and called her name, Esther had trouble standing up on her weak knees, but Gus's hand clutched her elbow and he helped her to her feet. As much as she didn't want him to see her fall apart, she didn't want to hear the news alone either.

She and Gus waited in her doctor's office. He was a young fellow, too young to be practicing medicine, Esther thought, but she'd been referred to him by her regular doctor.

"Stop looking like you're preparing for your own funeral," Gus grumbled.

Esther tried to picture Lizzie or Naomi sitting next to her, anyone with a more compassionate nature.

"Hello, Esther." Dr. Boone walked in wearing his crisp white coat and a stethoscope around his neck. Esther wanted to ask him how old he was, but she simply returned the greeting.

"Okay." He opened a file before scanning two pages, then looked at her. "You've got a nasty stomach ulcer, so you need to make some diet changes, and you'll need to take these pills, at least for a while. He pushed a small piece of paper toward her, a prescription she saw when she put her glasses on and looked closely.

"You mean to tell me, after all these tests and scaring the woman half to death, all she's got is an ulcer?" Gus groaned. "Seems a waste of money to me."

Esther held her breath, willing Gus to be quiet. "I don't have cancer? I'm not going to die?" she asked barely above a whisper.

Dr. Boone smiled. "Not any time soon. You're basically a healthy woman for your age, but your body is rejecting some of the food you eat. Here is a list of things you'll want to avoid." He handed Esther another piece of paper, larger and in color. "Your cholesterol is a little high, so I'm going to give you a prescription for that too." He began scribbling on another piece of paper.

"It's all a big scam for money, all those tests." Gus folded his arms across his big belly, but Esther ignored him. She had never danced in her life, but she was tempted to get up and give it a try, no matter how much Gus's comments embarrassed her.

"I'm afraid those tests were necessary to rule out other potential problems. But, Esther, you need to have regular checkups. And follow up with an eye doctor since it's been so long." The doctor stood, told Esther to call if she had any questions, then dismissed them, after Esther thanked him repeatedly.

On the ride home, Esther couldn't stop smiling. "I am so relieved. I've never been so relieved in *mei* life."

"How are you paying for all this? You and Lizzie don't seem to have financial problems, but you had a lot of tests, and MRIs ain't cheap." He raised an eyebrow. "You people don't have insurance, do you? Or Medicare?"

"We have a community fund that everyone contributes to for handling our medical costs. I chose not to use it. If a young person becomes ill, they might feel the financial strain, and I want there to be enough money in the fund for future generations. Lizzie and I are not wealthy by any stretch of the imagination, but our mother left plenty to sustain us." She paused. "I just hope I'm done with all of this."

"You best get off this irrational fear you have about your health. You're old and breaking down. There comes a time when you can't grease the parts anymore. They'll bust, and you either have to get new ones or do without. So you need to pay an occasional visit to a doctor for checkups. But eventually, you'll kick the bucket." He turned to her, frowning. "I thought your people were okay with death."

Esther didn't want to debate theology with Gus. "There is nothing you can say to ruin *mei* happy mood."

"Well, before you get too happy, you might want to check the foods you can't eat anymore."

"Whatever they are, I'm fine with it. I'm just relieved not to have anything seriously wrong." Esther took the list from her purse and scanned it. Most of it she could live with. She wasn't a fan of spicy foods, but there was one item on the list that caught her attention. "Oh dear."

Gus chuckled. "I'm gonna bet there's something on there about greasy food. You people gop everything up with lard and deep fry it."

She cut her eyes at him. "Say what you will, but I can change *mei* eating habits. Even if it means giving up fried foods."

"But is it really worth it? We're already old. Shouldn't we just enjoy ourselves? My blood sugar is off the chart, but I ain't giving up pie."

Esther lifted both eyebrows. "So I'm contributing to your poor health?"

"Probably not anymore. I reckon my pies will stop coming now that you don't need me."

She noticed a tinge of regret in his voice. "Gus, I have appreciated you driving me to these appointments, even though there ended up being only two." *Danki*, Gott. "But I will still bring you pie, maybe just not every day in rain or snow."

After a quick stop at Walmart to get Esther's prescriptions filled, it was a quiet ride the rest of the way—bumpy, but quiet.

276

By the time they returned home, Esther was still overjoyed, but also tired and in need of a nap.

She walked around the truck and waited for Gus to climb out and stand up. She looked up at him, then did something she never thought she would. "*Danki*," she said as she wrapped her arms around him.

He stiffened right away and kept his hands at his sides. After a few seconds, he patted her on the back.

"You're welcome," he said softly.

Gus would never be what Esther would consider a gentleman, but she'd seen a few soft spots. There was hope for him.

❧

Naomi peered out the living room window and raised her hand to her mouth.

Lizzie stood next to her, mouth agape. "Did I just see what I think I did? Was Esther hugging Gus?"

"*Ya*, I can't believe it either." Naomi watched Esther leave Gus. "I've also seen her coming from his *haus* before, and she was *smiling*."

"She's smiling now! And she's always taking him his mail or even defending him." Lizzie looked like the blood was being siphoned from her face. "Esther's lost her mind. I wouldn't touch that man with a ten-foot pole, and yet . . . *mei schweschder* is hugging him?" She looked at Naomi with wide eyes.

Naomi was having a hard time believing Esther could be

involved with Gus in an intimate way, but she sure had been spending a lot of time with him.

"Maybe we shouldn't say anything. It's her business." Naomi chewed on her bottom lip.

"Since when have Esther or I minded our own business?" Lizzie marched to the middle of the living room and clutched her hands in front of her.

Naomi followed and stood next to her, mirroring her stance.

Esther walked into the room with a smile that stretched across her face.

"Do you have something you need to tell us?" Lizzie lifted her chin, eyeing her sister as her nostrils flared.

Esther's cheerfulness didn't diminish. "*Ya*, as a matter of fact, I do."

Lizzie fell onto the couch, closed her eyes, and threw her head back. "*Gott* take me now. This can't be true."

"*Ach*, well, I don't know how you found out. Maybe there was a message on the machine, but it is certainly wonderful news that I'm happy to share with you now. Don't look so upset. I just didn't want you to worry until I was certain of everything."

Naomi wasn't sure Lizzie was breathing as the color continued draining from her face. Naomi put a hand to her forehead. "Esther, have you been keeping a secret from us?"

"*Ya*." Her joyous expression fell. "And I'm sorry about that. But I'm going to be okay, and I thank *Gott* for that."

Lizzie bolted from the couch with the energy of a teenager, her fists clenched at her sides. "How is being in the arms of that awful man going to make you okay? Exactly how long have you been carrying on with Gus?"

Esther's mouth fell open. "What?"

Naomi cleared her throat. "I-I saw you coming from his *haus*, happy and smiling one night. He's been driving you around, and you always take him pie or deliver his mail." She paused, waiting for Esther to say something, but her face turned as ashen as Lizzie's. "I'm afraid we figured it out after we saw you hugging him just now."

❧

Esther closed her mouth, bent in half, and laughed so hard, she hoped she didn't fall over.

"See, Naomi. I told you. Esther's lost her mind." Lizzie sat in one of the rocking chairs, rubbing her temples.

Esther finally straightened, but she couldn't stop laughing, and her eyes began to water. "You . . . you . . ." She pointed back and forth between Lizzie and Naomi. "You think I'm having a romantic relationship with *Gus*?"

The laughter started up again, until she finally forced herself under control. "I haven't been completely honest." She looked up. *Forgive me*, Gott. "But I assure you there is nothing inappropriate going on with me and Gus. The fact that you would even think that is . . ." She covered her mouth as another round of laughter built up.

Naomi grinned. "Too bad. I was hoping to lock you two in the basement."

"Stop. Stop. Stop." Lizzie stood up. "Then why have you been sneaking around and having him take you places?"

Esther didn't think she'd laughed so hard in years. This had been a good day in so many ways, and she couldn't leave Lizzie and Naomi in suspense any longer. She explained everything.

"You should have told us." Naomi frowned. "We could have been there for you."

Lizzie covered her face with her hands and shook her head, grumbling. After she lowered her hands, she said, "Don't ever keep anything like that from me again. I know why you did it, but don't do it again." She threw her arms in the air. "See how lying affects those around you! I almost had a heart attack thinking Gus Owens could end up being *mei bruder*-in-law."

Esther chuckled. "I can't believe you two even came up with such silliness." She raised a finger. "However, I did get to know Gus a little better, and as much as he tries to hide it, there is some *gut* in him, and——"

Lizzie covered her ears. "La, la, la, la. I don't want to hear it." She went into her bedroom and closed the door behind her. Esther turned to Naomi, who grinned and shrugged.

"It was hard to imagine." Naomi giggled. "But I'm just glad you're all right." After a big hug, Naomi asked to see Esther's food list.

"I can make some adjustments to our menu." Naomi eyed the items Esther shouldn't eat.

"*Nee*, don't make changes for me. Lizzie likes her fried and spicy foods, and I don't want her to be denied. I'll eat what I know I'm allowed and together we can probably come up with some new recipes." She shook her head, grinning. "Me and Gus." Then she roared with laughter again. "I'm going to go take a nap," she managed to say as she walked to her bedroom.

⁓∞⁓

Naomi spent the next few days preparing for the seven guests they had coming to stay at the inn, all *Englisch*. Lizzie and Esther helped, but Naomi handled most of the work by herself. It kept her distracted, but Amos still crept into her thoughts daily. She wondered if he thought about her too.

Their first visitors showed up near the three o'clock check-in time—two older women from Georgia who were traveling farther north. They were staying two nights. A group of three women, also older, arrived a bit later from Indianapolis. They were simply on holiday to "experience the Amish life." The other four guests would trickle in over the next few days.

After supper, Naomi cleared the table and made sure everyone had what they needed for the evening. Then she put on her heavy coat, readied her buggy, and left to meet Thomas for supper. He'd been good about giving her some time, and even though it hadn't been very long, Naomi had sorted out her feelings and knew what she needed to tell him. Postponing it any longer seemed cruel.

He stood up from the table at Gasthof Village when Naomi walked in. She'd insisted on meeting him there so she could control how long she stayed. The restaurant wasn't a place either of them frequented. It was mostly a tourist attraction tailored toward the English, but the food was good. Naomi also knew Thomas wouldn't hug her, try to kiss her, or show any public signs of affection.

"You look beautiful," he said as he pulled out her chair.

"*Danki.*" She willed herself not to cry and managed to order an iced tea when the server came, but once they were alone again, her bottom lip began to tremble. The restaurant had a lavish buffet with a variety of offerings, but neither of them moved.

Thomas's eyes began to water when Naomi's did. "Don't do this," he said in a shaky voice.

"I'm sorry." She blotted her eyes with her napkin. "I think a part of me will always love you, Thomas, but I don't want to marry you."

He folded his hands on the table and stared at them for a few seconds before looking up at her. "Is this because of Amos or because I left and was with another woman?"

Naomi still didn't know what *with* meant, but it didn't matter anymore. "I guess both." She paused, trying to recall the way she'd practiced the conversation in her mind. "I prayed for you to come back. I waited. It was all I wanted—to be your fiancée again. But if you loved me as much as you say you do, you wouldn't have left me in the first place."

"It's Amos." Even though tears pooled in the corners of his eyes, his face turned red. "He did this."

"Thomas . . ." She took a deep breath. "Amos is gone. And has been for several days. I don't know if I will ever see him again. But having another man show me attention gave me hope that there is someone out there for me, someone who will never leave me." Even though her feelings for Amos ran deeper than she was letting on, she didn't have the heart to share that with Thomas. It served no purpose.

"Naomi, I promise you with everything I am that I will never leave you again. You are *mei* number one, always and forever."

She bit her bottom lip so hard she feared it might bleed. When she finally opened her mouth to speak, her voice felt shaky. "But"—she twisted the napkin in her lap, as a tear trailed down her cheek—"you're not *mei* number one anymore."

His face reddened even more. "Then it *is* Amos."

"I honestly don't know. I haven't known him very long, and I don't know if I'll ever see him again." Naomi paused as Amos's face appeared in her mind. "Whether or not he is the one for me is not the point. I'm telling you that I know you are not the one for me, and I'm so sorry." She dabbed at her eyes, then noticed two servers, both young women, staring at them.

"Is it because I didn't give you enough time? I can give you more time."

Naomi recognized his pain. She could practically feel it boring into her heart. But it would be cruel not to be honest with him.

"I don't need more time." She spoke the words as firmly as she could. She slid back her chair, feeling like she was going to burst into a stream of tears any second.

"I'm sorry," she said again, then she walked out of the restaurant.

❧

Later in the evening Naomi decided to write Amos back. She was still confused by his letter. Parts of it sounded joyful, but also infused with regret. Was he sincere about giving her time to work out her feelings for Thomas? Did he even want to hear from her again?

She turned up the propane heater in her room, then scurried into bed and slid under the covers. After pulling a notepad and pen from her nightstand, she nervously tapped the pen against the paper as she tried to put into words how she was feeling. She hadn't thought she should write him until she had ended things with Thomas, but she'd been truthful when she told Thomas her decision wasn't because of Amos. Something had been lost between her and Thomas, even though it had taken her a while to see it and then to figure out that it couldn't be found.

She reread Amos's letter, then finally put the pen to paper. The red pen.

> Dear Amos,
>
> I regret that we weren't able to say goodbye, but I appreciate that you understood *mei* need to work through *mei* feelings for Thomas. I owed him that. In the end I came to the conclusion that he is not the right man for *mei*.

I want to be someone's first choice with no doubts. It was difficult to tell him I did not want to pursue our relationship, but it was the right thing to do. I no longer feel that he is *mei* number one so to continue our engagement wouldn't have been fair to him.

I am happy I was able to bring some joy and laughter into your life. Spending time with you allowed me to crawl out of the dark place I had been hiding in too. I can still hear your laughter. I can still see your smile. And I can picture that intense look you get when you paint—so serious. I, too, shall return to painting, but not without thinking about you. No more gray tints for *mei* either, only colors that lead me onto the right path, one filled with love.

She stopped and read his letter again. In some ways, there seemed to be a finality to it, especially what he wrote at the end—*To sum it up, you brought joy back into* mei *life, showed me how to laugh again, and helped me recapture a part of myself I thought was gone forever. I will always be grateful to you for that. I will pray for you. I will miss you. But mostly, I hope you find the peace in your heart that I know you are searching for.* Then he had signed it *Fondly, Amos.*

Fondly? She tapped the pen to the pad again. Then she wrote how she felt.

I am wildly attracted to you, pretty sure I'm in love with you even though we haven't known each other long, and I wish you'd get back here as soon as possible!

Growling, she squeezed her eyes closed, knowing she could never send such a letter. She ripped it up into tiny pieces and dropped it in the trash can by her bed.

If Amos wanted her to write him back, wouldn't he have said so? The finality of his words echoed in her mind, over and over.

TWENTY-TWO

Amos dialed the number for The Peony Inn, the same way he had every day for the past week. Like Esther and Lizzie, Amos's family had a phone in their barn. He hung up before the call went through. Again. Some folks had cell phones these days, but he didn't and neither did Naomi.

He'd been home over two weeks with no reply letter. She'd obviously stepped back into her role as Thomas's fiancée. Amos wanted to be happy for her, but he hadn't realized how much he cared for her until he'd been away from her for a few days.

He found himself loitering around the mailbox daily between two and two-thirty, the mailman's regular delivery time. Nothing. He hadn't been completely truthful in his letter to her. Yes, she'd shown him how to laugh again and to open his heart, but she'd also stolen a chunk of his heart.

He had tried to paint down by the creek, but when the

grayish tints started to show back up in his paintings, he gave up. Some days, he really was grateful to have known her. Other days, he wished he'd never met her. God had given him a glimpse of what a second chance could look like, but now all he could do was think about what he'd lost. Again.

He'd only loved two women in his life. He seriously doubted there would be a third. But could he really love Naomi after such a short time? Or was their only role in each other's life simply to bring the other out of the pit of despair they'd been living in? Each day without seeing Naomi seemed like one more step backward.

As he stared at the phone, he wondered what she was doing. Was she with Thomas? Was she still painting?

He had just pried open a can of glossy sealer so he could apply the final coat to a special-order table, when he heard the mailman slide to a stop in front of their mailbox. Instinctively, he set the paintbrush down to go check, then thought better of it. If he hadn't heard from her by now, he wasn't going to.

With Thanksgiving in a week, he reminded himself that he had a lot to be thankful for—his family, his good health, his business.

But his heart just wasn't in it.

∞

Esther and Lizzie were sipping coffee at the kitchen table after they said goodbye to the last of their guests. So far, they didn't have any reservations for Thanksgiving Day. That could change, but Esther suspected most folks would rather be with their families.

"Where's Naomi?" She asked, realizing she hadn't seen her since breakfast.

"She walked down to the pond." Lizzie sighed. "But she didn't take her painting supplies."

"She seems depressed again. Do you think it's because she and Thomas broke up, or because Amos is gone?"

"*Ach*, it's because Amos is gone." Lizzie smiled, dentures perfectly in place. "And I know that to be a fact. I was upstairs last week, and Naomi had written Amos a letter. I was emptying the trash, and I saw all these tiny little pieces of paper. One caught my eye because it said, *Dear Amos*." She lowered her eyes. "I tried to piece them all back together again, but it was impossible. There were just too many of them."

"Why didn't you tell me?"

"I did."

"*Nee*, you didn't." Esther reconsidered. Maybe Lizzie did tell her. Neither of their memories were what they used to be. "I considered calling Amos's *mudder* to see if she thought he was pining over Naomi, but since he hasn't called or written, I decided not to."

"They're meant to be together," Lizzie said. "Calling off the engagement with Thomas just confirmed what we already knew."

"I think Naomi would have eventually called off the

engagement anyway." Esther got up and poured herself another cup of coffee, then refilled Lizzie's cup. "Mary and John are coming over for Thanksgiving dinner."

Lizzie's eyebrows shot up. "Really? We ask them every year, and they always decline. It hurts *mei* heart to know they're alone on the holiday. Their families live so far away. I understand why they moved here for John's job, but no one should be alone on Thanksgiving."

"I'm glad you feel that way." Esther smiled. "Because Gus is coming this year too."

Lizzie slouched in her chair and closed her eyes. "The holiday is ruined! Why in the world did you ask him?"

"I've never told you before, but I've asked him every year, and he's told me a firm no every time. But this year he said yes." Esther smiled again.

Still slouched in the chair, Lizzie wiggled a finger at Esther. "Are you sure you and him aren't having some kind of—"

"*Ach*, hush now. Of course not." Esther chuckled. "I can't help but laugh every time I think about you and Naomi having that notion in your heads."

"Then why is he coming this year? You know he will be his rude, grumpy self. Doesn't seem fair to the rest of us, Esther." Lizzie rolled her lip into a pout.

"I don't know why he chose to come this year. But you are going to be nice to him. And I mean it, Lizzie. I'm going to have a talk with Gus about the proper way to behave, and I expect you to treat him kindly."

"I just won't talk at all." Lizzie held her pout as she ran a finger around the rim of her cup. "But I'm telling you, that man will never change."

Esther thought about Gus's references to God in the past. It sounded like Gus had a relationship with God at some point. Maybe he could find his way back to Him.

"Just do your best to be nice to him. I'm going to head over there now. It's supposed to freeze tonight." She went to the counter and picked up the slice of chocolate pie she'd already packed.

"And you take him pie most days." Lizzie let out an exaggerated sigh. "You're a *gut* woman, Esther. He surely doesn't deserve it."

"I'll be back."

Esther left Lizzie pouting in the kitchen and went to the living room. She pushed her arms into the sleeves of her heavy jacket and placed her bonnet on over her prayer covering.

When she arrived at Gus's cottage, he opened the door before she knocked. He was looking like the old Gus, a bit unkept, hair too long, beard scraggly, and wearing a stained white T-shirt. Esther saw Whiskers behind him, sleeping on a rug in front of the fireplace.

He held out his hand for the pie. "It's been three days."

"Gus, it rained yesterday. You're lucky I came today. It's cold out here, and tonight it will be even colder." She cleared her throat. "May I come in, please? I need to talk to you."

He pushed his chest out, squinting at her. "What about?"

Esther shivered. "I'll tell you when you step aside and let me in."

Grumbling, he moved out of the way. Things inside had returned to the way they'd always been and a strange odor hung in the air.

Esther glanced around for a place to sit and chose a rocking chair. Gus obviously always sat in the same spot on the couch since it was worn down and lower than the rest of the couch. A paper plate with a half-eaten sandwich was sitting on the end table next to that end of the couch, along with three glasses, a stack of newspapers, and a banana.

After she was seated, she said, "We are very happy you are coming for Thanksgiving."

Gus laughed heartily, jowls jiggling. He sat on the couch, then leaned forward. "I'm only going cuz it will upset Lizzie."

Esther folded her hands in her lap. "That's what I'd like to talk to you about. I have already spoken to Lizzie about this matter. I told her I expect her to be gracious. We all have a lot to be thankful for. And I expect you to show her the same kindness." She wanted to tell him to clean himself up but decided Gus was a work in progress, and she shouldn't push it.

"I've changed my mind. I ain't going." He crossed an ankle over his knee. "I don't know why I said I would anyway."

Esther stood and walked toward him until she was standing right in front of him with her hands on her hips.

"You will be there, Gus Owens. And you will be nice to Lizzie and everyone else in attendance. You will remember to say thank you and please, and you will be polite and grateful."

Gus's bushy eyebrows drew inward. "I don't like this bossy side of you, Esther." He shook his head. "I ain't going."

"*Ya*, you are." She grinned. "Or no more pie." She glared at him. "Ever."

She walked out, slammed the door to the cottage, and figured Gus would be a no-show for Thanksgiving. But she'd done the best she could.

⌒∞⌒

Naomi gazed at the sunset. Since the corn had been harvested, the orange rays no longer filtered through the green stalks, but it was still beautiful and worthy of a painting. She'd tried, but without Amos by her side, her painting had reverted to a dull picture of a lovely place.

Even so, she enjoyed standing by the water and watching the sun set. There was something to be said for serenity. When such peacefulness wraps around a person, it spills over into everything they do. Without it, things can never be as we want them to be, and that included painting.

She pulled her coat tightly around her as she recalled memories from her past. Her parents dying. Thomas leaving. Thomas returning. Amos arriving. Amos leaving. But the Thanksgiving season was upon them, so she squeezed her eyes closed and forced herself to think about the things she was grateful for. Her good health. Lizzie and Esther—and their good health. Her life in their house and the comic relief that came almost daily—and was a nice distraction.

Despite her heart having been shattered by Thomas, she'd thought love had found her again.

"Want some company?"

She turned around, surprised to see Lizzie, since she never came down to the pond. It was cold this evening and quite a trek for her older friends.

"*Ya*, sure. I'm just taking in this beautiful sunset." Naomi pointed in front of her as she and Lizzie sat on the bench. "When the sun is exactly halfway down against the horizon, the water twinkles like a million tiny stars floating on top of the pond."

Lizzie watched quietly beside her.

"See." Naomi smiled. "Then the water begins to dull as if preparing for nighttime, even though there are still twenty minutes before it will be completely dark."

"Why aren't you painting?" Lizzie looked her way. "Is it because Amos isn't here to paint with you?"

Leave it to Lizzie to be direct. "*Ya*, I think maybe it is." Naomi was surprised she admitted her true feelings to Lizzie, but there didn't seem to be any reason not to. Amos was gone, so Lizzie couldn't play matchmaker or lock anyone in the basement.

"Then why haven't you told that boy you're in *lieb* with him?"

Naomi turned to Lizzie. "Can a person really fall in love so quickly?"

"Of course. I met *mei* Reuben, then two weeks later we were promised to each other, and we married the following month." Lizzie smiled her perfectly white smile. "And we spent fifty-one years in *lieb*." She shrugged. "Sometimes you just know."

Naomi smiled. "I bet you miss him."

"Everyday. But I will see him again." She paused. "Um, he left you a letter. Did he say he loved you?"

"*Nee*. He thought I needed time to work out *mei* feelings about Thomas."

"Did you write him back? Did you tell him you called off the engagement?"

"*Nee*. His letter said I helped him find his way back to a happier place, but he didn't ask me to write him back. He basically wished me well." Naomi knew the letter by heart from reading it every night.

Lizzie groaned. "Then he doesn't even know you broke up with Thomas. It was clear that boy had feelings for you."

"He lives in Ohio. The geography doesn't work. And if he felt so strongly about me, he would have written."

"*Ach*, I don't think I believe that."

Naomi wanted to change the subject. "I heard Gus is coming for Thanksgiving next week."

Lizzie shook her head as she clicked her tongue. "That's because Esther has taken leave of her senses, or she's punishing me for something I'm unaware of. Can you even imagine how that man will ruin the holiday?"

Naomi agreed with Lizzie but felt like she should encourage her to behave. "Maybe it won't be so bad. And it seems important that we're all together. Even Mary and John are coming."

"That part, I'm happy about. But I don't even like to be around Gus, and we've never sat down for a meal together."

"I'm going to prepare some special side dishes, things Esther can eat that shouldn't upset her stomach." Naomi turned her eyes to the setting sun. "We better go back to the *haus*. It's going to be completely dark soon."

As they started back, Naomi glanced at Gus's cottage. "I'm going to go check on Whiskers. Gus seems to have adopted her."

Lizzie shivered. "That black cat and Gus deserve each other, although I'm surprised he's taking care of anyone besides himself, especially since it's a black cat that will give him nothing but bad luck."

"Gus seems to have had plenty of that before the cat came along." She waved at Lizzie as they parted ways. "I won't be long."

She made the short trek to Gus's house, knocked lightly on the door, and waited. He answered with a frown on his face. "What do you want?"

"I was just checking on Whiskers."

Gus pointed over his shoulder. "All it does is sleep and eat."

Naomi peered around him and saw the cat asleep in front of the fireplace.

"Is that all?" Gus looped his thumbs beneath his suspenders and raised an eyebrow.

Naomi was cold, but she didn't treasure the idea of going into Gus's house. "*Nee*. I also wanted to tell you that it is important to Esther for Thanksgiving to be a nice day. I hope you and Lizzie will be able to get along."

"This is getting ridiculous. You're the second person to

instruct me on how to behave at Thanksgiving. Esther already gave me a lecture. I'm tempted not to go, except I'd rather not eat another frozen turkey dinner out of a box again this year." He paused, grumbling. "And I can't control the way Lizzie treats people. Grumpy old woman."

Naomi pressed her lips together to keep from smiling. The man obviously had no idea that his nickname was Grumpy Gus.

"Well, I'm glad you're coming." Naomi smiled. "I best get back before dark."

"That cat is already causing me bad luck." He slammed the door, and Naomi started back to the main house. She prayed that Thanksgiving would be a good day and that Gus and Lizzie would be nice—or at least civil to each other.

Then she prayed for Amos, wishing him the best life had to offer. If she couldn't be with him, she could at least pray for him, like he said he would pray for her.

I hope you find the peace in your heart that I know you are searching for.

TWENTY-THREE

ESTHER HAD DECORATED THE HOUSE FOR FALL AT THE BE-ginning of the season, and the Lord blessed them with a beautiful day for Thanksgiving, filled with sunshine beaming through the windows. A wonderful aroma filled the air as she opened the oven to check on the turkey. Lizzie had prepared the bird, stuffed it, and basted it several times throughout the morning.

Lizzie and Naomi scurried around the kitchen. Dinner would feel more like a family affair this year. Esther had her concerns about Lizzie and Gus being at the same table for a meal, but she wasn't completely convinced Gus would show up. But it would be nice to have Mary and John in attendance.

She walked into the dining room. "The table looks lovely." Esther pressed her hands together as she eyed the good china set for six.

"Naomi gets credit," Lizzie yelled from the kitchen.

Esther headed toward the front door when she heard a knock. It was John and Mary.

"*Wie bischt*, and Happy Thanksgiving." She waited while they shed their coats, hanging them on the rack by the door. "We're so glad you could make it this year. Although, I'm sure you miss your families back home."

"*Ya*, we do, but we are happy to be here," Mary said.

They glanced at each other and smiled, then wished Esther a happy Thanksgiving. Esther was glad to see that the couple looked happy. So many times she'd sensed unease at their house, and she'd worried about the heartbreaking conversation she had with Mary recently.

"If you'd like to take a seat in the dining room, we're just waiting on Gus, then we'll fill the table with all the wonderful offerings *Gott* has blessed us with on this special day of thanksgiving."

Esther walked back into the kitchen just as someone else knocked on the door.

"He's here." Lizzie lifted her eyes to the ceiling. "Stay with me today, *Gott*. Don't let me sink to that man's disgusting ways."

Esther sighed and left her sister and Naomi in the kitchen. When she opened the front door, Gus was standing in front of her. His Amish haircut had grown out, but he'd brushed the thick gray mass to the side and tucked the rest of it behind his ears. He may even have trimmed his beard a little. He wore a red long-sleeve shirt that was tightly tucked into a pair of tan slacks, held up with suspenders.

"Welcome, Gus. We're happy you could make it, and you look very nice." Esther desperately wanted to get a pair of scissors and cut his hair again, but that was a project for another time, if Gus would allow it.

"Yeah, you look okay too." Gus went to the fireplace, looped his thumbs beneath his suspenders, and shook his head. "Women. Don't know how to build a proper fire." He lowered the screen, stoked the wood, and added three more logs from the carrier.

"*Danki*." She clasped her hands in front of her and waited.

"Yeah, okay. You're welcome. Now where's the food? I'm starving." He sniffed the air and moved like an animal following a scent until he was in the dining room. He nodded at Mary and John.

"Ha. Can't believe you two showed up. You're always looking all—"

"Gus," Esther said firmly as she gritted her teeth.

He took a deep breath, then pulled out the chair at one end of the table, the one usually reserved for Lizzie.

Naomi and Esther delivered the last of the food to the table, then joined their guests. After a few comments about the weather from John, Naomi looked over her shoulder as they all waited for Lizzie.

"Excuse me." Esther left the room and found Lizzie pressed up against the counter in the kitchen.

"I can't do it. I can't break bread with that man." She scrunched up her face as she tossed her head from side to side.

"You can, and you will. Stop acting like a child." Esther

tugged on Lizzie's arm and pulled her along until they were standing in the middle of the dining room.

With two chairs left to fill, one next to Gus and the other across the table, Lizzie chose to face off with Gus at the far end of the oblong table. She slowly eased into the chair, raised her chin, and squinted at him. At least they were as far away from each other as possible. And Lizzie wasn't making a fuss about Gus being in her chair.

Gus grinned as he stared back at her.

This might have been a very bad idea.

"Let's lower our heads in prayer and thanksgiving for this wonderful meal and for friends and family." Esther waited until everyone bowed, except for Gus.

She stared at him and after a heavy sigh, he lowered his head, and Esther followed suit.

Everyone silently prayed. When Esther lifted her head, everyone else did too at about the same time. Except for Gus. He either had a lot to say to God, which Esther doubted, or he was waiting for someone to lead the prayer, like the English normally do.

"How long do we stay like this?" He grumbled with his head down and eyes closed.

Lizzie snickered, which caused Gus to bolt upright.

Here we go.

Lizzie slapped a hand over her mouth and quieted her laughter. Gus snarled at her as he sat back down. Lizzie snarled back. It was like watching two wild animals summing each other up as prey.

Esther cleared her throat, and they both stopped gritting their teeth at each other. Lizzie would likely show her teeth a lot today, since she had gotten more comfortable wearing the dentures. Esther hadn't seen her moving them around in her mouth all morning.

"John, it's tradition in our family for a man to cut the turkey. Would you care to do the honors?" Esther nodded to the large bird at Gus's end of the table.

"*Ya*, sure." John rose from his chair just as Gus scooted back his own chair and stood.

"Boy, how many turkeys have you carved? And it's already right in front of me." Gus sighed.

Esther wondered when he had last washed his hands. Judging by the looks of his fingernails, not recently. He positioned the large fork and knife and began to slice the turkey with surprising precision.

"I used to work at a meat market."

Esther hadn't known that detail about him. Actually, she knew very little about Gus. He continued carving, then took a big breath. "This is one good-looking bird. It's juicy, cooked just right."

"Lizzie was in charge of the turkey." Esther smiled.

Gus froze.

Lizzie covered her mouth, coughed, and mumbled something under her breath.

"You got something to say, Woman?" Gus set down the knife and fork, glaring at Esther's sister.

Mary clinked her fork against her glass of tea. "Um, I have

something to say." She turned to John and smiled. "Actually, *we* have something to say."

Esther put a hand to her chest, thankful for Mary's perfect timing. She hoped and prayed it might be the news Mary and John had been waiting for.

"We are with child," Mary said as she sat taller, her eyes moist.

"*Ach*, sweet *maedel*, we are so happy for you." Esther softly clapped her hands. "This just adds to our celebration today."

Naomi and Lizzie also congratulated the young couple.

"Kids ain't nothing but trouble." Gus didn't look up from his work on the turkey, carving it as if his life depended on perfection. "First it's diapers and crying all night, then the next thing you know, they're sneaking out of the house, drinking, and partying. Oh, and stealing your car. Nothing but trouble."

Lizzie stood up and slammed her palm on the table. "You shut your mouth, Gus Owens. A child is a blessing! Esther and I would have given anything to have *kinner*. Just because you ruined your relationship with your *dochder* doesn't mean all children are trouble."

"Please stop!" Esther said loudly as her stomach began to churn.

Gus glowered at Lizzie. "I thought if I came today, maybe you'd have the good sense to keep your mouth shut. I should have known better."

Lizzie turned to Esther. "I told you so. He's a mean man, and he's never going to change."

He set down the knife and fork. "I don't need this. I'm

going home." He glared at Lizzie. "I'll send Whiskers back over here in my place, since I know how much you like the critters."

"Get out!" Lizzie yelled.

Instead of leaving, Gus turned to Esther. She could feel the tears burning the corners of her eyes, but she also saw the raw hurt in Gus's expression.

"I'm sorry, Esther."

"Gus, I appreciate that," she said, her voice trembling. "But please apologize to Lizzie and the others too."

He turned to the young couple, who both donned perplexed expressions. "Mary, John, I'm sorry." Then he looked at Naomi and apologized.

"Lizzie too." Esther took a deep breath as Gus's face turned bright red and he turned to Lizzie.

"Say it nicely," Lizzie said, batting her eyes at him.

"I ain't doing it!" Gus's jowls hung low as he bellowed at Lizzie.

"Because you're never going to change!"

"It's Thanksgiving. Stop!" Esther stood up. "Both of you be quiet. If you have nothing nice to say to each other, then don't talk."

∞

Naomi eyed the food on the table, a tremendous meal they'd worked so hard on. Esther had wanted this to be a special day, and Lizzie and Gus were ruining it. For all of them. She cringed as they continued to spat insults at each other, despite Esther's plea. It was a horrible display. Poor Mary and John, their eyes grew rounder and rounder. Naomi wanted to scream, but she didn't want to add to the chaos.

A loud whistle filled the room, and all the yelling came to an abrupt halt. Naomi looked in the direction the noise had come from and her jaw dropped as her heart flipped in her chest.

Amos.

He scratched his forehead. "I tried to knock, but obviously no one heard me." He glanced around the table. "Since everyone is yelling."

Naomi stood up, her heart thumping wildly. "What are you doing here?"

He grinned. "*Ach,* well . . . I was accepting your invitation for Thanksgiving. I only received your letter three days ago, and I got on a bus as soon as I could." He smiled at Naomi before his expression sobered. "I didn't know I'd be walking into this, but whatever is going on here, I'm happy to see you."

Naomi swallowed hard. "What letter?"

Amos reached into his pocket and held up a piece of paper. "The one you sent me."

"Um . . . I didn't—" She clamped her lips together as she rubbed her forehead. Then she saw Lizzie slouching farther and farther into her chair.

"There's your culprit!" Gus pointed to Lizzie.

Naomi stared at the woman, her heart still beating like a base drum. "Lizzie?"

She slouched farther into her chair. "You two just needed a little push. I saw the letter you wrote to him all torn up in your trash can." She shrugged. "I couldn't read it. It was in so many little pieces. So I did the best I could to recreate it."

"Lizzie! How could you?" Naomi laid her palms on the table and hung her head before she looked back at Lizzie. "How could you do something like that?"

"Well, that explains a lot," Amos said, frowning, and blushing slightly as he lifted the letter.

"Everyone is yelling at me!" Lizzie's bottom lip began to tremble.

Esther covered her face with her hands and shook her head.

"Amos, can I please talk to you in the other room?" Naomi pointed at Gus and Lizzie. "When we come back, this better be a room filled with love and thankfulness." She turned to Mary and John. "I'm so sorry you had to see all of this, but please, everyone go ahead and eat."

Mary and John waved her off, saying it was fine. Which, of course, it wasn't.

"Sounds like I made a long trip for nothing," Amos said when they reached the mudroom where they would have some privacy.

"I am horrified that Lizzie did this." Her stomach swirled and she was scared to read the letter, but seeing Amos tempered her nerves. "Can I please read the letter?"

"It didn't sound like you, but I was so excited to receive it . . ." He handed her the piece of paper.

306

Naomi took a deep breath and began reading the hand-written letter that didn't even resemble her penmanship.

My Beloved Amos,

I have missed you since the day you left here. I broke things off with Thomas. Lizzie was right, he's a cad. I don't laugh anymore since you've been gone. The truth is, I love you very much, and I belong with you. I don't paint either because you are my red color.

Naomi covered her mouth with her hand, really scared to go on, as humiliation filled her from head to toe.

There is no peace in *mei* heart without you here. You shouldn't have left without saying goodbye. Our heart armor is gone, so let's try to make a romance work. I'm willing if you are because I think you are the most hand-some man I've ever met. You work hard too.

Come back to *mei*, *mei lieb*. I'll be waiting with open arms. Can you be here by Thanksgiving?

All my love forever and
ever and ever and ever,
Naomi

She bent over, torn between laughter and tears. When she straightened, she didn't know what to say, and Amos was pale.

"I feel like a dunce." He pushed back the rim of his hat. "It didn't sound like something you'd write, but I wanted to believe it so much that I ignored the obvious. I should have known Lizzie or Esther wrote it."

Naomi started laughing. "You do know, only Lizzie would do something like this?"

"Did you really write me a letter, then tear it up?" Amos's expression was unreadable.

"*Ya*, I did. I didn't mail it because your letter sounded so final." She paused, taking a deep breath. "You didn't call or write."

"I assumed you were working things out with Thomas. I wanted you to have time to figure out what you really wanted." He stepped closer to her, his eyes locking with hers. "Is that part of the letter true, that you are no longer with Thomas?"

"That part is true." Naomi couldn't pull her eyes from his as the familiar longing to be in his arms consumed her.

"Do you want me to leave?" Amos's chest rose and fell as he spoke.

Naomi shook her head. "*Nee*, I want you to stay."

He tugged at his ear as he avoided her eyes. "I feel silly, thinking you wrote all of that."

She stepped closer to him, close enough to lean up and kiss him softly on the mouth. "It's a terribly written letter, and I would never write such things."

He eased her away, and when their eyes met again, she said, "But every single word of that letter is true." She'd put her heart out there, and she held her breath as she waited for a response. "So I guess I need to know how you feel."

He cupped her cheeks and brushed a gentle kiss on her lips. "Maybe I should show you just how much I *lieb* you." And he kissed her the way she remembered, and she went weak in the knees.

"Listen," he said after several seconds. "It's quiet in the dining room." Then he grinned. "I'm hungry."

Naomi laughed, and they walked hand in hand back to the dining room. Someone had already set an extra place setting on the table.

Amos walked to where Lizzie was still slouching in her chair. "Shame on you, Lizzie."

"I know, I know. I was bad." She squeezed her eyes closed and bowed her head.

Amos leaned down and kissed her on the forehead. "But *danki*."

Lizzie glanced at Esther, who was smiling. Then she turned to Gus. "See, you baboon. It worked!"

Gus looked directly at Esther, then he forked a bite of turkey and stayed quiet.

Esther glared at Lizzie, who threw her head back and groaned.

"Okay, okay." She sat taller and looked at Gus. "I'm sorry I called you a baboon."

"Apology accepted." Gus cleared his throat. "I've been waiting a long time to hear you apologize for the way you treat me."

Naomi braced herself for the explosion to come. Then Gus grinned. "You look nice today, Lizzie."

"*Danki*, Gus." The words seemed unnatural coming from Lizzie's mouth, as if someone was holding a gun to her head.

Naomi's mouth fell open, but when she looked at Esther, the woman winked. There must have been some coaching going on while she and Amos were away.

Lizzie turned to Amos. "Are you staying?"

He looked at Naomi and grinned. "Forever and ever and ever and ever, if she'll have me."

Naomi blinked back tears and silently thanked God for this second chance for her and Amos.

"I will," she said. "Forever and ever and ever and ever."

EPILOGUE

ONE YEAR LATER

ESTHER LIFTED THE TURKEY FROM THE OVEN, HAPPY TO have her family seated in the dining room for another Thanksgiving dinner. As she recalled last year's holiday, she cringed, even though the day had a happy ending. This year would be even better, and Gus and Lizzie had promised to behave.

The table was short two place settings this year. Mary and John had decided to move closer to their families after becoming pregnant. They were missed, but the timing had worked out perfectly for Naomi and Amos to rent the *daadi haus* after they were married. Esther was glad Mary stayed in touch and that she'd been gifted a healthy baby boy, whom they'd named Adam.

Instead of waiting until the next fall to say their vows, as was tradition, Amos and Naomi had married in March. Their decision had nothing to do with fear that one of them would leave. Amos simply needed time to move his construction business to Montgomery before the summer, his busiest time of year. Esther could still recall the way the couple looked at each other on their wedding day, and it warmed her heart every time she thought about it. God had surely blessed them with a second chance at love. Naomi continued working at the inn but not as many hours now that she was married. She and Amos traveled to Ohio to see his family as often as they could.

Esther enjoyed having her family close, even Gus. The man continued to be a work in progress, but Esther kept the faith that he would find his way to God and learn to be the best man he could be. She still took him pie often, and he thanked her every single time. Lizzie refused to dine with him except on Thanksgiving and Christmas. Luckily, last year's Christmas dinner had gone better than the disastrous Thanksgiving meal. Hopefully this year's festivities would be even better.

"Here we go," Esther said as she placed the turkey closest to Gus.

They each lowered their heads in prayer, including Gus. Esther had no idea if he was praying or just waiting. She'd tried to bring up the subject a few times, but Gus shied away from any talk about God. At least now he knew to raise his head and not wait for a prayer to be said aloud.

"Will you do the honors again this year?" Esther raised an eyebrow.

Gus grumbled, but for the second time, he carved the juicy bird with precision.

"Lizzie gets credit for the turkey again this year. It looks and smells delicious, *mei schweschder*." Esther paused. "Don't you agree, Gus?"

"Yeah." He didn't look up, but he didn't add anything negative either.

Amos ate like he hadn't seen food in a month of Sundays, and Naomi was glowing. Esther wondered if they were with child and didn't know it yet. Or maybe they did know and weren't ready to share the news. Either way, seeing Naomi and Amos so happy together filled Esther's heart even more.

"*Ach*, I have some news to share. And you don't even know because I just found out." Lizzie glanced at Esther, flashing her pearly whites. She wore the dentures every day now without shifting them around in her mouth as much. Esther had worked hard over the last year to adjust her diet, and along with the pills, her stomach had begun to heal. She rarely had problems or pain like before. She'd also stuck to her checkups like the doctor asked her to.

Esther straightened. "What news do you know that I don't?"

"Someone left a message on the answering machine requesting reservations for the spring. They said they'd firm up the dates later, but it will be an extended stay and there are a bunch of them!"

Esther calculated how many people they could house, even using cots and hide-a-beds. "How many is a bunch? If we fill each room to capacity, we only have enough beds for twelve people."

"I called the man back and told him that, and he said lodging for twelve would be fine." Lizzie's eyes grew. "They are coming all the way from Los Angeles, California." She smiled again. "I think he said they are with a big produce company. Fancy executives coming for a meeting or something."

"Well, it sounds like we will be busy." Esther was grateful the inn was making a name for itself.

⁓

Naomi glanced at Amos, and he nodded. In light of this information, she supposed they should share their own news. She cleared her throat.

"Um, we have some news too."

Esther gasped and moved her hands to her mouth. "I knew it!"

Naomi couldn't stop smiling as she reached for Amos's hand under the table.

Lizzie pushed her chair back, jumped up, and clapped her palms together. "Tell us! Tell us!"

"Amos and I are expecting." Naomi could feel herself blushing as Amos squeezed her hand. "In May. We were going to wait until I was farther along to tell anyone, but since you have a large crowd coming in the spring, I'm afraid I won't be available to work. It sounds like you need to hire someone new."

Naomi looked around at each of them. Her family. Even Gus had a pleasant expression on his face. Considering his reaction to Mary and John's baby news the year before, Naomi believed Gus was softening, even if just a little.

Lizzie rushed to Naomi and hugged her, then straightened and turned to her sister. "Esther! We're going to have a *boppli* to share!" She pressed her palms together again as she wound around the table and sat down.

"Well . . . there'll be no need for sharing." Amos chuckled before he reached for a slice of bread with his free hand.

Lizzie and Esther exchanged glances. After a few seconds Esther gasped. Lizzie was a bit slower, but her eyes widened as she caught on.

"*Ya*, it's twins." Naomi didn't think it was possible to reach this level of happiness. She didn't even know it existed and had always presumed no one earned it until they got to heaven. But God had blessed her and Amos in more ways than they ever could have imagined. They painted together almost daily, though they'd changed locations, which seemed fitting. Now they recreated the house and barn, and there was a lot of red in both paintings.

Esther clapped as she bounced up and down in her chair. She looked like Lizzie, who was doing the same thing. "A *boppli* for each of us, Lizzie."

"You both look like five-year-olds," Gus said with his mouth full. Once he'd swallowed, he actually smiled, which caused Naomi's heart to swell even more.

Naomi was thrilled to be expecting her first two children

with Amos. She prayed daily for healthy babies. She also prayed that Lizzie and Esther would continue to be in good health. They would finally be able to experience having a baby in the family—two of them.

Esther lifted her glass of tea. "I'd like to propose a toast." She waited until everyone held up their glass. "To Naomi and Amos, and to the two precious little ones coming into our lives."

Everyone clinked glasses, saying amen in unison. When Gus reached across the table and gently tapped his glass to Lizzie's, Naomi thought she might fall out of her chair. The two still sparred, but their coexistence was proof positive that God really was in the business of granting miracles.

Naomi rested her free hand on her stomach.

I can't wait to meet you both, mei *little ones, and to see what the future holds for all of us. Thank you,* Gott.

ACKNOWLEDGMENTS

A BIG THANKS TO MY PUBLISHER, HarperCollins Christian Publishing, for allowing me to create characters who are close to my heart and for giving me the freedom to step outside the box when it comes to this genre.

Much appreciation to my editors, Kimberly Carlton and Jodi Hughes. And for all of those important folks behind the scenes, a big thanks to you also!

To my agent, Natasha Kern, I'm so blessed that we are on this journey together. You are such an important part of my life, both professionally and personally. Xo

Janet Murphy—my friend, my assistant, my media/ marketing guru—you continue to rock. By the time this book releases we will have worked together about eleven years. Wow. Who would have thought that day we met at the Mexican restaurant would have landed us where we are today? I love and appreciate you.

Another round of thanks to my street team, Wiseman's Warriors! You gals are the greatest.

To all the folks in Indiana who have opened their homes and hearts—Amish and non-Amish—thank you for the encouragement, hospitality, and blessings. Indiana has truly become a second home to me.

My family and friends continue to be amazing, supporting me on every project. I love you all. Extra thanks to my amazing hubby, Patrick Mackey. I love you, Dear.

And to God the Father, saying thank you will never be enough for the many ways You have blessed me. I can only try to continuously follow Your lead and to write stories I hope entertain and glorify You.

DISCUSSION QUESTIONS

1. It's obvious Esther and Lizzie love each other very much. What are some of the ways that the sisters complement each other despite having such different personalities?

2. Naomi and Amos have both chosen not to pursue a romantic relationship. Eventually, they change their minds. Who begins to fall in love first?

3. When Thomas returned, did you root for him or hope he would leave Montgomery? If Naomi had chosen to be with Thomas, do you think it would have worked out, or would Thomas have left her again?

4. The sisters made a promise to their mother that Gus could rent the cottage for the rest of his life. Esther and Lizzie don't know why Gus's staying

in the cottage was so important to her. The reason is revealed in book two of this series. But what speculations do you have as to why Esther and Lizzie's mother made the sisters promise to let Gus live out his life in the cottage?

5. Gus's daughter, Heather, pays him a visit after not seeing him for forty years. More about Heather is revealed in the next book in the series. But what speculations do you have as to why Heather visits her father after all this time?

6. Naomi and Amos are both aware of their physical attraction to each other, but acknowledge that it takes more than outward appearance for a romantic relationship to ensue. Do you think most relationships begin with a physical attraction to the other person? Naomi and Amos become friends through their common interest in painting also. What romantic relationships do you feel are the most successful? Which order of courtship seems to work best? Or is there even a formula for love?

7. Despite Gus's grumpy disposition, there are some tender moments in the story, mostly with Gus and Esther. Can you name some of these scenes? What does this reveal to us about Gus?

8. There is a lot of tension between Gus and Lizzie. Do their personalities just clash more than Gus's other relationships—or lack thereof—with others? Do you

see anything past the obvious when it comes to Gus and Lizzie?

9. Most readers will be able to identify with Naomi, Esther, or Lizzie. Which one of these characters were you able to connect with the most? Or were you able to identify with Amos more than the ladies?

The Amish Journey Series

ABOUT THE AUTHOR

Photo by Emilie Hendryx

BESTSELLING AND AWARD-WINNING AUthor Beth Wiseman has sold over two million books. She is the recipient of the coveted Holt Medallion, is a two-time Carol Award winner, and has won the Inspirational Reader's Choice Award three times. Her books have been on various bestseller lists, including CBD, CBA, ECPA, and *Publishers Weekly*. Beth and her husband are empty nesters enjoying country life in south-central Texas.

∞

Visit her online at BethWiseman.com
Facebook: AuthorBethWiseman
Twitter: @BethWiseman
Instagram: @bethwisemanauthor